# DEVILS AT THE DOOR

*Also by Tessa Wegert*

*The Shana Merchant novels*

DEATH IN THE FAMILY
THE DEAD SEASON
DEAD WIND *
THE KIND TO KILL *
DEVILS AT THE DOOR *

* available from Severn House

*Knock Knock...*

# DEVILS AT THE DOOR

## Tessa Wegert

*Hope you enjoy spending time
with Shana!*

*Tessa W*

**SEVERN
HOUSE**

First world edition published in Great Britain and the USA in 2023
by Severn House, an imprint of Canongate Books Ltd,
14 High Street, Edinburgh EH1 1TE.

severnhouse.com

*British Library Cataloguing-in-Publication Data*
A CIP catalogue record for this title is available from the British Library.

ISBN-13: 978-1-4483-1138-5 (cased)
ISBN-13: 978-1-4483-1139-2 (e-book)

*All Severn House titles are printed on acid-free paper.*

Typeset by Palimpsest Book Production Ltd.,
Falkirk, Stirlingshire, Scotland.
Printed and bound in Great Britain by
TJ Books, Padstow, Cornwall.

# Praise for the Shana Merchant novels

"Wegert remains a writer to watch"
*Publishers Weekly* on *The Kind to Kill*

"Wegert does an admirable job of generating
mounting suspense"
*Kirkus Reviews* on *The Kind to Kill*

"[Wegert has] rightly earned the badge as one of the finest
talents of the past three years"
*The Strand Magazine* on *The Kind to Kill*

"A stunner of a thriller – both emotionally layered and a story
that keeps a riveting pace"
DANIELLE GIRARD, *USA Today* bestselling author,
on *The Kind to Kill*

"[A] standout crime thriller . . . Fans of DENISE MINA's Alex
Morrow will be pleased"
*Publishers Weekly* Starred Review of *Dead Wind*

"LOUISE PENNY meets RUTH WARE in this small town
mystery that bubbles with secrets and intrigue"
CHARLIE DONLEA, internationally bestselling author,
on *Dead Wind*

"An atmospheric, sophisticated thriller with layers
upon layers of secrets"
SARAH STEWART TAYLOR, author of the Maggie D'arcy
mysteries, on *Dead Wind*

"A bone-chilling mystery that crackles with suspense"
JOANNA SCHAFFHAUSEN, author of the Annalisa Vega
novels, on *Dead Wind*

# About the author

**Tessa Wegert** is the author of the Shana Merchant series of mysteries. A former freelance journalist, Tessa has contributed to such publications as *Forbes*, *The Huffington Post*, *Adweek*, *The Economist*, and *The Globe and Mail*. Tessa grew up in Quebec and now lives with her husband and children in Connecticut, where she studies martial arts and is currently at work on her next novel.

tessawegert.com
Facebook: TessaWegertBooks
Twitter: TessaWegert
Instagram: TessaWegert

For the good people of Alexandria Bay, NY

# PROLOGUE

*Burlington, Vermont*
*July 2001*

The wooded trail ended at the lip of the cliff. It was a near-ninety-degree descent to the pebbled beach where we'd stash our flip phones before wading into the water, scaling a rock, and jumping into the cold, black abyss. Down, then up, then down again. My stomach flip-flopped as we stripped off our clothes. I had my back to the others, conscious of my breasts and bare midriff. Suze peeled her tank top from her torso in slow motion, her dark, waist-length hair aglitter in the moon's hoary light.

'Jump out, not down,' Doug told us in a stony voice. 'There are about a dozen different ways this could go tits up – and, Shay? I really don't want to tell Mom and Dad you died tonight.'

I blinked at my brother, nodding in stunned silence, and followed the others into the lake. Eight long strides between triangular boulders veined with pearly quartz to where the lakebed dropped off, and then we were on our bellies, doggy-paddling toward the base of Lone Rock. The climb up twenty feet of slick, craggy stone was never easy, and I struggled to gain purchase, my fingers slippery and uncertain. In the distance, the lake was quicksilver, the storybook Vermont mountains beyond a wavy black line.

The wind was up. I hadn't realized it before, but perched atop the island, it buffeted my hair and body both. I folded my arms across my chest and willed myself to stay steady. Behind my ribs, my breath juddered.

A yelp, bright and affected. There was a splash, and just like that Suze was gone, sucked down into the water. All I saw when she surfaced was a flash of bone-white teeth. My skin exploded in goosebumps. 'I'll wait for you!' she called from below, still laughing.

'You're up,' said Doug's friend, his hand hot and moist at the small of my back. Below me the lake rippled and snapped, but I didn't hesitate. If Suze could do it, so could I. I inhaled so fast I choked as the earth fell out from under me, air rushing up from the water while I plummeted toward it. The lake closed up over my head like a sealed bag. Like a fist around my lungs.

Boggy darkness. No sign of Suze. No light from the surface either.

I'd grown up on Lake Champlain, but I wasn't a swimmer. The dark water was disorienting, and I summersaulted in desperation, searching for air, an escape. I knew I was starting to panic, and also what that meant, but I couldn't settle the chanting in my mind.

*I don't want to tell Mom and Dad you died tonight.*

When I tried to scream, my mouth flooded with water, my larynx spasming like a beached fish. Every futile kick speeding me to disaster as I spiraled into the deep.

# ONE

I t all started with two innocuous words.
*She's here.*
Tim's voice, hollow in the spartan room, reached me where
I stood by the window. This view was what I loved most about
our house, more even than the antique built-in china hutch. The
river outside was a creased sheet of midnight-blue silk, Boldt
Castle with its backlit towers and spires a black fortress more at
home in Romania than on an island in the St Lawrence River. I
let the curtain fall back and turned to face Tim just in time to
see him open the door. Already the house's cool, comfortable
silence was starting to fizz like a pot over flame.

Henrietta Della Merchant arrived in A-Bay carrying a duffle
as long as a body bag and wearing headphones smaller than
dimes. Gone was the Dora the Explorer bob and soft middle I'd
known when she was little. Hen was nearly as tall as me now
with hips, lean muscles, a narrow waist. The kid was practically
a woman.

I didn't know her at all.

We'd been in Canada, tasting wedding cakes at Sheriff Mac's
favorite bakery, when Doug put out the SOS. It was only recently
that I'd stopped being surprised when my brother's name popped
up on my phone screen. Our estrangement had lasted months,
and from time to time a familiar feeling of loss swelled like the
river outside. I'd wasted no time answering his call. 'Velvet isn't
a flavor. Tell me I'm right,' I'd said by way of greeting, because
Tim and I had just eaten our weight in frosting and still couldn't
see eye to eye.

'Velvet isn't the flavor,' Tim had muttered. '*Red* is.'

'Oh, sis,' Doug had said on the line. 'We need help.'

In a beat, the cake – all the carrot and chocolate and raspberry cream we'd consumed in service to our future wedding guests – had been forgotten and the pulse in my neck throbbed like a stubbed toe. Something had happened. Something was wrong. Was it Mom and Dad? Doug's wife, Josie?

'Tell me,' I'd said as the sickly-sweet icing in my stomach compacted into a leaden brick. I knew bad news; it was my bread and butter really, without which my job – and that of my fiancé – wouldn't exist. What I struggled with was the *anticipation* of trouble, the fear that it was on the way. As a child, I'd driven my parents crazy demanding reassurance that they'd come home safely after nights out, that I didn't have a life-threatening disease, that everyone I loved was healthy. *Promise?* I'd say, ever suspicious, as I thrust a small hooked finger into my mother's face to await the pinky swear that would release the pressure building around my heart. *Promise?* I'd asked when Tim swore to stick by me no matter what. Some threats I'd escaped. Others, I knew, were only beginning to bubble.

Doug had said, 'I could kill her,' and at once, I'd understood.

When I thought of my niece, I pictured her somewhere around age five, that thick curtain of bangs drawn across her forehead, her rounded belly wobbling when I gave it a playful poke. *Make the wind*, she'd demand whenever she wanted to see a tornado kick. I was new to martial arts back then, but my sensei gave thorough demonstrations, and I'd been practicing. Hen loved to watch me spin, my leg extending with so much force and speed that my pant leg whipped the air. If I did it right, a rush of wind would hit Hen square in the face and she'd stare open-mouthed at me as if I were a god.

The stories out of Vermont in recent months told of a vastly different child. Henrietta was newly sixteen, but in her last semester of sophomore year at South Burlington High School, she'd stopped turning in assignments and started skipping class instead. It wasn't uncommon for her to instigate screaming matches with her parents or brood in her room for hours. There were other problems as well, many related to Josie's disappearing collection of Sauvignon Blanc. But none of that had been enough to push my brother and his wife over the edge.

'She wrecked my car,' Doug had said with a groan the day he'd called out of the blue. 'Oh, and also the fucking house.'

Apparently, Doug's Jeep needed a whole new bumper, its shape now stamped into his garage door.

'What does her therapist say?' I'd asked, sitting with Tim in the parked car outside the bakery on King Street East. The therapy had been my idea; Hen was seeing a woman in Essex whom I'd researched and vetted myself. I credited my own therapy with helping me overcome PTSD, and the emotional check-ins I continued to conduct with Gil Gasko helped to clear my head.

'She refuses to go back there,' he'd replied, 'which is probably for the best. A hundred bucks a session, and Hen hardly said a word. She thinks therapy is bullshit. That's the word she used. *Bullshit.*'

I'd glanced at Tim then. My knowledge of his younger brother was limited, but I had a feeling Jean-Christophe's wild phase had nothing on this.

'That's why I'm calling,' Doug had continued. 'I'm terrified, Shay. We both are.'

*Shit.* My sister-in-law was way more patient than Doug. If even Josie's fortitude had become unglued, things at home must be really bad.

'She's like a different person.' Doug had whispered it urgently into the phone, as if worried Hen might be listening. Like he was afraid. 'The hair, her diet, all these horrible movies she's been watching . . . I don't even recognize my own kid.'

'Want me to talk to her?' My experience wrangling teens was extremely limited, but I couldn't bear the pain in my brother's voice.

Doug had cleared his throat and said, 'Actually, I was hoping for something else.'

I listened, mouth dry, knees turned to aspic.

'It's what she wants,' Doug had concluded, sounding as helpless as I felt. 'I can't for the life of me figure out why. Of all the places . . . but maybe, with you and Tim to get her back on track . . .'

So there it was. Hen was our responsibility now, at least for a little while. Her balled-up T-shirts would take up residence in the corners of her room, tattered sweatshirts pooling on every surface, her luggage lying open like roadkill with an empty, yawning maw. Tim would do his best to avert his eyes when she'd come downstairs in outfits so small they looked like hold-overs from when she was nine.

As my brother made his request, I'd thought of all the things he'd told me about Hen and the girl she'd become. Would she shut us out too? Creep around soundlessly, startling us at every turn? Blast her music late into the night? Already she had injected our lives with unwelcome mystery, and the uncertainty of the situation was an IV line I couldn't get free of, the needle stabbing deeper every time I moved. I loved my niece, of course I did, but how well did I know her? Especially after this past year?

That was three weeks ago, and now Hen was here, weighed down with luggage and making a point of distancing herself from Doug and Josie on our vast wraparound porch. Or was it the other way around?

'Hi, Hen,' I said, forcing a smile.

In an hour, once we gave them all a tour of the house and ate a lunch of grilled chicken with macaroni salad, Doug would tell Hen to *be good, kiddo*, and Josie would hold the girl to her chest with hands twisted into claws. After that, all that would be left was me, and Tim, and a volatile sixteen-year-old who now called our cavernous, run-down love nest home.

# TWO

'A twenty-one-count indictment,' Tim said, lifting the fork to his mouth. 'The guy had been stealing, defrauding customers and writing bad checks for years. We actually interviewed him, Shana and me, before the truth came out. We were considering hiring him to work on the house. Something felt off though – right, Shane?' There was always a gladness to the way he delivered the nickname he'd branded me with when I first joined the troop. A secret joy. 'Long story short, we said screw it and decided to do the whole renovation ourselves, and it's a good thing we did.'

It wasn't Tim's first time telling the story about the Watertown man whose crime spree spanned three counties. Even the punchline about our good fortune in avoiding the scammer was the same. We were running out of conversation starters, our coffers emptied of pleasantries and small talk, and still Henrietta stared down at her plate like we weren't even in the room.

Meanwhile, just a few hours into our new normal, I couldn't stop staring at *her*. After Doug and Josie left, she'd spent the afternoon headphoned and head down by the river, and after a few failed attempts at striking up a chat, I'd made the decision to give her some space. Prior to today, I'd last seen Hen over Easter, when Tim and I traveled to Vermont to talk about the wedding. The transformation she'd undergone in less than six months was disorienting.

With freckles a few shades darker than her haybale hair, fair eyebrows that were ruler-straight and deep dimples poked into ruddy cheeks, she'd always reminded me of a well-nourished Midwestern Swede. At some point though, Hen had tried to dye her blonde hair blue, the outcome of which was the current icy green. Her nails were long and sharp and painted green to match the hair, and her complexion was as colorless as ceiling paint. More concerning still: the girl was all angles; even under her sweatshirt and jeans, her boniness was impossible to miss.

I knew from Doug that she'd quit the swim team, swapping early-morning practices and three-egg omelets for Coke Zero and bloody stories secreted in the dark. Doug and Josie hadn't realized Hen was staying up late with her iPad until they clicked the wrong button on Netflix and found an old user profile they'd neglected to delete. Hen's watch history was hundreds of films deep, each more violent than the last. My niece had worked her way through Tarantino, Wes Craven, David Cronenberg. She'd watched movies about vengeful spirits and saw-wielding psychos, twisted bloodbaths every one. Other picks included the cultish first season of *True Detective* and the nineties neo-noir thriller *The Ninth Gate*, about a magic book that could be used to summon the devil.

'Hen,' I said, reaching for my glass of water. I waited until she acknowledged my voice with a tiny tilt of her spirulina-streaked head. 'How are you feeling about school on Monday? Ready to take this town by storm?'

Hen's gaze was hooded, limp strands of hair framing her washed-out cheeks. The light from the bulbs on the chandelier, an old-fashioned crystal one not at all my style, leeched the color from her eyes and for a second she looked like Aunt Felicia, irises and hair and skin all the same ghostly shade of curdled cream.

'I'm sure the kids here are great,' she said sweetly. 'Good people.'

'Right? Good people,' Tim repeated, pleased, though he knew full well the people of Alexandria Bay hadn't always been good to *me*. 'I'm sure you'll fit right in. There's no swim team, as you know – it's all ice hockey and basketball in these parts – but you'll find your friend group. And in the meantime, you can help with the house, and I'll teach you how to drive a boat.'

We'd need to keep her busy, Doug and I had both agreed. Take her to the library, teach her how to cook, maybe swing by the drunk tank so she could see bad behavior has conse-quences. With authorization from Doug and Josie, we'd already let Hen know she could drive Tim's car to school, and that – with express permission – she could explore the town, but we were hoping she'd do the latter with us. Between her time in class and with me and Tim, we'd have every minute of Hen's stay in Upstate New York covered so we could ship her back to Vermont safe and sound. An idle teen was a teen who went looking for trouble.

Hen's eyes were on her iPhone, which rested face-up beside her. Doug and Josie had a rule about phones at the table, but since she was only looking at the screen, not touching, I let it slide. When Tim's brother J.C. brought his phone to dinner, it was constantly lighting up with notifications: texts, TikTok posts, social-app messages. Hen's phone was black and silent. Softly, I said her name.

'Hm?' The kid steered her lips into a smile that didn't meet her eyes. 'Boating. That sounds so great,' she said, enunciating every word. Stretching out the *so* along with that ersatz smile. 'May I please be excused?'

My gaze hooked on Tim's; his wide eyebrows lifted. She'd hardly touched her dinner.

I said, 'You need to eat, hon.' That much was clear even without my brother's instructions, but he'd been adamant that Hen finish her meals and put some meat back on her bones. 'You like fish, right?' I said, encouraging. 'Tim made it especially for you.'

'I do,' Hen replied, head bobbing, 'and it's amazing. I just think all of this' – a wave of her arm, the cuff of her sweatshirt pulled taut over pale knuckles – 'is making me feel a little . . . I don't know. I'm just not hungry right now.'

'No problem,' said Tim quickly, though I'd seen how hard he'd worked on the dinner. 'It's been a big day. You can make it up at breakfast – right, Shana?'

'How about just a few more bites?'

As soon as the words were out, I winced. I was pretty sure I'd spoken them before, when Hen was in a high chair. She was looking at me with a mixture of disdain and amusement, like she couldn't believe I really thought I could sway her with a line like that.

Hen said, 'It's delicious – really! I feel so bad for not being hungry. You're a really good cook, Tim, but . . . make it up at breakfast?'

'Go ahead,' Tim said, watching as she lifted the beautiful plate of sole Florentine he'd lovingly prepared and set it in the kitchen.

Without another word, Hen retreated to the second floor, and we heard the door to the guest bedroom close behind her.

'Sucker,' I said when she was gone. 'I thought you said you knew teenagers?'

Tim frowned. 'What do you mean? She asked politely. Polite's good, right? Polite is progress.'

'She's playing us. *Good people? You're a really good cook?* Please. She was looking for an escape hatch, and you pointed her straight to it.'

Tim glanced in the direction of the stairs, disappointment blooming across his face.

'This isn't going to be easy,' I said, blowing out a breath. 'I can't look at her without seeing a child, but she's this autonomous being now, and totally . . . *unpredictable*. It makes me nervous.'

Outside, a ripple of wind caused the window to shudder. I rose from my chair and walked toward it. It had a built-in seat that concealed a deep chest we were currently using to store paint and tools. I lifted the lid and pulled out a bottle of red wine. After what happened to Josie's liquor supply, I didn't want Hen to see us drinking. Now I unscrewed the cap and, straight from the bottle, took a deep slug.

I had to hand it to Tim for agreeing to let Hen stay. We were still settling into our life as an engaged couple, still molding a routine. Every morning before work, we propped up our feet on the back patio and watched the river. It was always changing – bluer or grayer based on the sky, flatter or more bloated due to rainfall, wind. While sipping hot coffee, we studied it, along with the windswept pitch pines growing crooked on the shore and the boats gliding to and from the marina, with the curiosity of anthropologists. On warm days, Tim liked to cook breakfast in his boxers, and I had taken to bathing with the door open so he could pretend to happen across me and run his fingertips down my steamy bare arm. All of that had gone out the window the minute Hen walked in the door.

'You hid the wine?' Tim asked as I passed him the bottle. He pressed the mouth of it to his curled lips.

'I want to trust her. Really, I do. *Shit*,' I said. 'I'm supposed to be the *fun* aunt. The one who takes her shopping and gives her sweets.'

'*You* take her shopping?'

'I have,' I said defensively, snatching back the wine. 'A couple of times. OK, it's been a while.'

Tim said, 'You can't be that kind of aunt right now, but you will be again. As long as she's here, with us, you're her guardian, and keeping her safe and happy is what matters most. I'm sorry I let her pull that. You're right – she has to follow the rules. Think of it as practice,' he said with a playful smirk. 'A trial run.'

I blinked twice. The subject of kids had come up only once, shortly after Tim proposed. He wanted them; Tim had grown up with a sister, two stepbrothers and a large flock of cousins, all of them close. I wasn't opposed to children in theory, but in practice the idea of raising one jangled my nerves. Our control over kids, and the people they became, only went so far. It was rare, but sometimes raising kids went horribly wrong. I'd seen it happen for myself.

'I hope you're right,' I told Tim. 'Doug and Josie will never forgive me if I screw this up.'

'The only thing you're going to screw—'

'There's a *minor* in the house,' I purred, pressing a finger to his lips as I recapped the wine.

Leaning back in his chair, Tim groaned in frustration and chased the sound with a laugh. 'Maybe this wasn't such a good idea after all.'

# THREE

I woke with a start to a sound in the hall. The floors in our house were sloped and squeaky, cranky to the point where Tim and I had devised a game of mapping their landmines; skip the fourth tread on the staircase, sidestep the knotty board outside the bathroom door. He was better at the dance than I was, deliberate in his movements – Tim was more panther than pachyderm, while I tended to forget myself and thunder on through – but Tim was asleep beside me now, his breath soft and warm on my bare shoulder.

There was a time when such sounds would have jolted me upright, and my hand would have darted to the bedside table for my sidearm. Now and then I still dreamed of a figure looming over my bed, me unconscious and defenseless, him with a pocketknife angled at my face, but it had been a year and a half since I closed the door on my cousin for good, and I was finally getting better at not flinching when I felt Tim's arm snake over my hip, or pulling away and persuading myself that I didn't deserve his love. Abraham Skilton, the boy who became Blake Bram, was no longer a threat to me. And again I heard the growl of weight on a floorboard, just beyond our bedroom door.

I threw off the sheet and swung my legs out of bed.

It's incredible how completely a foreign presence can change the atmosphere in a place. One night in, and already our routine felt slippery and elusive, almost as if our previous way of living never existed at all. I still wasn't used to its new shape or Hen's cool presence. The idea of her creeping around the house at night made me itchy, uneasiness spreading over my skin like a hot red rash. Night was when Hen drank her mother's wine, and crashed the family car, and gave herself over to dark diversions, the bloodier the better. This was her first time sleeping in our home, and though we'd done our best to set up the bedroom, to make her feel welcome, she'd waited there like a mink in a den until we were out cold.

*Maybe she's hungry*, I thought, struggling into a sweatshirt, its hood snagging on my head to block my view of the door. When it was just us, Tim and I slept with it open, but we'd nudged it closed tonight to provide some semblance of privacy, stopping just short of engaging the latch. When I finally managed to yank my head free of the hoodie, the door stood wide open, the hall beyond it illuminated with an eerie silver light.

Bewildered, I crept forward. The house was old, but the floors weren't so crooked that doors swung open all on their own. What was Hen up to?

To my right, her bedroom door stood open too, her bed conspicuously empty, but the quiet in the house was deep and dark as the channel once more.

As I walked toward the staircase, skirting the loudest of floorboards, an object caught my eye. Outside the door that led to our study, a small former nursery that connected to the master bedroom, a black pearl earring lay on the hardwood, lolling gently as if recently dropped.

I recognized the earring; it was mine, left to me by my paternal grandmother when she died. Along with the rest of my jewelry, which I rarely had occasion to wear, I'd tucked it away in a wooden box on a shelf in the study closet. And now, here it was on the floor.

The human mind, I've often thought, is like one of those jumping fountains, a jet of water hopping back and forth across a swimming pool. We're somewhere and then, in a blink, we're someplace else, with an entirely different point of view.

As I stood in the hall, that lone earring clutched in my damp fist, I found myself in rural Quebec at a place called The Mystery Spot. Less than two hours north of Swanton, the tiny Eastern Townships hamlet of Huntingville had been a tourist destination when I was a kid, attracting visitors almost entirely based on the merits of a house that defied the laws of gravity. The story I'd heard was that the owners bought a parcel of land and discovered it had supernatural properties; beads of water rolled uphill, chairs balanced on two legs. The Mystery Spot house looked like an M.C. Escher painting, all tilted floors and slanted ceilings that messed with your mind and made you feel drunk. Tour guides told ghost stories about the *maison hantée*, and after my visit,

I'd returned to Vermont feeling like I'd experienced something paranormal, an inexplicable secret that fueled my inherent need to ferret out the truth.

The house I lived in with Tim, a beautiful Victorian antique he'd bought a year ago right before proposing, was no Mystery Spot. It was Hen who'd opened the door and dropped the earring; it had to be. We'd invited her to make herself at home, but I didn't like her sneaking around – and I sure as hell didn't want her messing with one of the few family heirlooms I had.

In the weak moonlight, I made my way into the study and felt around inside the cluttered wooden box. The velvet sack was still there, not quite empty, and with a sigh of relief I returned the earring to its partner.

Downstairs, I found the TV flashing a late-night infomercial on mute, blue light pulsing off the walls and ceiling, but there was no sign of my niece. The whole thing was starting to feel like a pre-Halloween prank.

'Hen,' I whispered in the kitchen, the mud room, under the stairs. I didn't want to disturb Tim, but I was starting to worry. Our house wasn't a ten-bedroom villa or island manse, but there were times when it felt sprawling, like when it needed to be cleaned. Or when I lost my niece. I'd just made up my mind to wake him when I heard another creak, this time directly above me. Inside Hen's room.

When I got back upstairs, I found her door closed. Slowly, with chills winding up my bare legs, I turned the knob and peeked inside. There she was, her body caterpillar-curled under a light blanket. She lay with her back to me, but her breathing seemed steady, so pillow-soft you'd never have known she'd set foot out of bed.

You can tell a lot about someone by the way they sleep. Tim sprawls out across the mattress, confident and bold, while I'm what he calls a small sleeper. For as long as I could remember, I'd tucked in my limbs like a gymnast and teetered at the edge of the bed, ready to spring into action at the smallest sign of danger or distress. Hen slept like I did, tight as a nut, and it made me question what else we had in common. I understand the origin of my own subconscious security system. What was Hen's?

I didn't know. Not yet anyway. But as I crept back to Tim's dependable exhalations and the refuge that was our room, I couldn't help but imagine Hen's lips curled just like her body as she stared through slitted eyes at the darkened wall.

# FOUR

'She needs friends,' Maureen McIntyre said when, on Wednesday afternoon, we packed up our pamphlets and posterboards to leave Geneva's Hobart and William Smith Colleges. We'd volunteered to visit the Finger Lakes region of Upstate New York weeks prior with the intention of looking for new recruits. Earlier in the year, the Thin Blue Line, as we were sometimes known, had been evaluated by the upper echelons of New York state law enforcement and found to be lacking. The big guns wanted diversity, equity, inclusion. Our femaleness made Mac and me attractive candidates for an enlistment effort. Our mission? To find a replacement for former BCI investigator Don Bogle, who was currently serving a prison sentence for criminal obstruction, among other things.

I had mixed feelings about the task. When Bogle was a member of my team, before he violated multiple New York state laws, he and I had been close. Despite what he'd done, swapping in someone new felt a little like betrayal. Still, Mac and I had spent the day talking to the young women on campus about a career as a state trooper, posing as role models for potential candidates with diverse backgrounds who might be interested in following our path. They could be investigators, forensic scientists, sheriffs, we said, though the candidates we met on campus wouldn't be qualified to work those jobs for years. Someday, though, they might well take the civil service exam, head off to the academy and join our ranks. As the first elected female sheriff in the history of New York state, and a trooper back when just twelve percent of them were women, Mac had a soft spot for campaigns like this.

Me? I needed a break from Henrietta.

At the beginning of the day, when Mac and I were setting up, I'd tried to romanticize our new addition. 'Hen tasted my scrambled eggs and said they weren't awful. She called the river view from the patio "cool."'

Mac could read between the lines though and had discerned the truth. By the time we handed out our last pamphlet, I was confessing all.

In the four days since her arrival, Hen had barely spoken a word to me and Tim, preferring to be alone with her earbuds and looking increasingly morose. The morning after finding the earring in the hall, I'd casually inquired about her creeping, holding back any mention of the black pearl so she had a chance to own up, but Hen insisted she'd been asleep all night. *I'd never do that*, she told me, broad-eyed with innocence. *I'm kind of a scaredy-cat to be honest, Aunt Shay.* This from the kid who watched movies about axe-wielding maniacs and drove a car into her parents' house.

If all went according to plan, Hen would live with us for four months – the entire fall semester. We had a single season to sort out my brother's kid before the all-important second half of her junior year, and chipping away at her defenses was like trying to fell a tree with a string of dental floss. Meanwhile, Tim and I were neck-deep in planning our pre-Christmas wedding, every room in our antique house was mid-renovation, and we were short-staffed at the barracks. I hadn't even made it to a karate class in months.

Not the perfect time to open our arms to a wayward teen.

'Friends would be great,' I told Mac as I stuffed a stack of printouts into my tote. 'Know any? Because Hen doesn't seem like the kind of girl who'll willingly bang down their doors.'

'Kids go through phases,' Mac reminded me. 'And hey, if the drunken altercation with a garage door's already behind you, it's bound to be nothing but blue skies ahead.'

'You're not helping,' I said with a withering look.

'What I'm *trying* to do is convince you this isn't as dire as it seems. She'll meet someone at school she likes and boom, she's got a social life. Hell, she could have a new bestie already. Teens make friends ten times faster than adults.'

'Those stats sound sus,' I said. 'I learned that word from Hen – when she used it to describe the lunch I made her.'

Mac laughed. 'Teenagers adapt,' she insisted. 'I have nieces too, remember? If they were closer to Hen's age, I'd suggest we hook them up.'

'A playdate,' I said, tickled.

A recent trim had left my friend's blonde hair extra feathery, and it shimmied when she laughed. 'Ah, no. Playdates are for babies. Hen needs time with her peers. Time away from *you*. Four months is eons, Shay. Kids need their freedom.'

'OK, but let's not forget who we're talking about,' I said, my mouth tight. 'Hen's last name is Merchant, same as mine. Everyone here knows me – and they sure as hell know *him*. No matter what Henrietta says or does while she's in A-Bay, she'll still be part of the most notorious family on the East Coast.'

Mac said, 'But it's been better for you lately, right? Less judgment from the restless natives? Time makes people forget.'

'Forgetting's a tall order,' I said, though Mac wasn't wrong. Since last summer, when a former reporter for the *Watertown Daily Times* launched a website devoted to the families of killers and published a sympathetic interview with me that went viral, the locals had been decidedly more hospitable. Of course, that was before my niece arrived to sit in a classroom next to their kids.

There was a note of reassurance in Mac's voice when she said, 'It won't be so bad. Some kids that age come off as jerks, but most are more compassionate than we give them credit for. And didn't you say anything's better for her than being back home?'

'*I* didn't say it,' I told her. 'Doug did. But I'm not sure I agree.'

Sending Hen to us, here in A-Bay, hadn't made sense to me from the start. I understood that the kids back home had shut her out. Even the swim-team girls she'd been closest to, whom she used to see three mornings a week at dawn for practice, kept their distance once word got out about Bram. Parents Hen had known for years started warning their daughters to avoid 'that Merchant girl.' But the name-calling was often much worse.

Doug and Josie told Hen it was just a phase. That, in time, everyone would forget. When they didn't, and Hen got drunk and crashed the car, fear and desperation took over.

'Doug thinks being a cop means I have unique powers of persuasion, like I can magic away bad behavior. He's wrong of course.'

But it wasn't just that. Part of me still couldn't believe Hen had actually wanted to come here. Here, of all places. The village

Bram had made his hunting ground. I'd been expecting Hen's first few weeks to be rough. New town, new school, a reputation so black it left a smudge on everything she touched. But every time she drove away from us to spend the better part of her day at the combined elementary, middle, and high school, I felt panic rising like an angry surge of tide.

'Give her a chance to forge her own path and prove she can be trusted.'

Hadn't she already shown us she couldn't be? A busted garage door was one thing, but Tim and I lived at the edge of a river that ranged from two to fifteen miles wide, and living as 'up north' as one could get without crossing into Canada could be dangerous. I'd grown up fearing the water, and despite Tim's boating lessons, it unnerved me still. One bad experience had left me traumatized, but it had also instilled in me an understanding of the water's dangers and a deep sense of respect. Henrietta was a swimmer and naturally unafraid. Couple her pluck with a disregard for rules, and that was a dangerous combination.

'Treat her like she's twelve and she'll resent you for it,' Mac went on as she shouldered open the door so we could step out into the warm September light. 'Your brother wants you to be a positive influence on her, right? Can't do that if she doesn't respect you.'

I blew out a breath. The sheriff was right. If I wanted to connect with Hen, she needed to see that I trusted her. Trouble was, I had no idea how to prove it. I couldn't help but think it was a matter of time before the bullies came for Hen here too.

Alexandria Bay had become synonymous with Blake Bram.

And we were throwing Henrietta to the wolves.

# FIVE

'I'm not going back,' she said that very afternoon, kicking off her sneakers and wrapping her arms around her chest.

Hen lived in flare leggings and massively oversized shirts with extra folds of fabric that swallowed her hands. Standing like that, it looked like she was wearing a straightjacket. *Hours from home, trapped in a strange house, it probably feels like she is.*

'The parents in the pickup line won't stop staring,' she told me. 'The teachers treat me like a bomb that's about to blow. The kids don't even try to hide that they're talking about me.'

Standing on a stepladder by the dining-room door, I tried to channel Mac's optimism. 'I'm so sorry, Hen. They'll come around.'

Our latest home renovation project was the moldings, two inches thick with deep, smooth grooves that ran floor to ceiling where they met with medallions of even more intricate millwork. Our doorframes were gorgeous, original to the historic home but coated in countless layers of old paint. As I stripped and sanded in my downtime, I found I could trace a room's evolution. White, then blue, then pinky beige and white again. We were aiming to get back down to raw wood. Tim had pitched the project warily, an apology twisting his lips, but despite the blisters and the heat-gun stink, I'd discovered there was comfort in chipping away the old stuff and starting fresh. I wished I could transfer some of it to my niece.

'*Come around?* You don't get it,' Hen said, batting a hank of hair from her eyes. She'd done a slapdash job of painting her nails fire-engine red, and it looked like her fingertips had been gnawed raw. 'Today this kid—'

She paused, mouth agape.

'What?' I asked. Something in her expression threatened to shift the conversation from gripe session to serious talk.

'Forget it.'

'No, I want to know. What did the kid do?' I couldn't imagine and didn't want to try.

Hen's eyes brimmed with frustration. She didn't say anything more, just marched toward me, cell phone in hand. A second later, I was looking at an Instagram post. Photos of Hen in the school cafeteria, head bowed, looking down at her lunch. Ugly red streaks snaked over her sandwich, the brown bag I'd packed it in that morning, and the empty span of table on either side of her chair.

'It's ketchup,' she said before I could get a word out. 'Someone I don't even know came up behind me and sprayed ketchup all over my lunch.'

My lips parted, but the words wouldn't come. I watched, mute and dumbstruck, as Hen peeled off her shirt to show me her back. Red smeared her fair shoulders and veined the crop top she'd worn under her flannel. It looked like she'd been flogged.

It looked like sprays of blood.

'Who,' I said, my voice rough with rage.

'I don't know. It doesn't matter.' She dragged a hand across her eyes and turned away from me. 'Kids play "Psycho Killer" when I pass them in the halls. In the bathroom, some freshman coughed Bram's name under her breath. Someone asked me if we were "kissing cousins."'

That last part hit like a shove, the words transporting me to my own high school where, nearly twenty years ago, I found the words *Abe + Shay = kissing cousins* scrawled on my locker door. He'd faced the wrath of fellow students who saw his strangeness as a personal affront – and because I was his kin, and we were friends, I was collateral damage. A freak by association. Condemned to a bilious state of humiliation that I had to shake off like the shackle it was.

'I'll call the school.' I'd forgotten all about the heat gun in my hand, my grip like a tightened vise. I set it down, tore off my splattered rubber gloves, and reached for my mobile. 'This is unacceptable,' I said. 'That kid should be suspended.'

Hen's eyes widened. 'No. You can't do that.'

'Don't worry, I can be discreet. They can't get away with this.'

'It's the third day of school,' she said. 'Day three of a

seventy-four-day semester. I already don't have any friends. You can't say anything about this. It'll be worse for me if you do.'

My finger hovered over the contact I'd created in my phone's address book, in case I ever needed to reach Hen's school in a hurry. I chewed my lower lip and let the screen go black. 'Hen—' I began, but I didn't know what to say next. I had no idea how to make this go away.

Or how to make her understand I knew exactly how she felt.

Before he was Blake Bram, he'd been Abraham Skilton. My first cousin and Hen's cousin once removed. He had brutalized more than a dozen women, held me captive for eight days, and followed me to the Thousand Islands before going out with a literal bang. There had been no keeping those facts close to the vest, not once the press got ahold of the story and our family was publicly outed as Blake Bram's next of kin. And when that happened, a target had been painted on Hen's back too.

Abraham Skilton was born to Felicia and Brett when I was six months old, still swaddled in a blanket patterned with yellow ducklings that had once belonged to Doug. Abe was sweet as a young child but exceptionally codependent, raised that way by Aunt Fee, who'd suffered crushing anxiety of her own. Later, it was me Abe clung to when his mother spat threats about the dangers lurking right outside the door. He was always steps behind me at school, so close our shadows mingled on cracked sidewalks, playground woodchips, kitchen floors. When I started watching *Murder, She Wrote* with Dad in between reruns of *Columbo*, Abe took an interest in sleuthing too. It wasn't until high school that I understood he'd compensated for the dearth of mysteries in our tiny town by creating crimes of his own.

It wasn't until I was a detective with the NYPD that I learned he'd reinvented himself as a killer.

If Hen had any knowledge of all that, it was rooted in rumor. She never met Abe when he was my strange, controlling cousin or – thank Christ – when he became Blake Bram. My niece was no more responsible for Bram's crimes than I was. But there were people who would always treat us like pariahs, friends of Bram's victims and folks convinced the rotten apple never falls far from the tree. We'd always been a family of outsiders in a way, both the Merchants and the Skiltons acquiring a murky sort

of homegrown fame. The judgment our family endured in
Swanton was thick as woodsmoke, especially now. Not many
New England towns could claim to have birthed a serial killer.
And Hen had hopped from the frying pan straight into the fire.

For a girl who was still molding her identity, trying to understand where she fit in, Bram's life and death and the role I played
in both was harmful beyond measure. I once read that while the
foundation of our personality is laid as early as infancy, it's
the teenage years that stabilize us. What happens when your
world is nowhere near stable and everyone you know associates
you with a sociopath? Hen was living proof of the damage that
could cause, both to a kid's state of mind and to their social life.

I took a step toward her and held her gaze. I hadn't noticed
before, but with her neat white teeth gritted against the pain of
her attack, I saw she was missing a molar. I knew from Doug
this was unusual, a kid her age still losing baby teeth, but Hen's
dentist had affirmed she had a young mouth. The sight of that
child-like gap hit like a reverse punch.

'What Bram did,' I said, 'is as bad as it gets. But that has
nothing – *nothing* – to do with you. People conflate us, people
who don't know the truth, and they look for excuses to punish
us because they can't process this terrible thing. Because there's
no one else left to blame. Those people aren't thinking about
how their actions affect you. The kid who did this' – I waved at
her clothing, the picture on her phone – 'lacks the emotional
intelligence to understand.' *Some*, I thought but didn't say, *don't
even try.*

'Whatever.' Hen didn't wait for me to reply before turning
away and sweeping out the door.

I sighed, tugged a hand through my hair, and looked down at
my fingers; at the paint under my nails and around my cuticles,
specks of white that remained despite routine efforts to scour
them away. The skin on my knuckles was rubbed raw from all
the sanding, and when I made a fist, my finger joints ached.

*This house.* As much as I loved it, it was wrecking me and Tim
both, forever blindsiding us with rotted wood or an unexpected
layer of hidden tile. Always demanding more. After the debacle
with the contractor, we could have tried harder to find help, but
restoration specialists were hard to come by, and there was the

issue of money. Tim was still bound to the cabin, which hadn't sold after a full year on the market. More than once, he'd gone to check on the place and discovered fresh graffiti. There, on the beautiful little home he'd built with his own, strong hands. That Tim had little to do with the bloodbath in his backyard didn't concern the vandals. According to the realtor, there was finally an interested party, a local who wanted to breathe new life into the cottage on Goose Bay. All we could do now was hope the potential buyer didn't come to their senses and pull out.

On more than one occasion, Tim had assured me the challenges we'd faced were simply life's MO. They left us ravaged, but that was temporary. Eventually, inevitably, my hands would be clean again. Henrietta's clothes too.

I didn't disagree. What worried me were the marks that couldn't be seen. That the lead dust Tim worked with would lodge in his lungs and cause cancer, or that we'd inadvertently uncovered asbestos and were breathing it in even now. One day, with any luck, all the trouble the house gave us would be a vague memory. But the aftereffects of this challenge could kill.

I wiped my hands on the thighs of my Carhartts, and turned to face the molding once more.

# SIX

Tim was on call Saturday night, so it was his phone that trilled on the bedside table. Garrick Dupont, the on-duty trooper, kept his voice low on the line, but beside Tim in bed, my bare feet slotted between his own, I caught snatches of the conversation.

'Suspected drowning,' my fiancé confirmed when he hung up, looking somber when he dropped a kiss on my forehead and slid out of our warm nest of a bed.

'ID'd?'

'Not yet.'

I nodded and slumped back against the headboard, knowing I'd be awake for hours now, wondering. Waiting for Tim to come home. I hadn't met everyone in town, not by a long shot, but with the high season over, it was likely the victim was a local. The majority of summer visitors had long since gone home, cable TV ads for sunscreen subbed out for school supplies.

I was contemplating getting up to work on the molding some more when, on the nightstand closest to me, my own phone lit up. A snatch of breeze from the open window snaked across the skin of my cheek. They were summoning us both – Tim to work the case and me to supervise. There was only one reason to bring in an off-duty senior officer at night.

This case was big.

We didn't know much. Garrick, who'd been dispatched to the scene by the 911 center, had reported a suspected drowning out on Devil's Oven Island. A still-warm body found in the night-dark water that couldn't be retrieved in time. We were silent as we slipped on our clothes. Ghosts as we padded past Hen's room and down the hall, careful not to wake her.

And when we got in the car and started to drive toward our docked police boat, Tim reached over the center console to hold my hand.

\*    \*    \*

'The story goes like this,' Tim said on the boat road to the island. 'Bill Johnston, a Canadian American river pirate, smuggler, and War of 1812 privateer, had a price on his head.' He'd been playing both sides, violating neutrality laws and evading the British and United States armies. He'd ordered the looting and destruction of passenger steamer the *Sir Robert Peel*, inciting General Macomb of the US army and British army commander Sir John Colborne to launch a joint expedition to capture Johnston. According to Tim, that's when the pirate, for whom a summer street festival was now named, absconded to the natural cavern that snaked through the center of Devil's Oven Island, purportedly hiding in his rowboat for weeks while his daughter, Kate, kept him in supplies.

It was a tale told on every river tour and ferry ride in the Thousand Islands, and I'd always assumed it was a fib designed to impress customers and eke out bigger tips. Tim had other stories to tell about the island too, ones he knew from personal experience were true. Craggy and uninhabited, yet just a five-minute boat ride from the A-Bay municipal dock, Devil's Oven used to be a popular hangout spot for teens that Tim himself had frequented while in the same high school Hen attended now. The town had since formally banned access, deterring teens from making landfall with a *No Trespassing* sign and *Keep Off* painted on the rocks.

Naturally, the warnings had the opposite effect. An isolated island just minutes from the liquor store? It was a teenage dream. Kids still went there to light bonfires, chug pirated beer, and dive off the cliffs, letting the water swallow them up like the mouth of a whale. Devil's Oven, Tim told me on our approach, got its name because of an anomaly of nature. In the fall, when the water cooled and the air warmed, the cave would fill with mist and steam like a stoked oven.

It was fall now. But what we saw as our boat glided up to the island, barely visible in the moonlight, wasn't steam. It was smoke from a fire.

We had come from the west and the dock where we kept our police boat. The sky over the river wasn't the velvety blue we got most nights but a toxic shade of absinthe green approaching black. Were it not for that wash of orange light visible through the trees, I would have figured the island for deserted.

As we drew closer, the far side revealed itself and a scene emerged, a cluster of boats coming into view.

'Whatever happened,' Tim said, 'looks like it played out by the cave.' He pointed to the activity on the eastern shore, where A-Bay EMS and coast guard response boats bobbed in the water.

'Tell me we don't have to swim for it.' I nodded at the rocks. The edges of the island were steep, almost vertical, inky black water lapping at ragged stone.

'Well, there's no dock, so most visitors drop anchor and get wet. Looks like someone beat us to it.'

A Jet Ski sat abandoned a few yards away.

Devil's Oven, I realized, was smaller than I'd thought. It looked imposing from a distance, but its mass was an illusion born of the mainland that stretched out behind it. In reality, the island was half the length of a city block, all vertical rock with a crown of warped trees just dense enough to conceal trouble.

My gaze trailed up to the fire behind the trees and the flicker of shadow that looked distinctly human.

'Can you let me off? Swing around over there to assess the scene? I think there's still someone up there,' I said.

A uniformed on-duty trooper, the village EMTs, and the coast guard were already on-site. My hope was that Tim could join them, while I secured the island's summit.

By now, I knew my fiancé's face well. I'd learned his expressions like a language, committing each eye crinkle and shift of the jaw to memory. Tim didn't like this plan. But if the first responders had eyes on our victim and I was still seeing movement up above, the crew in the water might have missed a witness – or worse, a second victim. In the grocery store, Tim liked to suggest we split our list. *Divide and conquer.* The strategy made sense now too.

'I'll shout if I need you,' I told him. 'Meet you at the cave in a few.'

'Right,' he said with a tight nod, and navigated the boat up to the shore.

Most of the island was sheer cliff face, but one spot had a natural upward slope about the width of a windowsill that I hoped

to shimmy along while gripping the flat expanse of granite beside
me. It was the same place where someone from town had mounted
the *No Trespassing* sign.

It was my way on to Devil's Oven.

The current was strong so close to the channel. Tim kept the
boat running until we'd nosed up to the rocks, constantly read-
justing his position to avoid a collision. 'You'll have to be quick,'
he said. Under our feet, the boat reared up like a struck horse.

I hoisted myself on to the bow, fighting to keep my balance
as I moved toward the gunwale. 'Ready,' I called, one boot on
the chrome corner cap.

Tim eased the boat closer, I aimed for the rock that looked
most like a step, and I jumped. Tim kicked the boat into reverse
the second I was airborne and, with a roar of the engine, swung
it around toward the rest of the team, leaving me in the dark.

Now that I'd made landfall, Devil's Oven reminded me of
someplace I'd been before. The name arrived like a pounce. *Lone
Rock*. That island was in Lake Champlain, on the Vermont side.
Not far from home. It wasn't meant to be scaled either. That
never stopped me. Lone Rock was famous for its geological
significance. A promontory separated by lake water from a yellow
cliff of dolomite and ancient shale. Lone Rock attracted expert
climbers, photographers, boaters, kids with drones. To us, back
then, it had been a cheap thrill.

I was still thinking about it when I heard a disembodied scream.

Tim was already out of sight around the corner, and I was
alone, pinned against the steep rock. The scream had been close.
Female. I picked up the pace, limbs taut as wire as a second
shriek pierced the night.

It's surprising how quickly people can move when compelled
by the threat of danger, even when it means ascending a rock
wall in the dark. I clambered upward, ignoring the bite of blade-
sharp stones against the flexed heels of my hands. Through the
ring of trees above I could see the flames clearly now, a small
bonfire sending hot orange sparks into the night sky. The clean
river air was replaced with a smell both smoky and sweet. Voices,
light and low, drifted toward me. Laughter too. What the hell
was going on?

When I reached the summit and parted the branches, two

figures came into view. A boy and girl, their bodies a tangle of limbs. Nothing about the girl I saw now spoke of harassment or fear. She was latched on to her companion, legs wrapped around his hips and mouth sealing his while thick blonde curls bobbed against her back. Entwined in the firelight, they looked otherworldly, like inhuman creatures from some dark fairytale. Siren and giant, conjoined in a lurid ritual of power and lust, alliance and revenge.

Slack-jawed, I watched them writhe, and when the boy buried his face in the crook of her neck, she screeched a third time, head thrown back in delight. His eyes were lidded as he groped inexpertly at the cleavage that spilled from her deep-cut top while she tugged at the jeans already slung low on his hips. Hers were movements of intention. But her cunning smile fell away like a rock dropped in the river when she spotted me.

Shoving the boy off of her, she scrambled to her feet.

'What the fuck? Were you *watching* us?'

'Who the hell are you?' the boy added, knocked off-balance as he attempted to zip up his jeans.

'What's going on here?'

What I saw made no sense. Nothing about the scene spoke of a fatal accident in the night, but we'd received a distress call from this island. There were multiple rescue boats just beyond the trees, yet it looked for all the world like this couple thought they were alone. The empty beer cans strewn about the fire, dozens of them, suggested otherwise. Had there been others here earlier in the evening? Where were they now? Based on their glassy eyes and sloppy expressions, it was clear these two were drunk, or high, or both. Did they really have no idea what was going on down by the cave? My confusion was heightened when the girl pushed back her hair and I felt a tingle of recognition. I was looking at Mia Klinger.

That was how she'd introduced herself in the summer, this curvy girl with starlet hair and a full face of makeup, meticulously applied. I'd met Mia because her family owned a business that gave ghost tours of so-called haunted hotels and businesses in town. They'd had an issue over Fourth of July with a tourist who reported a stolen wallet immediately following one of the Klingers' tours. I'd interviewed both the girl and her mother, and marveled over Mia's mature looks even then. Memories of my own face at that age were scattershot, the trifling moments of my youth forced out by bigger, badder things, but no way had I ever resembled this girl, with her pristine skin and bee-stung lips. Mia was Instagram-perfect, down to her tinsel-fine highlights in a dazzling shade of gold.

'Mia, right?' I said. 'Do you remember me?'

She blinked, looking more closely now. 'You're Shana Merchant.'

'That's right. I'm a senior investigator with the New York State Police. Were you the one who called for help?'

'Shana Merchant,' the boy repeated, his mouth slack. He was the opposite of Mia in every way: tall and muscled, with dark hair and copper skin. His eyes widened as he said, 'No fucking way.'

I wasn't unfamiliar with this reaction. My reputation preceded me. Still, the boy's expression didn't match the ones I usually saw. There was no consternation or dark curiosity in his gaze. What I saw instead was undisguised awe.

'What happened out here tonight?' I asked, glancing around.

'*See?*' Mia told the boy, looking triumphant. 'And look. Here she is.'

'Do you know about the accident?' I asked. 'We got a call—'

'We didn't do anything wrong.' Stumbling backward, tripping over a rock, the boy raised his hands.

'The accident,' I repeated. *Suspected drowning. No ID.*

'What accident?' asked Mia, tilting her head.

'Do your parents know you're out here?'

She shrugged. 'My dad lives in Rhode Island, and Tristan's mom's in prison.'

I looked to the boy for confirmation. He only stared.

'Shana!' Tim burst through the trees, his mouth falling open at the sight of the couple, the boy's belt still dangling from his jeans like a tire-flattened snake. 'You better get down there.'

'This is Tim Wellington,' I told the young couple. 'He's a plainclothes detective, and you're staying right here with him until I get back. We need details – age, address. Full names and phone numbers. We'll need to call your parents. Don't you know this island's off-limits?'

The kids watched Tim with wary eyes as he pulled a notebook

from the pocket of his State Police jacket. The boy's expression had finally morphed from astonishment to fear, but still I felt his eyes dart toward me as I pushed through the trees.

It was dark away from the fire, and I used my flashlight to illuminate my path. Unlike in the clearing, the ground here was littered with branches, tangles of brush punching up from soil that was packed between plates of stone. There was no trail to speak of, but I knew where I was going. *Down.* Somewhere below me was the cave, and the scene I'd been called to investigate.

My footfalls, muffled by moss and the carpet of pine needles twisting between the rocks, were accompanied by the murmur of voices. Male this time – and getting closer. Had the first responders really not seen the kids on the summit? How could they have missed the fire? I kept the beam of my flashlight on the sloped terrain, thinking about my conversation with Mia and the boy. If they didn't know about an accident, if they hadn't been the ones to call for help, then who had?

And who was in the water?

In my two years with the New York State Police's Bureau of Criminal Investigation, I'd made it around to dozens of the islands. It was important to familiarize myself with the area, and I'd learned early on that no two islands were alike. Whether large public communities or one-acre properties owned by a single family for a century or more, each had a unique topography and its share of challenges, be it an island's distance from the mainland or shallow-rooted trees that were easily felled by storms. As far as I knew, Devil's Oven had never housed a residence, though Tim had told me there was once a gazebo here. No one seemed sure who had built it or what purpose it served. In terms of topography, it was clear what set this place apart, and now I saw it for myself. The cave.

Its entrance loomed a few feet below me, a black crevice that cleaved the east-facing rock wall. Bobbing in the water nearby was the coast guard boat, and next to that, a Guardian-series Boston Whaler dive boat with *State Trooper* in metallic blue letters on a thick black stripe. Help had come from the east then, straight to the cave. They might not have seen Mia and her friend. EMS had their backs to me, and as I contemplated how to get down to the crevice, I heard another sound. It was the quivering voice of someone crying, and it was coming from inside the cave.

Steeling myself, I jammed my fingers into the cracks in the stone and lowered my body over the cliff edge. It was only eight feet or so down to the water, but I didn't want to take the plunge at night.

As I repositioned my hands and shifted lower, the echoey voice grew louder. Stretching, I felt the toes of my boots meet the rock at the mouth of the cave.

'Shana, over here.'

Garrick, the trooper who'd called me and Tim, noticed me making my descent. His voice sounded grim, but I didn't turn around to face him, not yet, because something had stopped me in my tracks. There was a kid inside the sliver of cave, crouched low. Feet in the water, back pressed to the cold stone wall. My mouth went dry when I saw her, and my hands started to shake.

It was Hen.

# SEVEN

'I am never fucking having kids.'

Those were my brother's exact words almost eighteen years ago, after our midnight jaunt to Lone Rock. It wasn't that Doug thought he'd make a shit dad, but he'd witnessed the nonsense teens could get up to.

And those teens had included me.

There were five of us that night: my brother and me, a nameless boy who loved the Tragically Hip, Doug's latest love interest, and Suze. It had been Suze's idea to go, and I couldn't say no to my brave, beautiful friend, even though I suspected even then that our relationship, built on chaos, wouldn't last. We'd gone to visit my brother in Burlington, where Doug was working for the summer before returning to UVM, and spent the evening at North Beach drinking canned beer and pink wine coolers Doug's friend called *lame*. All of that had been Suzuka's idea too. It was two years before she and I would graduate high school and go our separate ways. One year before I got my scar.

There was just enough light on the wooded trail that I could see the back of my brother's head. I could hear him too, sneakers scuffing the dusty earth, the occasional thump when Doug stumbled on a wayward root. *Don't take the path that forks to the right*, he'd warned before we set out, *unless you wanna swan dive off a hundred-foot cliff.* I'd stuck close to him after that. Up ahead, laughter. An errant, nervous giggle from one of the girls, and the frenzied movement of light from the only flashlight we had. We were getting close.

'No way in hell,' was what Doug said when Suze first suggested we go to Lone Rock, his eyes on the silhouetted headland beside North Beach. We all knew about the man who'd plunged seven stories to his death at nearby Red Rocks, along with the tales of blunt-force trauma and shattered spines. But Suze had already decided. For us. For me.

I watched Doug's freckled face as he assessed the situation.

His sixteen-year-old sister was planning something incredibly stupid. Suze and I were foreigners in Doug's college-age world, hangers-on out to impress; if she jumped, I jumped too. And there was something else. In the set of Doug's mouth, I sensed a trace of relief that I was here in Burlington with him and Suze rather than back home in Swanton with Abe. To him, anything was better for me than spending time with our cousin – even this. We'd all visited Lone Rock before, summer after summer, the ensuing adrenaline rush like a drug. Never before had we come at night.

I had nearly blacked out in the dark water by the time something grabbed my leg with a savagery that shocked me conscious, and then I was on the move, water dragging against my thighs, dry night air on my face. My brother's curses ringing in my ears.

Doug drove me all the way back to Swanton that night while Suze snored inelegantly in the back seat of his beat-up Honda Civic. It took both of us to rouse and coax her through the front door of her parents' house, and it didn't escape our attention that the light was on in Mr and Mrs Weppler's bedroom upstairs. Our own parents weren't waiting up when I got home, even though they'd warned me not to stay out past midnight, warned Doug to keep me – still a child fresh off my sophomore year of high school – safe. Whether they trusted we'd stick to our promises or they were gathering their strength for an epic scolding in the morning, I didn't know, but in my memory, their inevitable wrath was of no more concern to me than a bug bite or scratch from an unseen branch. All I could think about was my time in the water, and how close we'd come to the kind of trouble even my big brother couldn't make right. In my mind, it was just me and Doug at the lake, in the car, easing open the back door. Holding our breath and saying a prayer that the hinges wouldn't creak while a heady perfume of sand and algae clung to our skin.

'I am never fucking having kids,' my brother hissed when we parted ways in the hall, and I knew why. He was imagining what life would have been like for our folks if, that night in the lake, I'd been snatched away. My mother often accused us of trying to send her to an early grave, and I couldn't blame her. My behavior had been tremendously reckless. No concern for the ones waiting at home at all.

What happened at Lone Rock was worse than all the parties and drinking and teenage nonsense that followed, because if I'd drowned under Doug's watch? That would have killed him too.

She'd been in her bed – I was sure of it. Safe and warm at home. Yet here she was, soaked to her frail bones, huddled in a cave on an island.

'Hen?' I gasped in a rush of breath, and she looked up at me, her face a mess of emotions, rivulets of mascara streaking her cheeks. We'd made a plan to get breakfast at the diner in the morning. Spend a lazy Sunday together, maybe even teach her how to drive Tim's boat. How the hell had Hen gotten out *here*?

All at once, I understood. She'd snuck out. Hen had come here to meet Mia and the boy from the fire to . . . what? Drink? Have unprotected sex? Jump off a cliff?

Since Wednesday, when she'd come home spattered with fake blood and we'd talked a little, Hen's mood had improved. I'd kept my word and refrained from calling the school, and maybe it had paid off; it seemed like she'd turned a corner, thanking Tim for his dinners, even doling out the occasional smile. Now here she was, miles from her bed on a forbidden island in the black of night. Crouched on a bed of shimmery stones. They were mollusk shells, I realized as I adjusted my weight and felt them crunch beneath my boots, their tender clam and mussel meat long since devoured by muskrats or mink. Discarded and abandoned here in the dank cavern.

*Suspected drowning.*

Was my niece the missing person we'd been called to find? Was this another cruel cafeteria trick? Had Mia and her friend brought Hen here on the pretense of inviting her to party, only to push her into the water?

Was this some kind of sick punishment for being related to Bram?

'What's going on here?' I said, my voice low and urgent as my fingers roamed her face, arms, legs for signs of injury. 'What happened? How did you get out here?' Both my car and Tim's had been in the driveway. As far as we knew, Hen had no friends. But hadn't I noticed her eyes zing to her phone last night at dinner? There had been a row of notifications there, the tiny

white-and-yellow logo I knew from J.C. meant she was getting
messages through Snapchat. Had these kids been the ones who
were contacting Hen? Nothing made sense.

'Hen.' I gave her a shake, relief and fury colliding with enough
force to leave me winded. From the corner of my eye, I could
see the boats. Two EMTs huddled next to a coxswain and
officer on the coast guard vessel, the largest of the water crafts.
They were looking down at something. 'Hen,' I said again. 'Talk
to me.'

Her voice was a croak. 'He's dead.'

'What?'

'Dead,' she moaned, a terrible refrain. Her breath smelled sour
and hoppy.

A trickle of fear snaked down my spine.

'Who? Hen, *who?*' But she was silent and hollow-eyed, her
small mouth yawning into a silent wail.

'Stay here,' I commanded, releasing her. 'Don't move – you
understand?'

Turning to face the water, I picked my way down the stones
toward the river's edge. When I locked the beam of my flashlight
on the boat, two heads jerked upward. Two others, belonging to
the EMTs, stayed down, and so did Garrick's. The trooper was
on his knees, his head hanging heavy in a way that reminded me
of overripe fruit left to rot on the branch of a tree.

I plunged my boot off the rocks and waded into the cold St
Lawrence. I could feel the current even now, grabbing at my pant
legs. Jostling me forward and back.

'Hey!' I called, waving at the coxswain.

'Coming around!'

He steadied himself as he brought the bow of the boat close
to shore, and I waded farther out to meet him. Clutched the arm
that was thrust over the side and hoisted myself on board. Before
making landfall, Tim had tied our boat up to the State Police
vessel, which was next to the coast guard.

On the floor of the boat lay a boy. Another boy, different from
the one I'd seen with Mia, and I knew at once that Hen was
right. The kid's eyes were glazed, and he wasn't moving, his
arms loose as tossed coils of dock line. A hank of sandy hair
concealed one eye, his slack lips a terrible shade of blue. Even

so, one medic was doing compressions on the boy's chest while
the other worked the bag-valve mask. They would keep trying
to resuscitate him until they got to the hospital, though it
looked to be too late.

'Could have been under for twenty minutes,' Garrick said
thickly, deep-set eyes like empty holes under the ledge of his
pronounced brow. He was one of our newer state troopers, but
Garrick had kids of his own, and the pain of the discovery
had slackened his features and dulled his skin to the color of
bonfire ash. He cradled the boy's skull in his hands as though
protecting it from the boat's tumbled knocks. As if it wasn't far
too late for that. 'She says that's how long he was gone before
she realized and came looking,' he told me, nodding in the
direction of the island.

*She* being Henrietta. My head swam. 'Christ, he looks young.
Do we know who he is yet?'

'She isn't talking much,' the coast guard officer said. *Hen
again*. 'She refused to leave the cave.'

Garrick said, 'I haven't had a chance to question the others.'

So he did know about Mia and her friend.

'You found him in the water?' I asked as I watched the EMT
hold his fingers to the boy's carotid artery where a pulse should
have been. Hopeful. Hopeless.

The coxswain gave the signal, and the EMTs prepared to
transport the victim to the mainland. Together, Garrick and I
clambered off the boat and watched the coast guard rush back
to shore.

'By the time we got here she'd already found him,' Garrick
explained once we were back on the State Police vessel. 'Dragged
him out of the water herself. We brought him on to the boat.
Easier to treat him there than on shore, with the steep terrain
around that cave. There's a head wound. We think maybe he
jumped . . .' His voice trailed off.

'You said *she* was dragging him?'

Garrick nodded.

Hen had tried to rescue this boy. She'd been the one to call
911. Why hadn't she reached out to me? She must have known
I could rally the troops just as fast as dispatch. And why was
Hen the one pulling the victim from the river? The boy I'd seen

on the summit was three times her size. Even Mia Klinger had twenty pounds on my niece. But they'd stayed by the fire, ostensibly oblivious to what was happening by the cave. Why hadn't Hen called for help?

'The coast guard should spend more time patrolling this place,' Garrick said, solemn. 'An uninhabited island this close to town? It's a magnet for kids. Trouble. Then again, these kids should know better than to swim out here at night. Where the hell are the parents?'

*Snug in their beds while a cool September breeze rustles the curtains.* It had been the same for my own parents, decades prior, the night Doug and I went to Lone Rock. I knew what the trooper was thinking. The parents were at fault here too. They hadn't been paying attention.

And neither had I.

'I need to get back to the cave.'

'Hope you can get some answers out of that one,' said Garrick. 'The boy's family is gonna want to know what happened here.'

I took a breath. 'That one is my niece.'

'No shit?' He made a face and said, 'Maybe she'll talk to you then. Clammed right up when we asked for details.'

'Did an EMT check her out?'

'No time.'

I nodded and glanced at the cave, but it was too dark, Hen's figure fused to the shadows.

It was a struggle to get off the boat and back into the water, and I was terrified Hen might not be there when I arrived. I didn't need an EMT to tell me she was in shock, with that rapid breathing and pupils the size of bar-top coasters. There was a good chance she was drunk too.

'Hen, listen to me,' I said. 'I need you to tell me what happened.'

She began to rock, arms locked around her bent legs.

'The boy,' I said. 'Who is he?'

A shake of the head. She wouldn't look at me.

'You need to talk to me.' I scraped a damp hand through my hair. 'Jesus, Hen, you shouldn't even be out here.'

'I saw him,' she whispered, the words little more than a breath.

'Saw him where?' I asked. 'Was he swimming?'

'I pulled him out, but I couldn't . . . he wasn't . . .'

'Did you see what happened to him? *Hen?*'

My niece's eyes were dark in the half-light, her head turned in the direction of the mainland. Of home.

'Please,' she said, desperate now, those dark eyes suddenly locked on mine. 'He's my boyfriend.'

# EIGHT

Tim found me in the kitchen the next morning, banging cupboard doors like I was trying to wake the dead. I didn't notice him until I felt the heat of his chest against my back, his arms skimming the base of my ribs as they pulled my body close.

It had been a fitful night, my dreams shot through with horrible images. Mia Klinger, grinning like a deranged clown. A pallid body hauled from the river. When I got in close for a look, it wasn't the boy's face I saw but Henrietta's, her dark eyes wide and unseeing, lips unbearably slack. I started toward her through water thick as sludge, the distance between us widening with every passing second. My T-shirt was still damp with sweat.

Tim had it even worse. While I took Henrietta to the hospital, both to get her checked out and for a physician's report on the victim, Tim and Garrick had handled the death notification, one of the hardest of Tim's career. As it turned out, the boy, whose name was Leif Colebrook – Tim finally got a straight answer out of Mia Klinger – was the only child of a widower who'd lost his wife five years prior. When Tim told me about it later, once he'd finally dragged himself back to the house and into bed, he confessed that he and Garrick had to prop Ford Colebrook up when the man learned his son, the only remaining member of his family, was gone.

'There's coffee,' I murmured as Tim nibbled my ear and uttered a moan of pleasure that could have been about the coffee, my body, or both. From behind me, he ran his fingers over the seam in my cheek, a little fainter after a summer of weekends spent on the boat. Whenever my ex used to touch my scar, the mark left by Abe before he was Bram, I always flinched. Carson's fingertips had felt like hot pokers searing my skin, but Tim's touch was comforting and cool, and I melted into it.

A week ago, that touch would have led me to trip my fingers down the hollow of his stomach and lead him back to bed. We would have discarded a trail of clothing in our wake like impatient teenagers desperate to get each other naked before getting found out. Now, the image disturbed me. We had a teenager in the house, a sullen, grief-stricken girl who moved with a feline's crafty silence. It was likely she was still asleep, so emotionally drained not even a tanker ship's horn could rouse her. *My boyfriend*, she'd said. So little time had passed since Hen had arrived in town. How could she have a boyfriend already?

How could he be dead?

It was chillier outside this morning and the wind whipped the river into a choppy lather, causing the glass in our hundred-year-old windows to creak and hiss. I shivered a little as I looked out, grateful I'd thrown a cardigan over my tank top and plaid flannel pants. I turned around to accept a single heady kiss.

'It's the worst kind of lesson,' Tim said as he nuzzled my nose with his own and brought the coffee to his lips. 'So many tragedies are senseless, but this . . . folks around here will use it as a cautionary tale for the rest of their lives.'

He was right. Leif Colebrook's death would haunt the town for years to come. Parents and guardians would feel compelled to warn their children that bad decisions could result in an accident like Leif's – especially the parents and guardians of the kids who'd known him. My mind went to Aunt Fee, and I wondered if parents in Vermont used Abe as a cautionary tale too. No one would ever know how much Fee's mental-health struggles had impacted my cousin's personality and behavior, or the extent to which her parenting had distorted his moral code, but there were many who held her responsible for creating Blake Bram.

With Hen mixed up in Leif's death, I couldn't help but feel the way I handled this could impact the kid's whole life.

I said, 'I have to talk to Doug and Josie.'

Hen had been with us a week. Not only had we failed to rein her in, but she'd gotten into the most dangerous situation of her young life – and on my watch. She'd been given a clean bill of health, but it was also clear she was deeply traumatized. My brother had entrusted me with the person most precious to him in the world, and in my role as proxy parent, I'd proven to be utterly incompetent.

'This isn't your fault,' Tim assured me as he gave my arm a

squeeze and backed out of the room. 'You can't watch her every second. They'll understand.'

Pulling in a steadying breath, I flashed him a tired smile and dialed my brother.

'Sis, hey. All good there? I was going to check in for an update. Josie told Hen to call us every day, but of course that hasn't happened. Good thing she's got an overprotective aunt, right?'

'Right,' I said, biting down on my lower lip. I've never been good at hiding things from my big brother. Maybe because he blazed the trail to adulthood, making all the same mistakes as me but doing it first, the guy could read me like a street sign. I'd managed to fool my parents on the regular, but Doug could always sniff out trouble from a single word wrapped in a whisper of fear and doubt, and one word was all it took now for him to grow wary.

'Everything *is* good, yeah?' he said slowly. 'Hen's OK?'

'Hen's OK.' Let him spot the lie if he could. Our conversation was about to get a lot harder, and I needed him at ease for as long as possible.

'Doug, listen,' I said. 'Something happened last night. Tim and I, we're still trying to understand exactly what went down, but I'm going to tell you what we know, OK?' And I did. I explained that Hen had snuck out to a dangerous place with a group of veritable strangers, and that the escapade had resulted in the drowning of a young man who, somehow, Hen believed to be her boyfriend.

Unlike me and Doug, Hen had grown up in the water. She'd undergone lifeguard training, and I had a vague memory that, last summer, she'd been instrumental in saving a toddler's life at the community pool. Historically, Hen was competent and strong, but now I told Doug about her mood and state of mind on the island, how she'd folded in on herself like one of those paper fortune tellers Suze and I used to make from notebook pages, labeling each origami diamond with colors, numbers, futures: you will go on a dream date, you will meet your soulmate, you will fall in love. Henrietta's own fortune was undecided, her future in a state of flux.

My brother was known to get angry. Shout expletives, voice

throaty and sputtering, and wave his arms like a madman while he put me in my place. He always ran out of steam eventually, and we talked rationally then. I understood how Doug processed emotions. This time, I wasn't at all sure what to expect.

'Jesus.' By the hitch in his breath, I could tell he was pacing. Probably running a shaky hand through his hair as adrenaline flooded his bloodstream and filled him with an overpowering urge to escape the horror I had just unleashed on him. 'And she's not talking?' he said. 'What does that *mean*?'

'The doctor at the hospital told me it's shock. Temporary.' God, how I wanted that to be true.

'OK,' Doug said at length in the voice reserved for serious matters, most of which involved reining me in or cleaning up my mess. 'Wow, I don't even know what to say. Is Hen there? Can I talk to her? A kid her age, dead. She must be terrified.'

I said, 'She's still sleeping. It was a late night. But I can have her call as soon as she's up.' I hoped I wasn't overpromising. Would Hen be talking when she woke up? I had no idea.

'Right. Of course.'

'But, Doug,' I said, running the pad of my thumb over the rim of my mug, 'she's getting bullied at school – worse, I think, than in Swanton. I should have told you sooner, but I thought I could handle it. It seemed to be getting better.' And now, this.

Doug went silent, his mood unreadable on the line. What was he thinking? Did he blame me for Hen's behavior? Doug's daughter could have been killed, and it had happened on my watch. At home in Vermont, she'd been miserable and misbehaved, but at least she'd been safe.

'Does she . . .' Doug began, floundering. 'What does she want to do?'

That was the question. 'I don't know yet. But I'm guessing . . . if it was me, at that age,' I said, 'I'd want to come home.'

That was how I'd always felt staying over at Abe's, when things got scary. No one lost a life, not while I was there, but my aunt and uncle fought with the commitment of people in mortal combat, all or nothing, do or die. Aunt Fee and Uncle Brett would bellow at each other while my cousin Crissy screamed bloody murder about something as inane as being told she had a curfew, and Abe and I burrowed deeper under the covers behind the safety of his closed door. Needless to say, my sleepovers at the Skilton house were few and far between.

Silence on the line. I wondered where Josie was just then, tried to imagine what *her* reaction would be when Doug – tag, you're it – unloaded the mind-bending news.

'So you'll have her call us?' Doug said. 'Right away?'

'Soon as she's up, I promise. She'll be OK,' I told him through clamped teeth.

*She has to be.*

# NINE

Death pulls a cowl over a place with skeleton fingers dragging in the darkness with ease. The loss of a local is inescapable in a small town, dominating every moment, conversation, thought. But the death of a child is even worse. Loss of life that profound can smother so completely that an entire community is left gasping for air.

Such was the case when word got out that Leif Colebrook, age seventeen, had drowned at Devil's Oven Island. On a Sunday morning in September, while leaves reddened on their branches and locals poured their morning coffees, the residents of A-Bay tapped screens and shook open papers to receive the news. I was willing to bet that by the time the village's four churches flung open their doors, organ hymns bleeding into the street to beckon parishioners, there wouldn't be a person in Alexandria Bay who didn't know the Colebrook Boy was dead.

There's a protocol for sharing information about a crime, and it starts with Larisa Ruthers. As the region's public information officer, it was always Larisa who channeled our cases to the media and advised them on which details they could release. She organized press conferences and delivered updates while reporters snapped photos of the PIO in her trooper uniform, slate gray apart from the tan hat. Larisa covered seven counties, from Jefferson to Lewis, Oneida and Oswego, but the woman had a way of conveying deep regret while remaining a dry-eyed figure of authority. An autopsy had been scheduled, but Leif's death, she told the media, was being ruled an accidental drowning.

Drinking still more coffee with Tim, fielding impatient texts from Doug while waiting for Hen to wake up, there was nothing to do but look into the kids she'd been with the previous night and try to make sense of how my niece had gone from bullied loner to party girl in a matter of days. I rarely went on social media and always felt like a creep when I did, but the other three teens were easy to find on Instagram, and all had public accounts. While Leif's and Tristan's appeared to be placeholders, displaying a handful of photos that spanned several years, Mia's Insta was an open window into the kid's life. Even so, it came as a shock when I looked at her story, an ephemeral post that vanishes from the platform in twenty-four hours, and saw Hen's face. The photo had been taken on the island – same flickering amber firelight, same wall of trees. Mia's post was timestamped, time counting down to the moment Instagram would make the image disappear. I snapped a screenshot and saved it to my phone. At 12:30, Mia had taken a selfie with Tristan, Hen, and Leif, and I suspected she'd inadvertently captured one of the last moments of a young man's life.

It had been past three by the time I got Hen to bed, and though I had a lot of questions about what happened, I hadn't wanted to push her. But it was morning now, and somewhere else in town, Leif's father was suffering the most anguished moments of his life. Tim and I would need to make sense of this somehow. Give the man some answers and hope it eased his pain.

On the surface, the incident appeared easy enough to explain: Leif and Hen had gone swimming in secret, and the boy – drunk, disoriented by the dark water – got into trouble. Hen had tried to help, but her efforts came too late. It was, as Tim had put it, a senseless tragedy, and Hen had been in the wrong place at the wrong time.

When I looked closer at the story my mind had conjured, though, I saw it was shot through with holes. The river still hovered around sixty degrees, warm enough to swim in if you were hardy, but at night it got much colder. I'd checked, and it had dropped to fifty-one degrees the previous night. Neither kid had brought a towel or change of clothes. The ride back to the mainland, however short, would be miserable for someone drenched and shivering. Even drunk, even on a dare, swimming was unthinkably stupid.

Then there was the wound on Leif's head. We'd know more after the autopsy, but the physician at the hospital, who'd made his own fruitless attempts to revive Leif, said the laceration looked consistent with the island's rocks. Like maybe Leif had fallen.

Or, possibly, jumped.

Even more confusing was the Jet Ski we'd seen bobbing just offshore, which Tim found out had been driven by Tristan Laurier. According to Tim, four to a Sea-Doo didn't work. It was Tristan's brother's Jet Ski, and Tristan had given Mia, along with Hen, a ride – but both kids insisted Leif was already on the island when they got there. There had been no second personal watercraft though. No other boat either. Someone had dropped Leif off and failed to come back for him, and until Hen started talking, we had no idea who it was.

'This could get complicated,' Tim said now, idly eyeing the doorframes. There was so much more sanding to be done.

'She was found with the body,' I said. 'If anyone knows how this happened, it's her.'

Hen had willfully snuck out, traveled to an abandoned island and been involved in activities that had resulted in the death of a minor. But as the apparent only witness to a tragic accident, a scenario we couldn't reconstruct without her help, she had a chance to redeem herself.

'It's almost eleven.' Tim got to his feet, inspecting the molding up close. He'd already thrown on his work clothes, a paint-splattered shirt with faded jeans so holey I could see straight through to his boxers. 'Want me to come with you?'

Tim had more experience with kids, and more of an affinity for them too. Hen was my niece though, and I had Doug and Josie to think of.

'I'll be OK,' I told him, heading for the staircase. 'Wish me luck.'

Henrietta's bedroom smelled of artificial pineapple along with something foul and oniony that made me think of high-school gym class. On her pillow, a spray of greenish hair fanned out like beached seaweed. The girl was a faceless, unmoving mass.

I lowered myself on to the bed and lay a hand on the lump I thought must be her shoulder. *She's breathing.* It was my first thought, though there was no logic to it. Of course she was breathing. Why wouldn't she be? That dream though. The sight of Leif's body. I suppressed a shudder.

'Hen,' I said softly. 'Hen. Wake up.'

Nothing.

'Honey,' I tried, 'are you OK?'

'Go away.'

Her voice was a wet croak. Had she been in here crying all night? All alone? It hadn't occurred to me to check in sooner. What kind of aunt was I?

With a flexed palm, I drew jerky circles on the dune that was her back. 'I know last night was really hard,' I said, 'and so, so awful. What happened, what you saw, it's a lot. I just need to know you're OK – and not just me. Your parents too. They're worried. They want to talk to you.'

'I don't want to talk to anyone.'

My gaze trailed to the window by her bed and the river that roiled outside. It always amazed me how quickly the seasons wheeled by. A few days ago, it had been sunny and warm, and I'd stood on the patio drinking coffee without my coat. Fall was here now in earnest, Hen's room too cool. I envied her those blankets.

'Just . . . say hi,' I coaxed. 'Let them hear your voice. Then you can go back to bed.' Would that be confirmation enough for Josie and Doug that Hen wasn't mid-mental breakdown? I honestly had no idea.

When she didn't move, I took out my phone. Doug had texted twice more in the past five minutes. *Josie's losing it over here – she's minutes from getting in the car and driving over.*

I believed it. A four-hour drive would be nothing to a mother desperate to know her child was OK. Part of me was surprised they hadn't left already. It had been more than two hours since I talked to Doug. What were they waiting for? *Hit the road. Bring the kid home.*

'Your parents,' I said. 'They're coming to get you.' It hadn't been decided, not officially, but I couldn't see the situation going any other way. 'Do you want to wait? Talk to them once they're here?'

Hen went very still. Deep under the covers, her voice was too soft and muffled to hear.

'Hen? Should I tell them—'

'Tell them not to come.'

She pulled the blankets from her face and lurched upright. Eyes puffy. Nose shiny. She'd definitely been crying, but now my niece looked at me with an intensity I hadn't seen in her before.

'I'm fine,' she said, flattening her hair with her palms and sucking in a breath. 'I'll talk to them. OK? I don't want to go home. I can stay, right? Shana? I can stay?'

As I stared at her, stunned, my niece's head began to bob.

'I'm not going home,' she said, not waiting for my answer. 'I'm staying right here.'

# TEN

Dori Wellington and her long-time partner, Courtney, lived fifteen minutes away, in a Cape Cod-style home near the water. I always looked forward to visiting Tim's mom and stepmother's house, with its vibrant colors and cooking smells and so many monstera plants the place looked like Jumanji, every room a steamy jungle wonderland.

Dori was out when I arrived, getting groceries to make Ford Colebrook a meal along with half the other women in town, but it was Courtney I'd come to see. She'd heard the news too, and her eyes were the color of blood in water, stripes of crimson threading out from tear ducts plump from overuse.

She knew better than to ask for details about the accident, but Courtney listened intently as I explained what had been going on with Hen.

'I'm so sorry, Shana – I had no idea,' she said when I got to the part about the ketchup, pushing her silky straight hair behind her ear. 'I guess Hen wouldn't have thought to come to me about it. To her, I'm still a stranger.'

Courtney and Hen had met, just a brief hello before the start of school, the idea being that Hen would see at least one familiar face when she walked the halls. Tim's stepmother, who worked as the front office secretary, had assured us she'd watch out for my niece, and I could see how much the bullying upset her.

'Don't take it personally,' I said. 'Hen didn't even come to *me*. I had to pry the story out of her, and Leif's death is still a big fat question mark.'

'But she was there when it happened. That poor, poor girl. How's she doing?'

'Honestly? I don't know. I thought for sure she'd want to go home, but she doesn't. She begged us all to let her stay.'

I'd been shocked by how little pushback she got from Josie and Doug about that. I had a hard time putting myself in their shoes, imagining what I'd do in their place, but a kid had died

right in front of their daughter. I found it odd that they'd agreed
to Hen's request, and even odder that they hadn't driven straight
over to comfort her. Hen was fragile. In a delicate state. If her
parents weren't going to make her go back, I certainly couldn't
force her out the door.

'I think it may have something to do with the boyfriend thing,'
I told Courtney. 'If she cared about this boy, it might be hard to
imagine leaving town.'

'What boyfriend thing?'

'Last night, she told me Leif Colebrook was her boyfriend.'

'Oh. Really? But Leif was a senior.'

'I know. I'm as surprised as you are. I don't really understand
how it could have happened so fast. Regardless, Hen's a wreck.
We can't get a word out of her about that, but she called him
her boyfriend. I'm just hoping she can shed some light on things
for the father.'

'God,' Courtney said. 'As if that poor man hasn't been through
enough.'

'Do you know the Colebrooks well?' I asked.

Courtney brushed her long hair over her shoulder. Since I'd
known her, it had alternated between the strawberry gold of a
peach ring candy and salt-water-taffy-lavender striped with white,
but for the moment she was back to her natural color – a soft,
sandy blonde much like Leif's. I made a mental note to tell Hen
about Courtney's habits when – if – things quieted down.
Experimenting with hair color was something they had in common.

'I know them a little,' Courtney told me. 'Mostly because of
Geena, Leif's mom. She passed away, a few years ago now.'

Tim had mentioned that. First the man lost his wife, and now
this? I couldn't fathom it. 'What happened?' I asked.

'Diving accident. The Colebrooks have a dive business here
in town. Ford takes tourists down to shipwrecks in the area.'

'Even now?'

Courtney nodded. I could tell she was trying not to judge, but
we were both thinking the same thing. Wondering how a man
who'd lost his wife to scuba diving could continue to plunge into
the river.

'Did that interest extend to Leif? I'm wondering how
comfortable he was in the water.'

'You're asking if Leif could swim. I should think so,' she said, but I knew that living in close proximity to water didn't always guarantee a love of swimming, boating, diving. Even when it ran in the family. 'What I can tell you for certain is that the boy struggled the year he lost his mother. His grades slipped, he started skipping school . . . we had several administrative meetings about him to brainstorm ways to help. His poor father was too distraught to be of much help. Did you meet him? To break the news?'

'Tim delivered the death notification,' I said, 'while I stayed with Hen.'

'Imagine losing everything that matters to you in the span of five years, going from happy family to lone survivor. It's gut-wrenching,' Courtney said. 'Leif was doing so much better too. His grades were up, and he was applying to colleges.'

'Maybe it was the stress of all that,' I said. 'He was letting off steam. Or else it was just a bad decision. A night with friends gone wrong.'

'And you said Henrietta's been hanging around with Mia Klinger and Tristan Laurier?'

'Far as I can tell. They were out there with her on the island last night. Uh-oh,' I said when Courtney pinched her lower lip between her teeth. 'I don't like that look.'

Tim's stepmother sighed. 'It's just, neither of them is the best influence. Mia's a little strange. She lives alone with her mother, who runs the ghost tour in town. You must have heard about that.'

'I have,' I said. 'So she's into haunted houses. Sounds harmless enough.'

'She's into a lot of things – not all of them are harmless. Mia was suspended in the spring,' said Courtney. 'Five days of sitting in the main office as penance for her crime. Apparently, she wasn't ready for midterms, and took it upon herself to postpone them. There was a swatting incident. That's what they're calling it now. Mia phoned in a fake bomb threat to the school. Shut the whole place down for an entire day so she could blow off her exams.'

'I heard about that.' We'd dispatched several troopers to help the village police search the school. Law enforcement took threats like that very seriously. 'That was Mia, huh?' The idea that a kid Hen's age could have orchestrated such an elaborate and disturbing ruse slicked my insides with oil. Knowing what she'd pulled at school, I couldn't help but wonder if Mia had a hand in the wallet theft I'd investigated in the summer.

'What else do I need to know about this girl? Please don't tell me she's the local dealer.'

'No drug use, at least not that I'm aware of. But she's not your only problem. Tristan's been suspended twice for fighting.'

This was getting worse and worse. 'In school?'

'In the halls, and on the grounds. Tristan lives with a much older brother who came through the A-Bay school system too. Charles Laurier. Nice young man. Not sure where the father ended up, but I believe their mother's serving time at the correctional facility in Watertown. Charles is raising Tristan now, but it hasn't been easy.'

When my eyebrows lifted, she gave a sad nod. 'Poor boy hasn't had a very stable life. The superintendent could never prove it, but there was some speculation he might have been involved in that swatting business with Mia.'

'And Leif?' I hated to ask, but if the deceased associated with troublemakers and had a history of risky behavior, it might explain how he drowned.

'Leif was a good kid,' Courtney said without hesitation, 'and older than Mia and Tristan by a year. I didn't think he hung out with those two. Not at school anyway.'

'So we've got a lying ghost-hunter and a wannabe street fighter. Great.' I tipped back my head and heaved a sigh. 'Could be worse, I guess,' I said, though the decision was made. Hen would not be spending any more time with these kids.

'Well . . .'

'Uh-oh,' I mumbled for the second time.

'I wasn't going to say anything. It's just, there's a rumor. I don't know where it came from or how long it's been circulating, but I heard about it this week.'

'What kind of rumor?'

'There are always rumors. It's high school after all.' She was back-peddling. Trying to distract me from the look of distress on her face. 'But.' Here, she took a breath before saying, 'A couple days ago, I heard some kids talking about Bram.'

*Bram.* Would the day ever come when I heard that name and didn't feel like I'd just been shoved off a cliff? Would I ever stop hearing it altogether? It had been more than a year since my connection to Bram went public. That didn't matter though. Bram was no longer present in the way he'd once been, but he was woven into the fabric of this town, and his legacy was like a pulled thread. There would always be people who came along and felt the need to pick, and the more they tugged, the more visible he became. Hen's arrival in Alexandria Bay reminded people of him. Her classmates included.

I expected this story to be more of the same. Gossip about Hen's connection to a killer and speculation about why she'd moved to the town he made his target. Courtney's words, when they came, took on a shape that was unrecognizable. It was like anticipating your mother tongue and getting a language you didn't even know existed. Through my confusion, only a few words managed to dig in their heels. *A club. Meetings. I don't know where.* It wasn't until Courtney said my name that I managed to speak again.

'A club,' I repeated.

'A club for' – Courtney swallowed hard – 'for fans of Bram.'

'A fan club. You're saying there's a *fan club* for Blake Bram at the school?'

'It's a rumor,' she said again, showing me her palms.

I could picture them though: Mia and Tristan and Leif and – Jesus – even Hen in the dead of night on an island. I'd seen the awe in Tristan's eyes when Mia told him who I was. Courtney hoped the club was some sick joke with no basis in reality, and I did too. But I knew in my bones that wasn't the case.

As Abraham Skilton, a skinny kid with buck teeth and a home haircut, my cousin had failed to inspire. He'd been on the receiving end of every joke, teased and bullied daily to the point of tears. There was nothing about the boy anyone would deem impressive; Abe was a misfit with just one friend, a girl six months older, bound to him by blood. But Bram . . . Bram was a legend. A thief who stole unlucky women and whittled away at their flesh. Bram had eluded the police, myself included. He'd even outsmarted the FBI. In the end, when he ran out of exits, he still evaded capture, taking his own dark path instead. To most, Bram was a monster who'd earned a place in hell, their only complaint that he didn't die a longer, more agonizing death. But to troubled teens? Kids with underdeveloped morals whose tastes ran dark and who idolized those willing to take big risks? To them, Blake Bram might look like a god.

And if there were kids at the school like that, if their objective was to venerate Bram and celebrate his despicable crimes, their first step would be to enlist Henrietta Merchant.

# ELEVEN

'I know why you're here,' she said, locking eyes with every member of the group in turn to make sure the press of visitors felt seen. 'You came for the same reason they all do: for a story. Well, I'm going to give you one. Mine is a family of storytellers,' she went on, eyes aglitter, 'but not all stories are fiction, and the ones you're going to hear tonight are steeped in truth.'

Mia Klinger was dressed all in black. She wore a crop top that showed ample flesh both top and bottom, a short skirt over opaque black tights, a black cape, and platform Doc Martens in a deep shade of eggplant. Today, her bottle-blonde hair was swept into a ponytail that wended around her bosom like a cobra. I'm not a devout Christian, but there was something sacrilegious about this girl guiding paying customers through a church cemetery on a Sunday evening. A trickle of disquiet rolled down my back as I listened to her theatrical delivery, her voice somehow somber and cloying at once.

I was shocked to discover Mia was working tonight. Courtney had told me the girl gave many of her family's ghost tours herself, but not even twenty-four hours ago a boy she knew had lost his life while she got drunk and handsy with her boyfriend just a few yards away, and Mia didn't seem the least bit disturbed. She had led a group of twenty-two tourists around St Cyril's Catholic Church, weaving between lichen-specked gravestones rather than following the path. Moving with the gravitas of a priest on his way to a funeral. Her full mouth was burgundy red, eyes raccooned with liner, and when she arrived at the tombstone we stood beside now, she delivered a slow, sad smile.

'These stories may not be easy to take, but they're a part of this place now,' she explained, 'and it's important for you to hear them. You came to find out more about what happened in this sleepy Northern New York town, a town that went from anonymous to infamous in the span of just two years. Well, I'm going to tell you everything, starting with why the ghost of a handsome young man roams this graveyard at night.'

I didn't have much experience with teens, but Mia Klinger was a different breed from the kids I'd known growing up. My old friend Suze had been cocksure too, but her attitude was always about rebellion. In contrast, Mia had the kind of poise that inspired confidence. When she spoke, people listened.

In a cemetery in A-Bay, where she spun bullshit tales about my ex-fiancé's ghost, that was a serious fucking problem.

'Carson Gates was a local, born and raised. He left for a while, to work as a police psychologist in New York City, but eventually he came back.' Lowering her voice, she added, 'They always do, because look at this place. How could you stay away?

'He was one of the beautiful ones,' she said of my former fiancé, a man who would take almost an hour in the shower, grooming himself to a polished gleam. 'The kind of man who makes your heart flutter. But his light was snuffed out when our scenic town attracted another man, a monster with immense power. That man drowned Carson in Eel Bay, robbing his fiancée – and our whole community – of a kind, loving soul and a brilliant mind. Did Carson's perfection make him a target? Did notorious serial killer Blake Bram murder this innocent man because of jealousy, or simply because he loved a good challenge? Or maybe he was obsessed with death? We'll never know – unless,' she said, glancing surreptitiously around, 'Carson's ghost decides to whisper his secret in your ear tonight.'

My heartbeat had relocated to my head, the sound of its gallop deafening. I wanted to grab this kid and shake her hard, whatever it took to make her stop talking. I was starting to wish I hadn't come. Last year, Tim made regular visits to this churchyard in an attempt to reconcile his feelings toward Carson with the man's violent death. I didn't know about those trips until, one night after dinner, he confessed that he'd been lured here by guilt. This was my first time seeing the cemetery for myself, and I felt the heavy weight of remorse now too. Carson didn't deserve to be dead, but a kind and loving soul? No. Carson Gates had been cunning and cruel. He'd manipulated my emotions, and when they were kids living in A-Bay, he'd played havoc with Tim's life too. But Mia had got one thing right.

My cousin had killed him.

I felt the shift in atmosphere at the mention of Bram's name. It was past sundown, all of us bathed in the eerie light of dusk. The cemetery was old, its monuments stained and crumbling, but there was nothing so frightening as talk of the man who'd turned this town into a killing ground. *Jack the Ripper. Jeffrey Dahmer. Pedro López. Blake Bram.* Abe had earned himself a spot on the most vile of lists with more than a dozen victims to his name, and though he was gone, it was his ghost more than any other that haunted the town he'd left in shambles. The idea that the Klingers were now capitalizing on his notoriety and crimes made me feel ill.

'Before you,' Mia went on with a tilt of her pretty chin, 'you see Carson's tombstone. The groundskeeper here, who works for the church, told me in the strictest of confidence that this is no ordinary grave. What I'm about to reveal is something I've never shared with anyone, and for that reason, I must ask that you keep it to yourself. Almost every night,' she said, flinging the cape off her arms as she opened them wide, 'the ghost of Carson Gates can be seen roaming this boneyard, forever searching for just one more kiss from his lost love.'

Frail grass bent under my shifting weight as I listened, demurring to my presence. Carson's grave was heaped with flowers even now. Their crinkly plastic sleeves rustled in the fall breeze. I listened with increasing horror as Mia advised her guests to take multiple photos of every suspected sighting so they had a baseline image for comparisons. 'I want you to be on high alert,' she said. 'Our tour guests often see balls of light, known as ghost orbs, in this place. A chill up your spine might indicate the presence of a spirit as well.'

Mia was good. As she spoke in that ominous tone, her guests peered over their shoulders, clutching at each other while sporting grins and saucer eyes. As for me, I kept seeing things at the far edges of my vision. Unexplained movements. Sparks of light. I didn't believe in ghosts. And yet, there was something about Carson's grave that lifted the hairs on the back of my neck and set my skin to tingling.

'Next,' Mia said, 'I will take you to a former brothel haunted by a spirit who paces in the window, advertising her wanton wares to passing men.'

Mia gave a permissive nod, and the small crowd began to murmur, whispering excitedly as they scanned the graves. I watched them pass, hands flexing inside the pockets of my off-duty jacket, until Mia brought up the rear.

'You don't have a ticket.' There was no surprise in the girl's voice, and no fear in her eyes either as she looked me up and down. 'I would have remembered if your name was on the list.'

'No,' I said, 'I don't.' I'd made a point of hanging back behind the group in their sneakers and sweatshirts with iPhones at the ready to catch a ghost so Mia wouldn't notice me there, but now that she had, I wasn't sorry. 'I heard what you told those people.'

A shrug. 'I tell stories. It's entertainment. I'm not doing anything illegal.'

'Illegal? Maybe not. Just morally reprehensible.'

'Whatever,' she said, cheeks pinking. 'We had more customers this past summer than ever and they're still coming, even now that the season's done. I'm providing a service. Keeping Bram's victims alive.'

I cast a glance at the tour guests and forced myself to stay calm as oglers walked all over Carson's grave. 'What you're doing is defiling a victim's memory,' I said. 'Does his family know? Does Kelsea?'

Carson's most recent fiancée, the one he proposed to six months after I left him, was having a hard time with his death. I knew this because Kelsea was Tim's ex, and he'd made a point of trying to help her. Kelsea and I had never been close – it was awkward enough when she agreed to marry Carson, let alone after Tim proposed to me – but I was pretty sure she wouldn't appreciate a stranger making money off Carson's murder, even if Mia was painting him in a flattering light.

'Stories,' Mia repeated, and turned her back on me.

With her flock of tour guests growing restless – somehow, despite the promises, there were no ghosts to be found – Mia hurried to the front of the group to lead them to the next location. I knew where she was headed, and not just because I'd researched the tour. Rumors about A-Bay's Riverhouse Restaurant abounded. Not only had I already heard about the ghost in the upstairs window of the former brothel, but there was supposedly also a spirit in the dining room, forever seated at a corner table, gazing out a first-floor window at the street. Whatever happened in that building, it seemed the women who'd lived there wanted out. The walk from the church cemetery to the restaurant on Market Street was short. I had to work fast.

'Were Hen and Leif dating?' I asked when I'd caught up with her, keeping my voice low.

Mia snorted, but she looked surprised too. 'You're her aunt. She's living with you. Shouldn't you know stuff like that?'

'The kid who dropped Leif off on the island. Who was it?'

'How should I know?'

'If you're lying to me,' I began, but she cut me off.

'If I'm lying, then . . . what? You're gonna shut down the tour?' She said it with a dramatic flip of her cape.

'The thought had crossed my mind. Look,' I said, 'you can tell me what I need to know now, or I can call you and your mother to the barracks. It's your choice. But I should warn you, in meetings like that? A lot of things can come up. Like the alcohol consumed on the island by underage drinkers. Like your little club.'

Mia stopped. Bit her lip and gazed off into the darkness before swinging around to face me once more. 'Club,' she repeated, drawing out the word, giving it heft. 'I don't know what you're talking about. We were just hanging out. Me and Tristan, we only invited Hen to the island to be nice.'

'Not so you could brag that you spent time with a relative of Bram's?'

Mia's head dipped, but she opted not to answer.

'These stories about him that you tell your customers. Do you tell your friends at school too?'

'Why? You think I should charge them?'

'I think you should consider the dangers of treating a killer like a local celebrity.'

She laughed under her breath. 'That's what Bram is.'

To a certain extent, she was right. Last year, when word got out that Blake Bram was my cousin and had followed me upstate after holding me captive in New York, the media had glommed on to the story like zebra mussels with a sunken boat. Everyone knew Bram's name, and Mia's mother, the proprietor of Island Death Ghost Tours, wasn't the first to capitalize on the national exposure. The difference was that Mia was a kid in high school who'd immersed herself in my cousin's crimes. Crimes she took with her to school every morning as fodder for the *stories* she shared at lunch.

'You can't treat this like fun and games,' I said through my teeth. 'Carson was a real person, and what Bram did to him was more gruesome than you can imagine. Bram severed sons and daughters from their families. He obliterated lives. I'm appealing to you as a human being, Mia. I can't make you stop these tours, but I hope I can make you understand how hurtful they are, and how dangerous they could be.'

Mia had cocked her head as I spoke, but this time it wasn't charming. She was smiling with only one side of her mouth in a way that reminded me of Crissy. My cousin was one of the smuggest people I had ever met.

'After the brothel,' Mia said, looking straight at me, 'I'm taking them to the burned-out shell of Smuggler's Cargo, the second-to-last place Bram visited before he died. And if we're lucky,' she added over her shoulder, already turning away, 'we might even see a famous serial killer's ghost.'

# TWELVE

'Have you ever heard of hybristophilia?' Gil Gasko asked.

I was sitting in my dark car in the driveway, looking at the front door of our house. Inside, Hen was still acting distant and lethargic, preferring to keep to her room, but even though she wasn't wandering the halls, I didn't want to risk her over-hearing my conversation. I thanked my lucky stars that my long-time therapist had picked up on a Sunday night, but then he knew I didn't call unless it was important. I'd given him the rundown of the situation and gotten to the part about Mia Klinger. Leave it to Gasko to know her apparent condition actually had a name. I could picture him, dark hair slicked back from his widow's peak, small eyes attentive. I'd apologized for calling him unannounced, but Gasko was a sucker for a challenge, and while this one was a departure from the norm, my state-appointed therapist had never let me down before.

'It's a psychological condition,' he told me, 'a perversion, if you will, in which someone is enticed by a person who's committed a horrendous act. Some people refer to it as Bonnie and Clyde Syndrome. It's the reason Richard Ramirez and Ted Bundy had so many female fans.'

'Fans,' I said. My mouth was dry as ash and tasted stale. 'Of murderous criminals.'

'Unimaginable, I know, but believe me,' he said, 'it's a thing. It usually affects people with low self-esteem. Women who grew up without a father figure tend to be more susceptible to it too. And then there are the glory hogs, the women – because it *is* mostly women – who are obsessed with fame. They want a piece of the criminal's notoriety. A turn in the spotlight.'

'And this obsession, it manifests in a way that's . . . sexual?' I remembered Mia and Tristan in the clearing at the island's summit. The girl's white teeth glinting in the firelight, head thrown back in ecstasy.

'To some people, it's an aphrodisiac. Others think of it as an affliction that needs to be cured. A demon to be banished.'

'And how does one banish that demon exactly?'

'There's no definitive answer to that, I'm afraid. It's a mental illness, and like many others it's treated with therapy, occasionally medication. I know you can't go into specifics,' Gasko said, 'but I'm assuming this has something to do with Blake Bram.'

'How'd you guess?' The words slick with sarcasm.

'I was worried about that,' he said.

In some ways, I'd conquered Bram and the hold he had on my life. But trauma isn't so easily quashed. Trauma lingers.

'If it helps at all, this isn't uncommon. Bram's just the latest in a long line of criminals who turn women on. The good news is that, this time, they can't act on it. There will be no marriage proposals or conjugal visits. Not for him.'

'I wish I could say that made me feel better.'

'So do I.' Gasko's voice was a tender hand on mine.

'My niece is barely talking,' I told him. 'It's the shock, I guess. I just wish there was something I could do.'

'She'll come around. Retrieving a body, realizing he couldn't be saved, that's a harrowing experience. Don't be surprised if it takes a while for her to remember all the details. Blocking out traumatic memories is a form of self-preservation, as you know well. But if you're gentle with her,' he said, 'she'll talk eventually.'

Helping Hen recover was my priority, but protecting her was a close second. Should it have occurred to me that Hen's friends might be enticed by her connection to a killer? Maybe. Probably. The day my niece came home with ketchup on her shirt had shaped my opinion of her classmates. I'd convinced myself they had shut her out, and as unfair as that was, it made sense. I'd been shut out too. It's all too easy to cast the object of controversy in the role of pariah.

I believe most forms of judgment are rooted in fear. We look down on those who are different. Snub the people we don't understand. Just like at her old high school in Vermont, Hen was an outsider.

Until someone recognized her value, and glommed on to the very thing that compelled others to push her away.

# THIRTEEN

Arthur Daisy may have looked like my late grandfather, but his scalpel-wielding skills rivaled those of Tess Gerritsen's Dr Isles. As we spoke, I imagined him in scrubs, his crown of puffy white hair tucked under a cap. A-Bay had exactly one medical examiner, so I knew Art well. He responded to all unattended deaths, whether accidental or criminal, which made him a busy man.

All the more reason for his call the next morning to put me on edge.

Tim had phoned in an emergency appeal to his mom, who'd come to the house straight away. Hen hadn't met her yet, but I knew Dori would keep her safe and fed until we got home from work that evening. We had been about to head to the barracks when my cell phone rang. Now, in the study upstairs, I put the call on speaker so Tim could listen in.

'I have to tell you, Shana,' Art said with a note of distress in his voice, 'something about this death isn't right.'

We'd long since gotten past the irony of statements like that one. Death was rarely *right*, especially when it happened to a boy on the verge of adulthood. With a suspected drowning, the purpose of the autopsy was to confirm our theory and rule out anything else. From cases I'd worked back in New York City involving bodies dragged from the East River, I knew that for a forensic pathologist, drowning was one of the hardest rulings to make. It was difficult to prove by sight; there were no pathognomonic signs that enabled an ME to say, 'I see X, so drowning it is.' There are plenty of red flags, like froth around the mouth and nostrils, but what happened before the victim got in the water is hard to discern. It takes an autopsy to make that determination, and sometimes, an autopsy points to foul play.

'Talk to me,' I told Art, feeling my stomach start to twist.

Art said, 'Stop me if you've heard this one, but there are specific things I look for when a decedent's been found in the water. Overinflated lungs – kissing lungs, as we call them – is one. Foam in the airway is another. Watery gastric contents, fluid in the sinus spaces in your skull, sphenoid sinuses to be specific, and washerwoman hands if the body's been submerged for a while . . . these are all signs that a drowning determination is correct.'

'Art, I don't like where you're going with this.'

The man drew a rattly breath. 'There was water in the lungs,' he said. 'The kid definitely drowned. But I also found bruises on the victim's arms and neck.'

Tim and I exchanged a worried glance. 'The doctor at the hospital didn't say anything about that.' He'd pointed out the cut on Leif's head, which had looked relatively minor, but bruises hadn't come up in the conversation.

'Which makes sense,' Art said. 'Saturday night, the death was fresh. But I can see bruises accentuated up to forty-eight hours postmortem. As blood settles – you've heard the term livor mortis, yes? – bruises become more prominent. There's the laceration too of course, which indicates a minor fall, and other cuts and scratches consistent with the body being dragged out of the water and on to the rocks, but it's the bruising that concerns me most.'

'Wait,' I said, 'you said a minor fall. Could he have jumped from, say, twenty-five feet up and hit his head?' I saw the island's steep cliffs again. Remembered my own days as an often-injudicious teen.

'We'd be looking at much more damage if that was the case.'

'But there are bruises. Indicative of a struggle?'

'That would be my guess, yes.'

'Is there any way at all his injuries could have been self-inflicted?' I pressed. A fall could cause bruises of all kinds.

'I'm sorry,' said Art.

I glanced at Tim. 'Shit.'

'Yeah. It's a good thing we did an autopsy,' Art said. 'The father objected at first. I got a lot of pushback, even after telling him it's a must in cases like this. No adults around at all. An unreliable witness.'

*Unreliable witness.* He was talking about Hen.

Art was right about cases involving minors being complicated, though. Throw in some intoxicated juveniles and you got a whole new set of hurdles. Hen hadn't cooperated when Leif's death was ruled an accident. What would happen now that we were looking at homicide? Because that's what Art Daisy was telling us: Leif hadn't drowned all on his own. What would that do to a community still in the process of healing?

How could this town possibly survive another violent death?

Art promised to email me his complete autopsy report, and after thanking him and ending the call, I turned to Tim. While listening to our conversation, his expression had grown steadily darker.

'Another homicide,' he said, his tone equally grim. 'This is not going to go over well.'

The public would need to be told though – and soon. I'd been laying as low as possible over the past year, letting Tim take the lead on high-profile cases, of which there had been few. I was still his superior and the only Troop D senior investigator in the region, but in a lot of ways, Tim was better suited to the spotlight. Better with people. A trusted, familiar face. As a long-time local and esteemed member of the community, he was the logical choice when it came time to break bad news to the public, and I reminded him of that now.

'I'll prepare a statement,' he said, but his face was a jumble of emotions, and I sensed his black mood went beyond Art Daisy's report. 'But what about Hen?'

'What about her?'

'Shana, she was *there*. For almost the entire time you've lived in A-Bay, you've been shackled to someone else's crimes. Right or wrong, your name is synonymous with Bram's, and it took you flaying your secrets and saving multiple lives for the people of this town to really believe you have their best interests at heart. And now? Now, a blood relative of the notorious Shana Merchant is associated with a crime against a local. A *kid*. Can't you see how that's going to look after everything that happened here?'

I wanted to argue, insist that Hen had nothing to do with Leif Colebrook's death, but the words shriveled in my throat and turned to dust on my tongue. I *could* see how this would look – my new-to-the-area niece found at the scene of the crime. With the victim's body.

Tim said, 'I think you should step away from this case completely.'

I blinked at him, my mouth stitched tight.

'It might not even be up to us. You know how much the State Police cares about perception. They're not going to be happy when this goes public,' he said, 'plus, there's the ethics piece. You can't be a fair and neutral investigator when your own flesh and blood is involved.'

I'd heard that line before, first in Vermont when I was determined to find out who killed my uncle, then from the press when my connection to Bram came to light.

'We don't know what's going to happen here,' Tim said. 'All we know at this point is that Hen's a witness, and there's no hiding your relationship with her. For the sake of your duty to this community, to Leif's dad, I think it's the right thing to do.'

When I'd first met Tim Wellington in the State Police barracks on Route 12, he'd struck me as a pushover. A yokel who lacked sophistication and had little experience with violent crime. I assumed Tim had always leaned on personal relationships and provincial charm to sort out small-potatoes property disputes and the occasional sale of narcotics. Our first big case together, out at the posh Sinclair family home on Tern Island, proved me wrong. Over the course of just two days, I learned that Tim was earnest and honest with scruples to spare. He could turn on the backwoods boy act like a switch and used it to great effect. That made what he was telling me all the harder to hear. Yes, he was speaking on behalf of his friends and neighbors, who were owed an unbiased investigation, but he was trying to protect me too. Baring my past had been brutal, an act from which I hadn't fully recovered, and Tim was right to suspect my involvement with this case might leave an even brighter scar.

Since Saturday, I'd been haunted by the image of Hen lying on the floor of that boat instead of Leif. Both teens had crept out of their beds in the night. Both had ended up on the island. I couldn't shake the thought that our victim could just as easily have been Hen. By the looks of things, she had tried to help Leif, but what did we really know about the events that played out on Devil's Oven? I thought of Doug's reaction to the news that a kid Hen had known was dead, and I thought of Ford

Colebrook, whom I had yet to meet. I tried to imagine what he'd do when he found out his son was taken not by a horrible twist of fate but by someone else's hand.

'I want to tell him,' I said definitively. 'Leif's father. He needs to know we're going to find out what happened, whatever it takes. The fact that Hen was there, with Leif right at the end . . . I should be the one to do it. Whether I'm part of this case or not.'

'OK. I guess it can't hurt for him to know how committed the whole troop is to finding out who did this,' Tim said.

No, that couldn't hurt.

What hurt was the knowledge that if Hen knew more than she was telling, if – God forbid – she was somehow involved in a murder – she would get no protection from me.

# FOURTEEN

Finding Ford Colebrook wasn't easy. Despite the circumstances, there was no answer on his home phone. His dive business had no office or storefront, just a Facebook page that hadn't been updated in weeks. According to Courtney, there was just one place I could check if I hoped to find Leif's father, and that was the stretch of river behind the Cornwall Brothers Museum.

At the end of Market Street, the museum was one of Alexandria Bay's earliest general stores and the last remaining nineteenth-century waterfront landmark in town. It was a charming building of cream brick that had once received supply deliveries by way of the river. Ships would pull up to the back and unload their dry goods into the basement. It was steps from those basement doors that I saw the dive flags, red squares with a slash of white, strewn across the water.

Were it not for those flags and the mesh duffles dotting the shore, plus the cars parked nose to bumper along the curb, I would never have known there was anyone underwater. As I watched though, I started to see bubbles breach and ripple the surface. Like a raft of seals coming up for air, one masked head emerged, then another. Over the next few minutes, six bodies popped up in all, and I made my way over to where they were shedding their gear. At the sight of my State Police jacket, several of the divers shrank back. This time of year, when the weather was iffy, I kept it in my car; there was power in the blocky letters on the back, and I liked having the option of using it. Now, it occurred to me that I hadn't thought the jacket through. Every parent in town was still having nightmares about Leif. It would be hard for them not to imagine the same thing happening to their own kids.

*Wait until they hear this death wasn't an accident.*

A man with a goatee who was packing his dry bag pointed me to Ford, still in his wetsuit, back hunched under the weight of his electric blue tank.

'Mr Colebrook?' I said, introducing myself. 'I'm very sorry to bother you at work.'

He gave me a long, probing look before saying, 'Give me a minute,' and turning away.

I waited as he peeled off his wetsuit and, bare-chested, said goodbye to his clients. Ford Colebrook was the largest of the men by far, well over six feet with a full beard, cowlicked hair so dark it was almost black, and the solid blue eyes of the border collie my neighbors had when Doug and I were kids. That dog had a keen intelligence I'd been conscious of even as a child, and I wondered if the same was true of Ford. There was something about the way he held the gaze of each diver he spoke with, accepting their quiet words of sympathy with a stoic nod. His solid, serene presence was impressive. That he was working again so soon after his son's death boggled my mind, but who was I to judge? Maybe descending into the river's silty silence was his way of coping. Maybe it was the only way he could.

When at last the divers had dispersed, driving off in the cars lined up along the road, Ford ducked behind his truck. It was a shiny black pickup with a retractable tonneau cover to protect his gear and a sticker that read, *Proud A-Bay High Dad*. I felt a stab of sadness at the memory of Courtney's report about Leif. *His grades were up. He was applying to colleges.* When Ford appeared again, he was dressed in worn jeans and a tan Henley shirt. He'd made no effort to fix his hair, still as wild as a young boy's.

'You doing OK?' I asked when he approached me, watching him closely for signs of distress. Some people put on a good show only to break down the minute they're alone. I couldn't conceive of the pain this man must be feeling.

When Ford didn't answer, I said, 'It's an impossible question, I know. I'm happy to see you out of the house though.'

'Mind if we walk?' he asked. 'I get antsy after a dive. I need to keep moving.'

'Of course.' I gestured toward the road, and we set off side by side. It was a cloudy day, the sky like milk glass and the air viscous with cool humidity that dampened my skin. On this Monday in September, Alexandria Bay was a ghost town, its streets bereft of life.

'It helps,' he said, kicking a pebble with the toe of his boot. 'Working. Doing what I love.'

I nodded. Ford Colebrook's voice had no edges. He spoke in a permanent sotto voce that made it seem like he was confiding in someone. In me. Hard not to get lost in a voice like that.

'Been doing this for a long time? Diving, I mean,' I said.

'Since I was fifteen. My parents made me wait till then to get my certification. I would have done it younger if they let me.'

I nodded. 'Did Leif dive too?'

The man faltered. It was disarming, the way he was looking at me. Intense. 'No. He used to, but he quit. You're not from around here,' he said, and there was a hint of pity in his sad smile. 'Leif stopped diving because of his mother.'

'I heard about what happened to your wife. I'm so sorry.'

'She was an experienced diver, but accidents happen,' said Ford. 'After that, though, Leif didn't want to go back.'

'But you did. Were you with her?' I asked. 'When it happened?'

A shake of the head. 'She was with friends. For Leif, because of that, there are some bad associations, I guess. But for me, diving does the opposite. It calms me. Shuts out all the noise. And it reminds me of my wife. I have a lot of good memories of us diving together. Plus, you know,' he added with a shrug, 'it's my life. My summers would be miserable without it. Leif,' he said suddenly, his mouth now a grimace. Blue eyes like tide pools boring into me. 'Are you here because you have some news?'

I swallowed the lump in my throat. 'Actually, yes. We have some new information about the cause of death. I'm sorry, Mr Colebrook, but based on the autopsy results, we suspect foul play.'

Ford stopped walking. The way he turned to me, his expression so blank it was like he was seeing me for the first time, made me shudder. 'What are you saying? Someone else was involved in my son's death? How? *Who?*'

'We're still working to figure that out.' I explained Art Daisy's findings as delicately as I could and watched them seep into Ford's skin like a toxin. When I got to the part about the head wound and bruising, he raised his grief-stricken face to the sky and closed his eyes. He stayed that way for a long time, breathing through his nose and flexing his fingers. I couldn't tell if he wanted to crumple or drive his fist through a wall.

This next part was going to be rough.

'I'm sorry to ask,' I said, 'but was there anything suspicious about your wife's drowning? Now that we know more about the circumstances, and given your wife's cause of death . . .'

Ford nodded. 'No, I understand. I see how this looks. There's no hit out on my family, if that's what you're asking.' The corner of his mouth twitched. 'Geena's death was an accident. She took a couple of friends to the *A.E. Vickery*, a wreck off Rock Island Lighthouse. It was a regulator failure. No air.'

The picture in my mind was horrifying. How had the two people who'd mattered most to this man both ended up in the river?

'Your niece was there that night,' Ford said as we walked on. It wasn't a question. 'Kim called me this morning to . . . give her sympathies. She said Henrietta tried to save him.'

'Kim?'

'Kim Klinger. Mia told her what happened. Is it true?' Ford asked. 'Did your niece really do that?'

'It looks that way,' I said. 'Henrietta – Hen – she's a swimmer. She has some lifeguarding experience too.' *She might have been able to help*, I thought. *If only she'd been sober.*

'Hen.' Ford spoke her name with reverence. 'How old is Hen?'

'Sixteen. She's a junior. New to town.'

'Sixteen years old. And she risked her life for him.'

I hadn't thought much about that, focused as I was on the life that had been lost, but I supposed Ford was right. Hen had put herself in danger to help Leif, and though she'd called him her boyfriend on the island, he was practically a stranger to her, someone she'd only known a few days. It was clear based on Ford's reaction that *he* didn't know Hen at all. If she and Leif were really dating, Leif had kept that from his father. Just like Hen kept it from me.

'Kim's daughter, Mia,' I said slowly. 'This might sound crazy, but do you know anything about a club she might have started?'

'What kind of club?'

I hesitated. 'Possibly the kind that's interested in serial killers.' It sounded ridiculous to my ears, but after seeing Mia's tour for myself, I was starting to believe the gossip was founded on fact.

'Ah. Blake Bram.' He studied me before going on. 'A lot of people were interested in that news. I don't know about any club. Sounds dark.'

'It is. So to the best of your knowledge, Leif wasn't a member?'

'I've never known him to be into something like that.' Ford's brow furrowed and he said, 'Is that why they were out on Devil's Oven?'

'We don't know yet. But we intend to find out.'

'Whatever you need,' he said, coming to a stop, 'I'll help you. I have to know who did this to my son.'

I reached into my pocket for my card. 'You're not alone. We've got help coming in from Oneida.' I'd already put in a call to Lieutenant Henderson at Troop D headquarters to formally request a hand with the investigation, and he'd assured me someone was on the way. 'We'll find out who's responsible,' I told Ford.

But even as I said it, all I could picture was Hen's anguished face inside that cave.

# FIFTEEN

When Tim asked how it went with Leif's dad, I told him the truth. It was hard. The man was shattered. But I'd managed to get the job done.

In my office, I closed the door and slumped down into the chair. My next conversation wasn't going to be any easier.

'Homicide,' I said, the phone close to my face. 'This complicates things, Doug.'

I told him what little I knew and let him vent. The news couldn't have been much worse.

'Fuck. That poor kid – and God, his *family*. Hen's not part of this though, right?' Doug said suddenly, quickly. 'She's not, like, a *suspect*.'

'Nobody's saying Hen was involved. But she's a witness,' I said. 'There will be interviews, and I can't be the one who conducts them.'

'OK.'

He sounded relieved, but a little scared too. *You should be*, I thought. Nothing about the situation would be simple.

'And, Doug,' I said, 'there are rumors here about some kind of fan club. It has something to do with Bram, and the kids on that island with Hen might be involved. I know you were hoping that coming here would put some distance between her and all that, but she's even more conspicuous in A-Bay than back home now, and it's only going to get worse. She'll need to stay a while,' I explained, 'at least until the interviews are done, and maybe longer depending on what happens with the case. But then I think she should go home.'

*Say you agree*, I thought. *Tell me you understand*. It wasn't as if I hadn't tried to get Hen's life in order. My request had nothing to do with our sudden lack of privacy, or the constant sense that we were being watched, or the ever-present fear of what Hen might do next. Being here wasn't good for her.

As that fact loitered in my mind though, it was accompanied by another. Henrietta was very likely more than I could handle.

And that was saying a lot.

'I haven't been honest with you,' Doug said before I could come clean.

I tipped my head. What could he possibly have to confess? It was me who'd screwed up by giving Hen enough rope to hang herself. Expecting her to be something she wasn't because it was convenient, far easier than actually parenting the girl whose life suddenly ran parallel to my own.

'There's something I haven't told you,' Doug said. 'God, this is all so . . . look, Shay. Josie's pregnant.'

'What?' For a second I was sure I'd misheard. Conception hadn't come easily to my brother and his wife the first time around. Without enough savings for in vitro fertilization, it had taken years for them to get pregnant with Hen. They'd married young, so despite the delay, Josie had Hen in her twenties, but she was over forty now. They were having a *baby*? 'That's . . . Jesus, Doug, that's incredible. I'm speechless.'

'Believe me,' he said, huffing air, 'we were too. It was the last thing we expected. But somehow, it happened.'

'Wait a minute. Hen hasn't said a word about this.'

Here, my brother cleared his throat. 'She doesn't know. The doctors, they're considering it a high-risk pregnancy. You know how crazy things were before she came to you. Josie was out of her mind with worry, and stress can impact everything from gestation to birth weight to—'

'You haven't told her? Shit, Doug.' Not only were my brother and Josie keeping the baby from Hen, but it sounded to me like they feared her very presence could hurt their unborn child. But it wasn't as if shipping Hen away could completely alleviate Josie's fears. In fact, that decision had made everything worse. 'This is messed up,' I said. 'You're shutting Hen out. This baby's going to rearrange your entire family dynamic. You have to tell her.'

'We will, we will, just . . . not quite yet.' A note of shame had crept into his voice. It turned his deep, clear way of speaking viscous.

I said, 'So this, sending her here to us, it wasn't just about rehabilitation. You needed her gone for a while.'

'She was on board with it,' he insisted, his voice thicker than ever. 'We would never have done it if she hadn't agreed.'

'Oh, Doug.'

I knew a thing or two about guilt, and having to choose between his daughter and the health of his wife and baby had to be torture for Doug – but me? It only strengthened my resolve. Despite the chasm that existed between me and Hen, regardless of how much her behavior kept me up at night and, frankly, creeped me out, I couldn't give up on my niece.

I was going to get Henrietta back on track if it killed me.

# SIXTEEN

'I'm looking for Shana Merchant.'

There was a woman standing outside my office door, and she wasn't smiling. No more than five-foot-two with dark eyes, a small nose, and wavy black hair gathered into a low ponytail, she stood with one hand on her hip as if short on both time and patience.

'You found her,' I said, because I knew exactly who this was. Lieutenant Henderson's special investigator from Oneida – Valerie Ott, come to take over my case.

Come to investigate Hen and her friends.

'Welcome,' I said, inviting her to take a seat. 'This is all a bit tricky, as you may have heard.'

Was she sizing me up? It was hard to tell. I didn't know how much Henderson had told the woman, but Tim had been right about the New York State Police's stance on perception. When I'd called Troop D headquarters to fill Henderson in on Art Daisy's findings, he'd wasted no time removing me from the case. 'You've got a reputation to rebuild,' he'd said, sounding displeased. Henderson had never been a fan of mine. 'The last thing we need is for people to assume you're giving your niece special treatment, especially after your very public connection to Blake Bram.'

I'd been working hard to dispel falsehoods and set the record straight about me and Bram. I had a cousin who'd grown into a killer, but I'd also put my life on the line to hobble him and do whatever I could to make things right. While my story had ingratiated me to some, others continued to view me as a scourge on the community. Henderson, whose troop served seven different counties through more than twenty-five stations across Upstate New York, had no desire to field another round of complaints about an investigator who'd already given him nothing but headaches.

'Small-town crimes are a bitch, am I right?' Valerie let her gaze drift to the window, the expanse of dying grass and empty highway outside. 'I'm here to be fair and impartial. I won't get in your way.'

'I appreciate that,' I said.

'I get it,' she continued, re-crossing her legs. 'I'm not from Oneida, you know? Grew up in a tiny Northern Michigan town after moving from the Marquesas Islands – French Polynesia – when I was two. I lived there for twenty years before coming east, so believe me, this is nothing new. Close communities make it damn near impossible to be objective. There was a workplace sexual harassment case once involving my parents' next-door neighbor – this is Michigan I'm talking about, one of my first cases on the job. Every time I looked at the guy, I was sure it was all some big mistake. This was the man who let me borrow his bike pump! His was the only house that gave out full-sized candy bars on Halloween. But you know what? That asshole was guilty as sin.'

I nodded. Said, 'The witness is my niece.'

Valerie sized me up with a tilt of her head. 'I recognized your name,' she told me. 'You're kind of famous, huh?'

*I get that a lot*, I thought bitterly, but said, 'So you know about my connection to Blake Bram. This is a delicate situation, being related to a witness. Given who I am.'

The look Valerie gave me next was swathed in sympathy. 'Let me handle it, OK? Put it out of your mind. I've got this,' she said.

And I believed her.


'God, I wish I knew how to drive a boat.'

Valerie Ott was grinning, one hand braced against the police boat's T-top as she stared goggle-eyed at the river. We were coming up on Devil's Oven, the rocky island awash in sunlight. Me, Tim, our fellow investigator Jeremy Solomon, our forensics tech Owen, and Valerie on the boat. It would be so much easier to explore the island in daylight. The place that had just become the scene of a homicide.

'I used to say the same thing,' I told her. 'Ask Tim.' I nodded toward where he stood at the wheel, his legs in a wide stance, lips forming a tilted smile.

'She was clueless,' he said, 'which can be a problem when you work up here. Now she's as proficient as any of us.'

'Speak for yourself,' said Owen, a stocky man in his mid-forties who I noticed had a tight grip on the nearest grab rail.

'Then we'll leave the driving to these guys,' Valerie told him, 'and just keep enjoying the view.'

As we bumped across the water, I gave Valerie the lay of the land – or, in this case, water. Some parts of the St Lawrence were a long way from the channel, and that distance created a lake-like stillness that almost made you forget this same river flowed all the way from the Great Lakes to the North Atlantic. Not too far north it was home to whales – blue, humpback, beluga – some of which sometimes made their way down to Montreal.

Here beside the channel, where the water was an otherworldly shade somewhere between sapphire and teal, the river was all chop and current. It wasn't just recreational boating that made the seaway boil but the constant freighter traffic. Massive cargo ships hauled tons of iron ore, steel, and grain along this route daily, passing right by Devil's Oven, and as rough as the water had been on Saturday night, it was worse in the daytime. Now, the crosscut waves were downright wild.

'I'll get as close as I can,' Tim said as he drew the police boat parallel to the island. No dock meant there was no way for all of us to make landfall without anchoring and taking a swim, so we'd made a plan. This time, Tim would idle the boat near the rocks, while the rest of us toured Devil's Oven.

'I've always wanted to check this place out,' Sol said as the breeze lashed at his thick gray buzzcut and turned his fleshy cheeks pink. 'From what I've heard, it was party central back in the day. All we ever had where I grew up in Elmira were abandoned barns.'

'We partied in barns too,' Valerie put in. 'The more run-down and remote the better, because that meant we were less likely to get caught.'

'When I was in high school here,' said Tim, 'the hot spot was Boldt Castle. This was pre-renovation, when it was still on the verge of collapse. The gnarled old-timers who lead the boat tours now say it has three hundred and sixty-five rooms, one for each day of the year; twelve wings, one for every month; and fifty-two bathrooms, one for every week. Honestly? They're not far off. The place was creepy back then, but it served its purpose.'

'To conceal your misdeeds?' asked Owen, who was looking a little green.

Tim said, 'To keep us dry, and at least a little warm. This island is awfully exposed.'

That was true. The kids wouldn't be able to come here for much longer. In late fall and winter there was no venturing out on the deadly-cold water, even for teens who'd been boating since they were ten.

'What did you do out there?' I asked. 'At Boldt Castle?'

'Drank, mostly.'

He sounded sheepish. Tim was funny like that. Everyone had a past; I didn't know a single person who hadn't done something nefarious at some point in their lives. When it came to Tim's youth though, his sinful days were a source of embarrassment – and I knew for a fact his definition of sin was more conservative than most. The exception was the time he'd spent with Carson Gates, who'd coerced him into deeper trouble than Tim liked to recall.

'From what I've heard, it was way more fun out there in the sixties and seventies,' he said, 'right before renovations started up. Teens used to play hide-and-seek in the castle. Make out. Write their names on the walls.'

'How about you, boss?' Sol said it with a mischievous grin.

'What did I do as a teen? Hung out in the woods mostly,' I told the group. 'On the outskirts of town. Like Valerie said: the more remote, the better.'

*Nothing good happens in the woods.* That's what my mother used to tell me, and she'd been right. I'd heard plenty of stories to corroborate her theory, even lived a few of them myself. Alcohol poisoning was a real concern. Sexual assault too. As that thought crossed my mind, my stomach did a flip. Could that be why Hen wasn't talking? *No.* The ER doctor had checked her out. There was no sign at all that she'd been attacked.

'It was stupid, what we did,' I told them. 'You can get turned around in the woods. Break a bone. Be left behind.' My own cousin, Bram's sister Crissy, had once been missing in the woods for days. I was thirteen at the time. I'd been sure that she was dead.

'Doesn't look like you could get lost here,' said Owen, observing the island, but that didn't make it safe, and we all knew it. This rock was just as perilous as any barn or forest or crumbling castle.

'I really thought the worst we had to worry about with Hen was keeping her out of the liquor,' I said. 'I still can't believe she was even here.'

'Snuck out?' Valerie asked.

'Like a pro,' I replied. 'The stress of having this kid around, I can't even tell you.'

'Monica's desperate for kids,' Sol confessed. 'We've been married three years, we're not getting any younger . . . I've heard every line in the book. Sometimes I think I'm ready. Sometimes I'm even excited about the idea. But then something like this happens, a kid gone, survived by his father, and I just can't put it out of my head.'

'You have to compartmentalize,' Valerie told him. 'Leave the trauma at the door. Otherwise, it's impossible to live our lives without being in a constant state of fear.'

'Easier said than done when kids turn up dead. I swear,' I muttered grimly, thinking of Hen's willful disobedience, and Mia and Tristan with their pants down while their friend lay dying just a few yards away, 'this whole thing's enough to make me opt out of parenthood for life.'

The words were out before I could process them, and I felt a crushing wave of nausea once I did. When I turned a hangdog look Tim's way, his expression was waffling between distress and disbelief. Of course Tim was upset; he had every right to be. At the same time, the sentiment felt disturbingly authentic. I was on my way to look for evidence that one teenager had taken another one's life, and the last thing I wanted in that moment was to bring a child into such a world. Even as my chest swelled with regret for hurting Tim, I knew it wasn't the first time I'd felt that way.

'Wow,' Valerie said after a beat, her voice flat. Sol and Owen just stared.

'Joking,' I said with an awkward laugh, desperate to move

past the moment. 'Let's just get this done and get back to the barracks, yeah?'

Tim nodded, but I knew the truth. He wasn't fooled.

After a few hairy minutes fighting the waves, Sol, Owen, Valerie, and I clambered on to the rocks off the boat's starboard side and Tim backed the vessel away from the island. Moments later, I'd scaled the east-facing cliffs to the summit.

'This way,' I told the others, taking the familiar path along sloped rock and up the cliff face. It was doable in the daylight, but Mia, Tristan, Hen, and Leif had come when the sky was a day-old bruise, the water black as ink.

We started in the circle of trees. Owen, as he prepared to process the scene, warned us to skirt the perimeter, though countless feet had already trampled the area on Saturday night. The sun-warmed stones on the ground were smooth with the odd crevice, one of which had been used as a fire pit. It was filled with charred wood, its silvery ash swirling up from a pile in the breeze. Empty cans of Bud Light, some artfully crushed, lay scattered around the pit, sunlight glinting off their metallic blue skins when I nudged one with the toe of my boot. They brought memories of my teenage transgressions all over again.

Owen was looking for surface scatter that would help Valerie and Sol reconstruct events surrounding the incident. The weather had been stable, and apart from the minks I suspected lived inside the cave, there wasn't any interference from animals to complicate the search for evidence. I watched as Owen kneeled down and, with a gloved hand, bagged a crumpled cigarette butt. I was pretty sure the lipstick on the filter matched the color Mia had been wearing the night of Leif's death.

To Owen, Valerie said, 'Anything you can find that might help us reenact the events of that night would be useful. How did Leif get in the water? Where did the struggle take place?' She crouched down near the sticky, sooty rocks. There was so little soil on the island, so little earth to be disrupted. Uncovering evidence of a scuffle wouldn't be easy.

'The cave's down there,' I told her.

'You know, there's a legend that Bill Johnston hid in there for a week,' said Sol.

I smiled. 'So I've heard.'

I started to pick my way down the rocks toward the water, Valerie following close behind. Tim had already pulled the boat around and was rocking in the waves close to shore.

'The thing to note, I think, is that the cave is hidden,' I said. 'Whatever happened down here wouldn't have been visible to anyone on the summit of the island.'

'And this is where you found your niece?'

'Right here,' I confirmed. 'Inside the cavern. Garrick – he's one of our troopers – said she dragged the body up on to these rocks. I can't get her to talk about how Leif got into the water. Not yet anyway.'

'What's that?'

Valerie had stepped across the mouth of the cave and was leaning against the rock face on the other side.

'Find something?' All I could see from where I stood was the sun glinting off vertical stone.

'There are scratches on this rock. It almost looks like . . .'

'What?' I stepped over to see for myself.

'What is it? What did you find?' Tim called his questions from the boat, but I didn't turn toward his voice. Valerie's discovery had left me paralyzed.

The woods of Vermont, Sol and Valerie's countryside barns, Boldt Castle and Devil's Oven all had one thing in common: they were secluded. Apart from the few kids who had the balls to come here, the island was abandoned. There was no possibility of a parent or neighbor stumbling on to this place. Which meant that nobody else would see the message etched into the stone.

But Valerie had. 'That's interesting. We'll need a picture of this,' she said. She didn't know what the graffiti meant. But I did. The same message had been written in a letter with my name on it, left for me in my mailbox. Signed *Love, Abe.*

There were only two words, but together they buckled my knees.

*Good game.*

# SEVENTEEN

Courtney's story had been just that: a story. An unverified account acquired secondhand with questionable ties to the truth. Even if she was right, and someone at the school had corralled all the murder-obsessed teens to worship Bram and make Hen their queen, there had been no apparent ties to the island. But the way Mia and Tristan had looked at me on Devil's Oven, the nonsense words Mia had spoken – *See? And look. Here she is* – clung to me like a bad odor. My appearance had provoked a reaction they couldn't hide, the unvarnished reverence in their eyes impossible to veil. Mia and Tristan shouldn't have known me, a State Police investigator twice their age. The fact that they had could only mean one thing: they knew about my link to both Bram and Hen.

And that gave Courtney's story teeth.

'But how,' Tim asked as he turned his pint glass on the bar top. It was too early for cocktails, not yet five o'clock, but if ever we needed a stiff drink, it was today. The Brig was our new hangout, the bar Tim, Mac, and I had started frequenting after Matt Cutts closed the Riverboat and moved his traumatized family out of town. It didn't offer much in the way of ambiance, but the place served gin and tonics with dried juniper berries, and Tim liked the beer selection. That was good enough for me.

'Nobody else has seen that letter,' he pointed out. 'No one but us.'

For a long time, it had just been me. I wasn't sure if I should show it to Tim, even after we got engaged. It was the letter that ended it all, the final clue in the game my cousin and I had been playing since we were kids. A simple message that was meant to hint at one last kill.

Not long after I'd read it, Mac had called to tell me Carson was dead. I'd almost shredded the letter then, had thought of burning it countless times since, but the need to unburden myself of the guilt I felt for receiving what amounted to a deathbed confession led me to unfold the note and press it into Tim's hand. After that, keeping it became a form of penance, its closing sentence doomed to echo for all eternity in the dark.

*Good game. Love, Abe.*

'We know how,' I said through my teeth. '*Goddamnit*, Hen.' I hadn't touched the letter in over a year, not since pleating it into a tight little knob and storing it in the wooden box that held my small collection of jewelry. I was pretty sure it had been there when I put away the earring I'd found on the hallway floor, which meant Hen had taken a picture. Shown the letter to those kids.

'That doesn't sound like her,' Tim said.

'Doesn't it? What do we really know about her?' My stomach soured even as I said it – this was my niece, my flesh and blood – but wasn't it true? I didn't know this introverted and devious new version of Hen at all. 'She did some bad things back home, things that scared the shit out of Doug. How do we know she isn't capable of this too?'

'But she only just got here,' said Tim. 'A few days ago she knew no one, and now she's got a psycho bestie and a boyfriend?'

'Courtney warned me that Mia and Tristan were trouble. When I got to Devil's Oven those two knew me, Tim. They knew exactly who I was. It was almost like they'd been expecting me. You know, I don't think I really believed Doug's stories about Hen were as bad as all that. So she dyed her hair and developed a taste for horror – so what? Even when she was poking around in my stuff, I thought OK, she's curious. No harm done. But scaring us half to death by sneaking out – and to a place like *that*? Betraying my trust by sharing that horrible letter with people she hardly even knows? I swear, this kid's going to give me a heart attack.'

Tim's pint was halfway to his mouth, but his hand froze mid-air. 'Did you mean it?' he asked, setting down the glass. 'What you said on the boat?'

I glanced around us. Monday afternoon, and the bar was almost empty. Still, I said, 'This may not be the best time.'

'The wedding's three months away, and my fiancée just told me she doesn't want kids. Seems like the perfect time, actually. You know how much having a family means to me.'

'I do. I just . . . sometimes I'm not sure I feel the same way.'

'Hey there.'

We looked up with a start to see Valerie Ott standing next to the bar. She was dressed in dark jeans and a blazer, her jet-black hair arranged artfully around her face. It had been my idea to invite her. Get to know her a little but also gauge her stance on the case. I'd warned the new investigator I had a few things to tell her, and that they couldn't wait.

Tim jumped up and offered her his seat, moving farther away from me, and we got Valerie set up with a whiskey sour. No sooner was she settled than Tim excused himself, heading for the bathroom. Not looking back.

'So,' Valerie said when he was gone. 'You and eyebrows, huh?'

I blinked twice. 'You mean Tim?'

A twitch tugged at the investigator's Cupid's bow lip. 'Right, Tim. You're an item?'

'We . . . yeah. We're engaged.'

'Ah.' Her smile faltered as she processed the information. What did she think about the fact that I was planning to marry one of the investigators from my dwindling team? I wanted to push the question aside, convince myself I didn't care. Valerie could judge me if she liked; her opinion of my relationship had no bearing on the case she'd come to work. I knew that to be true.

So why did I find myself squirming under her cool gaze?

'What about you?' I asked in an attempt to gain the upper hand. If Valerie could probe into personal issues, then hell, so could I. 'Are you married?'

'Divorced. I don't recommend it. Don't recommend marriage in general, frankly. Probably not what you want to hear.'

I shrugged off the comment and said, 'How many kids?'

Her brow dipped in confusion, but then she reached for her wrist and twiddled the friendship bracelet there. 'Good eye.'

'If I'd noticed sooner, I would have kept my thoughts about procreation to myself.' My gaze flitted to the bathroom. Still no sign of Tim.

Valerie chuckled. 'It's fine. I've just got the one – Bobby. She's a girl. My ex picked the name. She's staying with him while I'm up here.'

'Ah. Is your ex in Oneida too?'

'Verona. Will's in the horse game. Trains 'em, sells 'em, coaches riders. He loves those horses more than anything. Certainly more than me. But enough about that,' she said, slapping the bar top. 'You said you had something to tell me.'

Tim was back. He pulled his beer toward him and settled in to listen.

'This is going to sound crazy,' I said, 'but there's some information I didn't include in the file. It might be relevant.'

Valerie took a long sip of her drink and told me to fire away.

I had done some research since talking to Courtney, and what I'd found was alarming. Article upon article addressing the phenomenon of true-crime clubs where killers were treated like rockstars. But that wasn't the worst of it. Some had members who didn't just sexualize and glamorize violence but committed it themselves. Club participants, who were often teens, sought to emulate acts they saw as fearless. Others described violence they'd seen their peers commit as 'chic.' I filled Valerie in on the rumor at the school and my fears about its connection to the island.

'I wondered about the island's name,' she said, poking at an ice cube with her straw. 'Any satanism around here?'

The question stopped me short, because I hadn't made that association. I'd heard about Devil's Oven long before Saturday, so it was just another name to me, no different than Dark Island, Fire Rock, or Grindstone. Was the ominous moniker what had drawn Mia and her cohorts to the rock? Or was it a happy accident that the closest uninhabited island boasted the perfect name for a satanic club's headquarters?

'I can't say I know of any devil worship or cults in these parts,' I confessed. 'But I'm no expert. Tim?'

'Not that I've heard about,' he said. 'And I've been here a long time.'

'Yeah, that stuff's not as trendy as it used to be,' said Valerie. 'There was a big case in New Jersey in the seventies involving some so-called devil's disciples, and Ramirez and his Night Stalker slayings back in the eighties – supposedly he was drawn to music about devil worship, and his crimes mirrored some of the lyrics. Google Satanic panic,' she said, just as flippant as if she was recommending a recipe for cookies. 'Black Sabbath, *Rosemary's Baby*, it was a whole thing.'

Abe had liked that movie as a kid. We'd watched it together more than once.

As Valerie spoke, I took out my iPhone and perused the search results. 'That Jersey case in the seventies,' I said, staring down at the screen, 'this says the cliff where the victim was found is called Devil's Teeth.'

Valerie shrugged. 'Probably a coincidence. It's not like these local kids named the island.'

'But Mia Klinger chose it,' I pointed out, suppressing a shiver. The similarity to Devil's Teeth made my own tingle.

'Listen,' said Valerie, 'I'll level with you: I'm probably not going to pursue this serial-obsessed, Satan-worshipping angle. I'm not saying you're wrong about Mia Klinger's creepy hobby, and a club like the one you're describing may well exist. I just don't believe it has anything to do with this crime. A boy drowned in a river in the middle of the night. The kids were all drinking. There were girls around, no adult supervision. I suspect our vic got caught up in some altercation and the witnesses, well, they freaked. Honestly, if Tristan and Mia were as hot and heavy as what you described in your notes, the fight could have been over that. Mia's an attractive girl. Maybe Leif had a thing for her too. We'll see when we get to the interviews. But Shana, it would help if we were straight with each other. This devil stuff isn't why you brought me here.'

*Of course it is*, I thought. *Weren't you paying attention?* 'The club—'

'Cut the shit. This is about your niece.'

The woman's smile was thin, and I didn't like it, not the smug satisfaction in her eyes or the insinuation that I was trying to sway her opinion and influence a homicide case. I was starting to think Valerie was the type who liked to test boundaries, crafty and just shy of devious. I'd met people like that. They weren't my favorite.

'Contrary to what you might be thinking,' I said, 'we all want the same thing. A boy – a young man really – is dead, and if Hen has information that's relevant, I want you to know about it.'

'*Does* she have information that's relevant?' Valerie lifted her glass to her lips.

I could feel Tim watching me. Waiting to hear what I was going to say.

'You want me to be straight with you?' I shrugged and said, 'I don't know. She hasn't told me a thing.'

'Leave it to me,' said Valerie. 'I'll get to the truth.'

I nodded, but the assurance didn't make me feel at ease. Valerie Ott didn't know this town, or Bram, or how his crimes had impacted the community. Bram's influence on A-Bay ran so deep that here I was, a full year after his death, speculating that a group of high schoolers might not just see him as an icon but a guide to the dark arts. I couldn't make this woman follow a lead she put no stock in.

But Valerie Ott couldn't stop me from picking apart this godforsaken club like a vulture with roadkill either.

# EIGHTEEN

I found Hen in the same place she'd been for nearly forty-eight hours, nestled deep in the blankets of our guest-room bed. Her back was to me, but I sensed she was awake, either crying or just staring at the moon outside. The window next to her bed led to the roof of our covered porch. That answered the question of how she'd snuck out, which, in the chaos of the past forty-eight hours, I hadn't thought to ask. The hinges on our heavy oak front door screeched like a witch, and I'd trained myself to listen for intruders. That window, though, told no tales.

'Hen?' Lowering myself to the edge of her bed, I put a hand on her shoulder. 'Henrietta, we need to talk.'

I waited for her to stir or at least acknowledge my presence. Nothing.

'I know this is hard,' I said, returning my hand to my lap. 'What happened was really scary. You just got here, you were just getting settled, and now everything is turned upside down.' Drawing a breath, I continued. 'I'm not sure how much you know about police procedure, but a death like Leif's has to be investigated. Based on what we've found, what we now know, we don't think it was an accident.'

Hen's body tensed. If nothing else, I had her attention.

'You seem to be the only witness to Leif's death. That makes you really important. It means I'm going to need your help.'

In the silence of the room her wet breaths rattled like beans in a can, but even after what I'd told her, she was quiet. I had to find a way to get this kid to open up.

Three years ago, after my abduction and narrow escape from Bram, I'd been in a similar state. My department had assigned me a police psychologist, and I'd sat across from Dr Carson Gates hating his office, his haircut, his novelty socks and plotting strategies to get away as fast as possible. *I bet there are a dozen places you'd rather be*, he'd said that day. He'd been right. But he also told me I could do this if I just took it slow, and I did, because that's what was required of me. Because I knew I had no choice.

Taking it slow wasn't going to work with my niece, who seemed content to never speak or eat or leave this room again. What I needed to do was recreate what I'd felt in Carson's office. Convince her that cooperating with me was her only option.

Playing the odds, I said, 'I think we should call your mom and dad again.'

Hen flinched, but I continued.

'We can do it together,' I told her, reaching into my back pocket for my phone, its screen casting the dark room in a soft blue light. 'You don't have to confide in me, but you do have to tell someone. Explain it to your dad, OK? I'm sure he'll understand why you snuck out and—'

'No.' Hen's voice was a croak.

'Your mom then? If you'd like to talk to her instead—'

'I don't want to talk to either of them. I won't.'

'Leif was your boyfriend, right? Can you explain how—'

In a flurry of movement, Hen flipped over to glare at me. Her skin was a swollen patchwork of crimson and white, her eyes and nose puffy and pink. Even her lips looked twice their normal size from all the crying, so red and raw they must have hurt.

'My *what*? Leif wasn't my boyfriend. I barely knew him.'

I shook my head. Had I misunderstood? 'When I found you in the cave, you said he was your boyfriend.'

'You're wrong,' said Hen. 'You don't know what you're talking about.'

'Then set me straight. Explain it to me. Hen, a boy is dead.'

'Don't you think I know that? I was right there. He was cold and blue and his eyes were . . .' She twitched and squeezed her own eyes shut against the memory. 'But I didn't know him, and I had nothing to do with him dying.'

'Then who did?'

Hen folded her arms and broke my gaze.

I would need to try a different tack. 'How do you know Mia and Tristan?' I asked. 'How did you meet?'

'English. Mia's in my class.'

'I thought you said you didn't have any friends at school.'

She shrugged.

*So this is what it feels like to be a parent*, I thought as I stared at my niece. I'd heard the teenage years could be excruciating, and the rumors were clearly true. I'd put my own folks through their share of grief, but in the grand scheme of things, they'd had it easy. At least until I grew up, and they got that phone call from New York telling them I'd disappeared.

I had a smattering of experience with juveniles who lacked moral fiber and impulse control, boys and girls whom I encountered at their low points through my work, but Hen's breed of rebellion felt different. She was, as Tim had noted, likely scarred by Leif's death, but she had to understand that what she'd witnessed was critical evidence.

She told me as little as possible. Whenever I'd start fishing, casting in her direction, she would intentionally evade my line. What possible reason could she have for dodging my questions? Again and again, I'd asked her what happened on the island. Again and again, she returned to that same, vague story: she'd stumbled on to Leif, a virtual stranger, in the water and hauled him to the shore.

'I think she's lying,' I told Tim later, once I'd given up on Hen yet again. He was in the living room reading a novel and drinking a cup of tea – peach, by the sweet aroma wafting from his cup. 'Why would she lie? Garrick confirmed that she tried to help Leif – and she was the only kid on that island who did – but Hen won't go into details, no matter how hard I push. It's obvious she's hiding something. And why did she call Leif her boyfriend if that isn't true?'

As I spoke, Tim lowered his book to his lap. He was wearing his thoughtful face, eyebrows cinched and lips pursed. 'Everyone her age lies. I did too,' he said, 'when I was sixteen. But most of the time, I wasn't doing it to protect myself.'

'Then what—' I began and stopped short. Dammit, Tim was right. Kids Hen's age lied to cover their assess, but their duplicity wasn't only about self-preservation. Sure, they lied to keep themselves out of trouble.

But they also lied to protect their friends.

'Go easy on her,' Tim said, wincing as he sipped his scalding tea. 'She's just a kid.'

'So was Leif Colebrook,' I replied.

# NINETEEN

'Shana? There's someone here to see you.'

In the doorway to my office, Tim took a step aside and Ford Colebrook appeared behind him.

I hadn't expected to see Leif's father again so soon. No doubt Valerie would want to arrange an interview, but it was the kids who'd be in the hot seat today. I wondered briefly if Ford had come in the hopes of seeing Mia and Tristan; by all indications, one of them was responsible for his son's death. It was also possible he was here to see Hen. I didn't like that thought at all.

'Mr Colebrook,' I said. 'It's good to see you. The investigator who's working Leif's case isn't in yet, but if you'd like to wait . . .'

'Actually,' he said as Tim closed the door behind us, 'I came to talk to you.'

I offered him a seat across from my desk. Ford had to know he was beautiful, but he was one of those men who was either very modest or very good at hiding his confidence. Resting his elbows on the knees of his jeans and leaning toward me, he didn't make a move to push the hair from his eyes – hair that was damp and tangled and smelled faintly of the river. He'd been diving again. I could understand that it reminded him of his wife and brought him some semblance of comfort, but given the nature of Leif's death, I couldn't imagine the resolve it must take for Ford to lower his body into the water every day.

I smiled at him and said, 'How can I help?'

'Well,' Ford said, 'it might be nothing, but I was thinking about that club.'

*You and me both.* 'Oh?'

'Leif never mentioned it,' he said, 'but I wanted you to know there were some . . . stories . . . going around about his mom's death.'

I felt my head tilt. 'What kind of stories?'

'Just rumors,' he said, already downplaying what he'd come

to say. 'Geena's death was an accident, like I told you, but people sensationalize things, and there were those who convinced themselves her death wasn't so cut and dry. It was ridiculous. Hurtful, really. I tried to protect Leif from it. He was so young when Geena died, not even thirteen, and I didn't want to confuse him. But if Mia Klinger's obsessed with crime, she might have found out about all that. Asked Leif about it maybe. It's the only explanation I can think of, because to be honest, it's kind of strange that Leif was out on Devil's Oven with Mia.'

'Did they not get along?' I asked.

'They just didn't hang out. Not that I was aware of anyway.'

Courtney had said the same thing. But if Leif and Mia weren't friends and rarely socialized, why had Leif gone to the island? It took some effort, as we knew, and he hadn't ridden with Mia, Tristan, and Hen. We had yet to determine how he got there.

'I don't know if that helps,' Ford said. 'I wanted you to know.'

'It definitely does. I'll make sure to share this information with the team. Thank you.'

'Of course.'

Ford got to his feet, and I did the same.

Walking the man to the door, I sensed a tension in his limbs. He seemed nervous. Twitchy.

As I reached for the knob, promising him I would keep in touch, his weight shifted. Years of karate had enhanced my reflexes, sharpening them like a whetted knife, so that when someone so much as jerks in my direction, my instinct isn't to flinch but block them. Protect myself at all costs. Couple those reflexes with years of being shadowed by a killer, and it's not easy to get close to me. But suddenly, somehow, Ford's arms were around my torso, his breathing warm and slow on my neck as he held me in a tight embrace.

It wasn't the first time I'd been hugged by the grieving relative of a victim. It isn't public knowledge, but witnesses, even the occasional suspect, ask for hugs on occasion. The crisis intervention and tactical communication skills taught at the academy are designed to de-escalate potentially volatile situations, and for desperate, inconsolable, or inebriated individuals, that process can be emotionally draining. I'd been trained to use empathetic listening, instinct, and compassion to build a rapport. The BCI discouraged physical contact, but the exception to that rule occurred when a touch was initiated by someone else. If a distraught father or sister goes limp in an investigator's arms, extricating ourselves is a delicate process. That was the situation I found myself in with Ford.

*He's hurting*, I thought. *Alone.* Maybe I felt I owed it to Ford to ease his pain because my niece had been out there with Leif when he died. And so, for just a minute, I let him hold me.

What I couldn't explain was the way my pulse picked up when he did.

# TWENTY

'How well did you know Leif Colebrook?'

Valerie clasped her hands as she spoke, and the position read as both anticipatory and placid. The interview table was intentionally small, but even though she and Sol were mere inches from the Klingers, Mia didn't shrink away. To the contrary, the girl with the meticulous makeup, tiny crop top, and high-waisted jeans held Valerie's level gaze.

'The balls on this kid,' I whispered to Tim from where we were observing through the double-sided glass.

'Makes you wonder if she's overcompensating. Covering up how she really feels,' he said.

'It certainly does.'

'Leif went to my school,' said Mia, her voice honeyed and light. 'He was a year older though.'

She hadn't answered the question. Valerie said, 'Were you and Leif close?'

Kim Klinger straightened up. 'Like she said, he's a year older. I don't remember too many senior boys wanting to hang out with juniors when I was in high school – do you?' Kim's smile died on the vine. A blonde like her daughter, with long bangs and too much eyeliner, she wore knock-off Uggs covered with purple sequins and her skintight Radiohead T-shirt was splashed with the words *I'm a creep*. Wherever Mia got her cool demeanor, it wasn't from her mother. Kim was pasty and sweaty. She looked petrified.

'No, we weren't *close*,' said Mia. 'Not like our parents.'

'Me and Ford are old friends,' said Kim, flashing Valerie another tense smile.

Mia said, 'I only invited Leif out there because of Hen.'

*Fuck.* I knew Hen's name would come up, that it would be recorded along with the rest of the conversation and added to a growing file of evidence, but hearing it now, during this formal interview, made my knees weak. It was abundantly clear that

Valerie Ott was a new breed of BCI investigator, exactly the kind of recruit Mac and I had failed to find in Geneva. She had the confidence of someone twice her age and the grit of a street fighter who'd seen it all. Today, her button-down was sky blue with a metallic sheen, her slacks perfectly tailored, the frayed friendship bracelet peeking out from her cuff the only part of her not polished and primped. I hoped the fact that she was a mother would work in Hen's favor. Right now, she could use every advantage she could get.

'That's interesting,' Valerie said. 'Help me understand that, Mia. Did Leif want to go because of Hen or vice versa?'

'Because of Hen,' she said. 'I thought Leif would want to meet her. You know, because of Bram.'

Before he could rein in his emotions, Sol's mouth tipped into a grimace.

'Blake Bram,' said Valerie. 'Hm. Was Leif interested in him?'

'A lot of kids are.'

'A lot of kids?' I said to Tim. 'Not according to Hen. Most kids want nothing to do with her.'

'A lot of kids?' Valerie repeated on the other side of the glass.

Mia nodded. 'It's pretty cool.'

'Pretty cool.' Valerie unfolded her hands and jotted something on the notepad in front of her. That was when Kim spoke up again.

'You have to understand,' Mia's mother said, 'I own a ghost tour business – Island Death? Right here in town? This interest Mia has in death and murder and all, it's because of the tours. She helps me give them – did you know that? She does a great job – people love her. The tips this kid makes! I can't compete. And this has been going on for years, so I can promise you it's completely harmless.'

Valerie didn't move. Beside her, Sol was watching the investigator as much as Kim and Mia. Waiting to see what she would say next. Valerie Ott's composure was mesmerizing.

'Let's talk about Blake Bram,' she said, as if the thought had just occurred to her. 'Seems like you're pretty interested in him too.'

'Yeah. I'm into him.'

*Into Bram.* Like my murderous cousin was a comic book or

pop band. Without taking his eyes from the window, Tim rubbed my arm, stiff as a rod.

Mia said, 'I'm into all crime stuff, like my mom said. I want to be a criminal psychologist.'

Kim said, 'You never told me that.'

Mia ignored her.

'That's great,' said Valerie. 'It's good to have goals. Was this, like, a club meeting out at the island?'

Mia's eyebrows shot up. 'A *club*? Um, no.'

Valerie nodded. Jotted. 'What were you doing out there?'

Another apathetic shrug. 'Just hanging out. Talking about Bram.'

Mia was not going to make this easy.

'And having a few beers? Let me be clear,' Valerie added, 'we aren't here to talk about underage drinking. I couldn't care less about that right now. But was there? Some drinking going on?'

'Maybe a little.'

'OK,' Valerie said. 'That was the plan then. Drink a little, talk about Bram. Is that what Leif was doing too?'

'Sure. And then he just, like, wandered off.'

'Why?'

'I guess he got bored?'

'What time was this?'

'I don't know,' Mia said. 'Close to one maybe? I didn't see him again after that.'

'You didn't see him again,' said Valerie. 'Not at all?'

'Not at all.'

'And what about Hen?' Valerie had leaned forward ever so slightly, shrinking the distance between them even further.

'Hen?' Mia Klinger said with a blink of her long, lush eyelashes. 'She followed him.'

# TWENTY-ONE

'That girl,' Sol said from his desk chair. 'I swear I've never seen a person less moved by death. I wouldn't necessarily expect her to break down crying, but man. The kid was cold as ice.'

I couldn't have agreed more. Cocksure Mia Klinger hadn't seemed remotely concerned about her involvement in a homicide case. To the contrary, I would swear she was enjoying herself.

'What about Tristan?' I asked Sol. I'd wanted to observe that interview too, but Tim had advised me to tread carefully. It was Valerie's case now, and while she seemed willing to accommodate my interest given my relationship with Hen, I didn't want to push it. So, while Tristan had fielded questions, I'd designated Sol my inside man and driven home to pick up Hen.

'Tristan was more upset, definitely,' he said, 'but that might have been because of his brother. Charles Laurier can't be older than twenty-five, but he's Tristan's legal guardian and he runs a tight ship, especially since Tristan got in trouble at school last year. Tristan strikes me as kind of a pushover. No backbone, you know? Putty in the hands of a girl like Mia. He definitely regretted taking that Jet Ski out to the island – and as much as he may like having a girlfriend, he turned on her in seconds flat. Said the whole thing was Mia's idea.'

'What did he have to say about Leif?' I asked.

'Same as Mia: they weren't close. Makes you wonder why Leif went out to that island, huh?'

*To talk about Bram and ogle Hen.* That was Mia's story anyway. At the moment, I was more concerned about how Leif got there.

'Valerie's going to track down that other kid, right?' I asked Sol. 'Whoever it was that dropped Leif at the island?'

Tim, who'd been listening with his hands sunk in the pockets of his work pants, said, 'She's got to. The whole village is talking about Leif's death, even more so since it was reclassified as a homicide. Weird that the driver hasn't come forward.'

'Weird,' I said, 'and alarming. If it was my case—'

'Which it's not,' said Tim.

'But if it *was*, finding our mystery ferryman would be priority number one. Let me know what Valerie gets up to, will you, Sol? Just . . . keep me in the loop? This case hits close to home.'

'Don't they all?' he said, running a hand back and forth over his bristly hair.

'You girls ready?'

Valerie had appeared down the hall, where she stood with arms folded and a too-cheerful smile. I'd left Hen in my office to work on a project for English, something about class divide in *The Great Gatsby*. The clock on the wall read five p.m., and I was about to take a seat in the interview room not as an active investigator but as Hen's civilian guardian.

'Just be honest,' I'd told Hen on the drive back to the barracks, doing my best to prep her for what was to come, 'and for God's sake, don't talk back.' Valerie didn't seem like the type to take shit, but Hen, like Mia, knew how to give it.

'Ready,' I said.

'How well did you know Leif Colebrook?'

It was the same question Valerie had asked Mia, but put to my niece, it had added heft. Hen shouldn't know Leif at all. She'd only been in town for a week. I wanted to tell Valerie to back off, that she was making unfair assumptions, but I couldn't. I couldn't say anything like that, because my niece was being questioned about a young man's murder, and because Hen, despite recanting her statement, had called that young man her boyfriend.

The interview had started out soft enough, with Sol offering Hen something to drink and Valerie telling her the indication of a crime meant Hen was now an essential witness. I watched Hen closely, observing her fine Nordic features as she struggled to keep whatever she was feeling and thinking under wraps. If she was upset, if she missed her parents, it didn't show. Whatever state of shock she'd been in had passed. She was Hen again, her breathing controlled, that aloof expression giving nothing away.

'Answer the question,' I told her when the silence stretched on.

'I didn't know Leif,' Hen said. 'Not at all.'

I swallowed. Summoned all my strength and said, 'Remember, you have to tell the truth.'

'That is the truth,' said Henrietta.

Valerie smiled without showing her teeth. 'She's going to be very helpful, I can tell,' she said, and though it wasn't clear which of us she was addressing, an uncomfortable prickle at the base of my neck told me Hen was being played.

I felt hot and useless, sitting by while Valerie sweet-talked my niece. *It's a style thing*, I told myself. *A strategy, nothing more.* Everyone had a different approach to dealing with a difficult witness. What mattered was that we got what we needed from her, and if that meant undermining my authority – what little I had left – then I would shut up and take it.

'We've got all the time in the world, Henrietta – can I call you Hen? So let's go back to the beginning,' said Valerie. 'Why don't you tell me, in your own words, what you remember about Saturday night?'

Hen twisted a strand of greenish hair around her finger. Examined a chipping red nail. The barracks always reeked of stale coffee and printer ink, both aromas baked into the chair upholstery and cheap wooden desks, but the interview room smelled of the cleaning solution used by the night janitor. Lemony fresh.

Hen said, 'I didn't see what happened. I didn't know something was wrong until I went looking for Leif.'

'And why did you do that?' asked Valerie.

'Mia and Tristan were all over each other. It was gross. And Leif had been gone for a while.'

'Did you have reason to be worried?'

'Not really,' she said.

'I understand he'd been drinking.'

'Everyone was.' Hen didn't bother to look embarrassed, though she must have clocked the disappointment in my side-eye.

'Everyone,' Valerie repeated. 'Does that include you?'

'I had some beer.'

'How many beers would you say you drank, Hen?'

'A few.'

'Enough to get you drunk?'

Another shrug. *Good God, this kid's going to end up in prison.* At least she was finally talking.

'OK. What about the others?' asked Valerie. 'You're new to town, right? They must have known Leif better than you did. Why didn't they check on him instead?'

Hen said, 'You'd have to ask them that.'

'That's fair. Why do you *think* they chose not to go?'

Hen paused and worried her lip before saying, 'Maybe because Leif was pissed.'

'Pissed at Mia and Tristan?' I asked.

Valerie shot me a look as Hen shook her head.

'Just at Mia.'

I couldn't say whether Hen had caught the subtle shift in Valerie's aura, but I did. The pretty investigator, her long black hair looped into a low bun, had tensed like a spinning reel.

'Why was Leif pissed at Mia?'

'Mia and Tristan had been talking about ghosts.'

'Ghosts.'

'Yeah,' said Hen. 'Mia's into all that paranormal stuff.'

'And Leif? Was he into ghosts and *paranormal stuff*?' Valerie made air quotes with her fingers.

'No. He didn't seem to like it. That's why he left. I guess Leif's mom died not that long ago.'

Geena Colebrook. My brain kicked into gear as I remembered what Ford had said in my office about Geena's death. *If Mia Klinger's obsessed with crime, she might have found out about that. Asked Leif about it.* Ford had referred to the stories as rumors. He'd also implied that Mia might be interested in them. Had she been questioning Leif about the circumstances surrounding Geena Colebrook's death? Was that the reason Leif had taken off?

I tried to catch Valerie's eye, but she wouldn't look at me. When I glanced at Sol, he lifted his eyebrows. The man hadn't gotten a word in since asking Hen if she wanted some water, and had apparently given up trying.

'Did Leif talk about his mother's death at all?' asked Valerie.

'No. He didn't want to. When Mia brought it up, he left.'

'What exactly did Mia say? Do you remember?'

Hen's eyes darted away. 'Not really. She was talking about famous murders, and then she mentioned Leif's mom. I don't know.'

'And then Leif left.'

'Yeah.'

'And you went after him?'

'Mia did,' Hen said. 'They talked for just a minute, behind a tree. Then she came back to the fire.'

'But not Leif?'

Hen shook her head.

'And then *you* left? To find Leif?'

'After a while, yeah.'

'Alone?'

Hen nodded.

*Shit.* Did she really not see she was setting herself up to be a suspect? 'Don't forget about the other kid,' I said.

In unison, Hen, Valerie, and Sol's heads twisted my way.

'Leif didn't come to the island with Hen, Mia, and Tristan. Someone dropped him off.'

'Do you know who dropped Leif off, Hen?' Valerie asked.

With another brisk head shake she said, 'I didn't see. He was already on the island when we got there.'

'No worries,' said Valerie. 'I'll look into it. You probably already know this from your aunt, but I'll be talking to everyone who might know what happened out on the island that night. The reason I do that is to compare stories. Investigators can't know for sure if someone's telling the truth. So we listen to everyone's stories, and we look for discrepancies.'

On our side of the table, both Hen and I were perfectly still.

'And if someone's lying,' Valerie said, flashing that thin, toothless smile, 'we find out.'

# TWENTY-TWO

The ride home was quiet, Hen's face shuttered as she stared absently out the window at the farmland flickering by. Try as I might, I couldn't get a read on what she was feeling. I kept imagining myself at her age, going through what she'd just been through. I would have been scared shitless. Unlike Abe, I'd been a kid who could hold my own with adults, cheeky and unafraid, but to sit before two New York State Police investigators and field questions about a murder? To know I'd disappointed the people who loved me most? How was this kid so relaxed? Where the hell did she get the mettle?

'My money's on Tristan,' Valerie said before we left the station, calling Tim and me into the interview room once I'd settled Hen back in my office to wait. 'All three of these juveniles are reluctant to talk, but I think they're covering for each other. Hen said Leif was pissed at Mia, but both she and Tristan were talking about a subject that upset Leif. And both Mia and Hen made a point of minimizing Tristan's presence. It's a bit odd that none of them have bruises or marks of their own suggestive of a struggle' – Valerie had, I knew, done a cursory check, making the kids roll up their sleeves and lift the hair from their necks for inspection – 'but Tristan has a history of violent behavior, isn't that right? I'm thinking the boys got in a fight, which is consistent with the bruises on Leif's body and neck. My guess? They got carried away and Leif – who was drunk himself – ended up in the water. As the only one in the group with lifeguard training, Hen tried to help.'

I'd be lying if I said I didn't feel some sense of relief. The new investigator liked Tristan for the crime, which ostensibly put Hen in the clear. But it wasn't that simple. I hadn't observed Tristan's interview, but I'd talked to the kid the night of Leif's death. Seen him fondling Mia by the fire, drunk and happy, not a care in the world. Tristan had been in trouble before, but his mood on the island had been jovial. It would take a stone-cold killer to attack a classmate, leave him to die, and keep making out with his girlfriend. If I didn't point out the chasmal flaws in Valerie's theory, someone else would, and I'd learned the hard way that things swept under the rug rarely stayed undiscovered.

'Do you really think Tristan's capable of murder?' I asked. 'Hen didn't mention anything about seeing a fight.'

'Like I said, she's covering for her new friends. And Mia's covering for her boyfriend,' said Valerie.

'But why would Hen protect Tristan over Leif?'

'She said she didn't know Leif.' Valerie's head was askew. 'What am I missing?'

All throughout her interview, I'd waited for Hen to confess she and Leif had been dating. Every time Leif's name was mentioned, I had held my breath in preparation for a confession that could alter the course of the investigation. But that loaded label – *boyfriend* – hadn't come up. Apart from a few disjointed words spoken while the girl was in a state of emotional shock, there was no record of a relationship between Hen and Leif. My eyes darted to Tim, the only other person in the room who knew what Hen had said that night on the island. He gave a nod.

'She was in shock,' I said, speaking slowly, 'but when I got to the island, I thought I heard Hen say something about a boyfriend. But I asked Leif's father about it, and he didn't even know who Hen was – not until Kim Klinger told him it was Hen who pulled Leif from the water.'

'We'll ask around,' Valerie said, nodding at Sol, who wrote the task on his to-do list. 'Seems like Hen would be quick to rat out the killer though, if she had a thing with Leif. This is going to be tricky.' The investigator blew out a breath. 'If it's Tristan, we'll need a statement from Hen or Mia to justify a criminally negligent homicide charge. Given Tristan and Mia are dating – that, we know for a fact – Hen may be our best bet.'

I couldn't see Hen agreeing to that, but I didn't have a chance to point it out. Already, Valerie was heading for the door.

'What about the other kid?' I asked.

'What other kid?'

'The kid who dropped Leif off at the island.'

'All three juveniles say they didn't see who it was.'

'But someone dropped him off,' I said, my frustration mounting.

'For however long, someone else was at that island. Which means there might be someone else who knows what happened to Leif.'

Valerie's lower lip slipped between her teeth then, just enough to warp the shape of her pink mouth. 'I'll look into it,' she said simply before pushing open the door.

It was too hot in the car. Warm air blasted my face and the back of my neck felt clammy as I rehashed the conversation with Valerie in my mind. Fall comes early in the North Country, and some of the trees were already going bare. Yellow leaves, parched and curled, bounced across the empty stretch of road. We were almost home by the time I spoke to Hen.

'You took something from me. You deceived me, Hen, and I want to know why.'

From the corner of my eye, I saw her chin dip toward her chest. She had to know what I was talking about, but we were back to the silent treatment again. She reminded me of someone just then, her heedless apathy and bone-deep ennui enough to boil my blood, but I couldn't think of who it was.

'I know about the letter,' I told her. 'We're family, but you're also a guest in our home, and you had no right to go through my things. You certainly had no right to take something so . . .'

I paused. *Personal? Horrible?* How to describe my cousin's final missive, the blinding words that haunted me still?

'Good game.' I spat out the words like a broken pill, their chalky alkaloid insides coating my tongue. 'Was it you? Did you scratch those words on the rock at Devil's Oven?'

That caught Hen off guard. 'You know about that?'

'Yeah, I do. Was it you?'

When she didn't answer I gave a snort, equal parts furious and appalled. 'What the hell, Hen? You sat by and let them talk about Bram like he's some kind of star to be worshipped?'

The radio was on, I realized, the music barely audible. A meaningless whine.

'At least they were talking,' she said. By which she meant, *at least they were talking to me.*

'This club,' I said, 'who's in it?'

'It's not a club. Not really. Just an excuse to hang out and drink.'

'And you were the guest of honor, there to give them the inside scoop on a killer.'

Mia must have started the rumor Courtney heard, spreading the news that she had an all-access pass to Bram's kin. It was on-brand for a girl whose tastes ran dark, and as I thought it through, I realized it was possible Hen, not Bram, was the impetus for the trip to the island, if not the whole twisted fellowship. I had no doubt Mia had been into Bram before that, reading stories about him in magazines. Digging up dirt on his crimes. When – hallelujah – his blood relation arrived in town, mining Hen's insider knowledge had been too tantalizing a prospect to resist.

'Mia's obsession with him isn't healthy,' I said, 'and it's not right. Bram killed people, real people who were part of this community. We're not talking about decades-old crimes with victims whose immediate families are dead and gone. This town is full of people who knew Carson Gates, and Trey Hayes, and every other innocent man and woman and kid he terrorized – or worse – and Mia's celebrating that. She's giving tours of his victims' graves.' I bit down on my lower lip. Pulled a breath through my nose. 'How could you do it, Hen? How could you agree to something like that?'

Hen turned her face toward the window and stared out at the falling darkness.

'That day, with the ketchup?' my niece said at length. 'I was really upset. Like, so upset I almost lost it right in front of everyone. And then Mia was there. She gave that kid hell. She made *him* look like the loser. Mia stood up for me. The next morning, she stopped me in the hall and asked about Bram.'

A gob of bile caught in my throat. I winced as I willed it back down.

'What was I supposed to do?' Hen asked sincerely. 'If I didn't want to spend every day completely alone here, cursed to be a total reject like I was at home, she was my only hope. Mia said you must have some stuff lying around at the house, since you and Bram were friends.'

*Friends?* My God, was that what she thought?

'Bram was not my friend,' I said. 'He was unhinged, a psychotic killer who took countless lives – literally. The FBI is still trying to tally all the women he erased from this earth. He was ruthless and deeply disturbed. Bram and I were not *friends*.'

Hen shook her head. 'I read the articles. You were *best* friends. Until he tried to kill you.'

It wasn't uncommon for me to forget about the ugly scar across my cheek. When I wasn't looking in a mirror, or seeing the dark curiosity it incited in others reflected back at me, I hardly thought of it at all. Abe hadn't wanted to kill me when he gored my flesh with a rusty nail and tore open the side of my face, and it had taken a lot of therapy for me to accept that. He'd wanted to hurt me, yes. To punish me for abandoning him. But kill me? That was never his intent. To the contrary, my cousin wanted me alive to bear witness to what he'd become – and what he would do next.

'Nobody should have read that letter, not ever,' I said. 'It's dark and twisted and seriously fucked up, and it should never have seen the light of day.' Hen's eyes widened, but I didn't slow my pace. 'The words on the rock. Was that you?'

Her reflection in the window was ghostly white. She crooked her leg, rested her chin on one knobby knee. Mutely, she gave a miserable nod.

The idea that Hen and Mia had been romanticizing Bram's crimes, swooning over the way he dragged his knife through the skin of the innocent, made me queasy. I knew firsthand that obsession was a brambled path, clawing at your flesh every step of the way. Most took the thorns as a sign: stop, turn back, beware – but there were those who kept walking, pushing through those barbs to emerge enraptured and bleeding. Had that path lured Henrietta? Was she already through to the other side?

'Listen to me,' I said. 'These secrets, this subterfuge, it stops now. Valerie Ott isn't kidding around. If you know anything else about what happened to Leif, anything at all, you need to tell me.'

She'd been picking at a tear in her jeans, the hole that spanned her thigh so frayed it framed a white net of spiderweb-fine threads, but now her fingers stilled.

'Mia and Tristan were by the fire all night. They had nothing to do with what happened to Leif. He was already dead by the time I got there.'

The rush of tires on the empty road. That music, either classical or the smooth jazz station, turned down so low I was almost convinced it was playing inside my head, the memory of a tune I'd heard in the grocery store or coffee shop. Now, it blared in the silence between us.

Hen had taken the letter. She had shown it to her friends, whether to fit in or because she felt she owed Mia for telling off a bully. Hen, despite knowing how much it would hurt her family, had gone along with the plan to meet at the island to talk about Bram.

What else had she done to impress Mia Klinger?

I looked at her for a moment longer before returning my eyes to the road.

Lying is like hunting. In the woods, you set a trap. Pry open the foothold and check the pan, the trigger. Lying can get you what you want . . . until someone calls you back to the clearing. Then you have to retrace every step, or it's you caught in that trap's jagged teeth.

# TWENTY-THREE

I could have stayed home. Nuzzled Tim in front of the TV and attempted to talk through the problems we were having. Reconnected in bed. But thoughts of Bram were haunting me. I was terrified about what Hen had done, and livid about the club, and I couldn't bring myself to sit still. And so I told Tim I was going for a quick drive, and headed back downtown to Walton Street.

Island Death Ghost Tours had no visible signage, just a pink neon light shaped like a Pac-Man ghost dangling in its front window. It was situated in an old brick building that looked mostly abandoned, its façade blackened in places as if damaged by fire. The only other commercial storefront on the main floor had cracked windows that had been papered over, and the second and third floors looked to be apartments long past their prime. The place was, in a word, depressing.

It surprised me that the Klinger family had made such an inconspicuous choice, especially in a tourist town that relied heavily on foot traffic and impulse buys. Walton Street was almost entirely residential, with nothing to offer visitors beyond a CBD dispensary and a church. This wasn't New York or Chicago with their hip back-alley speakeasies vaunted by glossy local lifestyle magazines.

Through the window, I could see Kim supplemented her tour income with retail sales. A shelf against the wall held Tarot cards, Ouija boards, and books of ghost stories: *The Shining*, *The Haunting of Hill House*, and a number of titles specific to the region, including one about the ghost of someone called Billy Masterson. On the counter, a stack of tri-fold brochures shone like a beacon. If Carson Gates's name was in it – or Blake Bram's for that matter – there was going to be hell to pay.

I pushed open the door.

The space was hot and dark and had the air of a shoddy psychic reading room. Flocked velvet drapes and purple wallpaper patterned in black roses. A vintage chandelier, also black, covered in layer upon layer of cheap flapper fringe. Scuffed floor, salvaged ticket counter, mismatched chairs along the wall. Mia had claimed business was booming, but I saw no evidence of that here. Someone had tacked up a tapestry behind the counter that bore the name of the tour, and that was edged in fringe too, the snagged strands twisted and uneven. Kim leaned against the counter's edge. Her eyes were concealed by her wing-like bangs, her head bowed over a cell phone.

'Welcome to— Oh,' she said when she looked up.

I'd stayed hidden from her at the barracks, so I shouldn't have looked familiar, but her eyebrows rose at the sight of me all the same.

'You're Detective Shana. I saw you in the paper last year. Are you here for a tour?' She said it with a nervous laugh, long nails picking at a loose thread on her shirt, but then her expression darkened. 'Or to talk to Mia?'

Confused, I asked, 'Is she here?'

'We live upstairs,' Kim told me, and when she nodded toward the back of the room, I noticed a hallway, the staircase to the second floor just visible in the dim light. 'The glamorous life of a single mom. We already talked to the police,' she said. 'I heard your niece did too. It's so terrible about Leif, and for the girls to be out there when it happened. You never get over something like that, and they're so young – just babies really. Death can really mess with someone's head.'

Some people are naturally nervous around cops, and Kim Klinger appeared to be one of them. It would explain her unease in the interview room. Her erratic way of speaking.

'I know my colleague interviewed all three kids – Mia, Tristan, and Henrietta,' I said. 'Thanks for your cooperation with that. What I'm here to talk about, actually, is Mia's interest in Blake Bram.'

On the drive over, I'd convinced myself that inquiring about Bram fell outside the purview of the case. Valerie had made it clear she wasn't interested in pursuing Mia's obsession. From where I was standing, that made it fair game.

'I caught a few minutes of Mia's tour on Sunday night. She talks about Bram quite a bit.'

'Well,' Kim said, relaxing a bit, 'that's kind of what we do.' She pointed at the Pac-Man sign as she said it, as if anyone could have missed that pink, pixelated ghost. 'I keep a scrapbook of deaths in the area, especially the unnatural ones, so when Bram came to town . . .' She shrugged as if to imply the whole thing was out of her control. 'In my line of work, you can't really ignore an event like that.'

I said, 'Was it Mia's idea? Talking about him on the tour? Letting people tramp all over Carson Gates's grave?'

'We're a team.' Her voice was flat now, as unyielding as ice. 'Mia has a lot of good ideas. Look, she already talked to those detectives, so I don't know why any of this matters?'

*It matters because I knew Carson*, I thought, *and he's been reduced to a stop on some tawdry excursion.*

'I can't make you take Carson's grave off your tour,' I told her. 'But I would ask that you at least consider his family.'

She narrowed her eyes. 'They haven't complained.'

'Maybe not,' I said. 'But I have.'

'I'll think about it,' Kim said after a beat, though I doubted that was true. If incorporating Bram's crimes into the ghost tours was drawing more customers and Kim Klinger's storefront still looked like this, I didn't think it likely she'd turn the knob down on their barefaced sensationalism. A lot of businesses kept reduced hours in the off-season, but Kim's was open on a Tuesday night in September. Something told me she and Mia would have taken paying customers ghost-hunting at midnight, or five a.m., or in a sideways hail storm as long as the price was right.

My plea was falling on deaf ears.

'By the way,' I said as I turned to go, 'I heard you had some nice things to say about my niece to Leif's father.'

That teased a smile out of the woman with the blonde curtain bangs. 'Mia told me all about it,' she said. 'I thought Ford should know. He and I are old friends.'

*Old friends.* They were the same words Kim had used in her interview, and I had no reason to doubt them. Kim had called Ford to give her condolences and let him know about Hen's attempt to save Leif, and Ford hadn't seemed surprised that she'd reached out. I barely knew Ford, but I had a hard time imagining him hanging out with Kim. Ford was gentle and nuanced, while

Kim ran a business built on drama. I wondered if she'd been closer to Geena and had simply inherited Ford's friendship now that his wife was gone.

'Ford loved that boy more than anything,' Kim told me. 'I hope you find out how this happened.'

'How do you think it happened?'

The words were out before I could stop them. I instantly regretted asking, but at the same time, I couldn't get a fix on what was going through this woman's head. We'd already determined Leif's death wasn't an accident, and as far as we knew, there had only been three other kids on that island. One was Kim's daughter, the other Mia's boyfriend, and here was Kim singing Hen's praises. Who the hell did she think had killed Leif?

'You know,' she said, tapping her long, painted nails against the counter, 'the detective we talked to never asked me that? Kind of surprising really. Maybe you can pass this along. I don't for one second believe that Leif Colebrook was murdered. I think his death was an accident,' she said. 'Just like his mother's.'

# TWENTY-FOUR

When I called Doug and Josie early the next morning to get their read on sending Hen back to school, they said they were all for it. I'd been surprised when the school hadn't cancelled classes despite the shocking news of foul play, but Courtney had filled me in on the administration's reasoning. Leif's funeral had been scheduled for Saturday, and Courtney expected half the school to turn out for it, but until then, recovering some semblance of a routine seemed to make sense. 'Better to keep the kids busy,' she'd said. 'Help get their minds off things as much as we can.'

I'd allowed Hen to stay home on Monday and Tuesday, but the principal had called in extra grief counselors, going so far as to set up a 'chill zone' for kids who were feeling scared and overwhelmed, and Hen could use that kind of help. While I didn't like the idea of her interacting with Mia, who'd no doubt be reveling in her notoriety given her penchant for dark things, I liked the thought of her spiraling into depression at home even less.

Hen had answered a few of Josie's concerned texts, which felt like progress. I'd been keeping my brother up to date by text too, letting him know how Hen was doing, though I often wasn't sure what to say. *Hen's been stealing from me* and *Hen's duplicity is making me question whether I want kids with Tim* were off the table, so I settled for something less alarmist. *Hen's coming around*, I told him, and left it at that. I couldn't help but wonder what the students who graduated from A-Bay's school in a year or two would be like as adults, raised in a town with as much fear as this one. But then I remembered Swanton, and Valerie's description of her own small-town youth. Tragedy didn't discriminate.

Courtney had offered to drive Hen in, so while we waited for her to arrive, Tim showered upstairs and I sat with Hen at the kitchen table, uncertain what to say. All I wanted was to get through to her. To make her trust me enough to open up, not just about Leif but everything else she was hiding too. But Henrietta Merchant was a freshwater mussel with a shell sealed against my advances, small and cold and hiding deep in the river's silt. She didn't talk to me while she ate her cereal, her phone once again face-up by her side. The icons indicating Snapchat messages were visible on the screen. She was still talking to Mia then. Maybe Tristan too.

'Did I ever tell you about my friend Suze?'

Hen eyed me, shook her head, and went back to listlessly chasing Cheerios around her bowl.

'Suze was a real piece of work. She was wild,' I said, cracking a smile. 'Like, really wild. She wasn't always the best influence on me. One summer, in the middle of the night, she convinced me to jump off Lone Rock.' I pictured it now, the night air rushing across Lake Champlain to snatch at my hair and sting my bare skin, and shivered. 'Have you ever been?'

'Dad won't let me. He says he was never allowed to jump so I'm not either, but I think he's lying.'

'Oh,' I said, weighing my options. 'You want the truth? He is.'

'I knew it,' she said, her grin like a dying spark, already gone.

'He's right about it being dangerous though. I had a scary night out on that rock when I was around your age.'

'Gram and Gramps let you do that?'

*Shit.* I'd been so excited to get Hen talking that I'd neglected to think the story through. 'They didn't exactly know,' I said. 'I may have snuck out once or twice.'

'Hypocrite.'

'Not so fast. I would never, ever have snuck out without letting them know.' When she gave me a baffled look, I said, 'Every time I did it, I left a note on my pillow.'

'Really?' Hen's green-tinted head was fully lifted now. 'What did it say?'

'Oh, you know. "I snuck out, but I'm OK. You can punish me later." Something like that.'

She barked out a laugh. 'Seriously? *Why?*'

'Because I love them,' I said. 'Because I didn't want them to worry. As far as I know they never found it, but it always made me feel better, knowing they wouldn't freak out if they found my bed empty in the middle of the night.'

I still remembered that feeling, the push and pull of guilt and anticipation and pure, golden delight. At sixteen I was forever torn: I didn't want to miss out on the fun, but I also didn't want to cause my loved ones grief.

'I know what it's like,' I told her, solemn now and holding her gaze. 'Discovering someone you care deeply for has vanished in the night. I wouldn't wish that on anyone.'

'Wow,' Hen said with a snort. 'I was so wrong about you.'

'Meaning?'

'I always thought you were kind of a rebel. But you're a total nerd.'

I smiled. 'Wow. Thanks.'

'Well, maybe not a total nerd. I read the articles – including the long one on that blog that went viral. You almost died, like, four times in the last three years. But you're still doing the same crazy dangerous job.'

She had me there. 'I did quit once, right after the abduction. Right before I moved up here. I had to go back to it though. This isn't just work to me. It's my life.'

Courtney's knock at the door interrupted us, and as Hen left for school, actually making a point of waving goodbye, I felt the kind of lightness I hadn't experienced with her since she was a little girl. Then I remembered our first meal with her and how skilled she'd been at manipulation. Was this more of the same?

There were no more shower noises coming from upstairs, the rush of water in the pipes gone quiet.

'Tim?' I called from the staircase as I pulled up a contact and dashed off a text message on my phone. 'I'll meet you at work, OK? I'm taking a quick trip to Watertown.'

When he replied that he'd see me later, not asking where I was going or why, the ennui in his voice rang in my ears.

# TWENTY-FIVE

'That family's been through the wringer,' Cunningham said. 'Two deaths just a few years apart? It's like some endless living nightmare.'

I hadn't seen Jared Cunningham for months, though we talked on occasion, and when I had the time, I made a point of visiting his website. Surviving the Crime had evolved from a sparsely populated blog to a full-fledged media platform devoted to sharing stories not of murder victims, but the families of those who'd been compelled to kill. It was my own story that had launched the endeavor, but the long-time newsman turned online magazine editor had since hired a small team of interviewers and writers to help.

Cunningham wasn't entirely surprised when I texted him a breakfast invitation. The former *Watertown Daily Times* reporter liked to play detective, and he had his finger on the pulse of crime in Jefferson County. I knew it was likely he'd heard about Leif's murder. I also knew he'd have some thoughts about another death in Alexandria Bay.

'It's not my case anymore,' I explained. 'Conflict of interest. The new investigator's keeping me in the loop as a professional courtesy, but my niece's involvement means I'm benched.'

'Makes sense,' he said, 'after everything with Bram.' Cunningham's fingers fluttered across his strawberry-blond comb-over as he spoke, making sure every feathery hair was in place. 'Believe it or not, I didn't accept your invitation so I could dig for dirt.'

'Really? I don't believe it, frankly.' I smiled as I reached for my coffee. I'd ordered a breakfast sandwich to go with it, but all that remained of that was a smear of yoke on the plate. Cunningham had suggested we meet at Watertown's Paddock Arcade, a historic covered shopping mall not far from where he lived. Few of the arcade's original Gothic Revival elements remained, but the first floor still boasted a checkerboard steel-and-wire glass ceiling that filtered light from the glass roof above, and the restaurant Cunningham picked had seating in the old-fashioned main thoroughfare, café curtains printed with forks and spoons and an ancient-looking standing placard out front advertising a Friday Night Fish Fry. I'd liked the place even before tasting the sandwich.

'So what did you find on Geena Colebrook?' I asked.

'Well,' he said, drawing out the word, 'hearing that name jogged my memory. I actually wrote about Geena Colebrook's death.'

'Did you really?' I'd been hoping that was the case – there weren't many crime reporters at the local paper – but I still felt a jolt of anticipation upon hearing the news.

'Dive accidents happen,' Cunningham said, 'more often than you'd think, especially around here. River dives are pretty dangerous, from what I've heard. Poor visibility and all that. In the Colebrook woman's case though, things were a little different. I remember there was no autopsy – strange but not unheard of. Here's what's really interesting: not long after the news broke about the accident, I got an anonymous email saying Geena's death was murder.'

'You're kidding. Her husband didn't mention that.' Ford had implied there were rumors to that effect, but an email claiming the drowning was a crime? That changed things.

'There were two friends on the dive with Geena,' Cunningham said. 'I wrote down their names.' He took out his phone. 'Some kind of girls' adventure, I guess. Here we go. Looks like her friends were both local to Alex Bay. Mandy Vance and Kim Klinger.'

'Kim Klinger? She was on the dive with Geena when she died?'

'That's right. And the email I got claimed she was responsible for Geena's drowning.'

My mind was reeling. 'And you said there was no name on the message?'

'Nope.'

'It doesn't make sense. Why didn't Ford push for an inquest,' I asked, 'if someone cried foul play?'

'Couldn't tell you. I did call the State Police at the time, just in case there was some truth to it all. I was told they were looking into it.'

'Well, you can bet I'll look into it too.'

'There's something else,' Jared Cunningham said as he continued to tap away at his phone. 'As I was looking back through my old stories, I found another one mentioning the Colebrooks that you might be interested in.'

He handed over the device, the article already cued up on the screen. It was a *Watertown Daily Times* piece, just a few hundred words, and the headline instantly pulled me in: *Treasured Islands: River Rats Find Fun and Friendship in Gananoque.*

The story was feel-good fluff about four couples from Alexandria Bay who called themselves the River Rats, a term often used to identify the hard-core locals born and bred along the St Lawrence. The article talked of a group of friends who, every summer, spent a weekend together at a rental on the water in Gananoque. At the time of its publication, in June 2008, their tradition of getting away to Ontario had been going on for ten years.

Some of the names in the story were familiar.

Ford and Geena Colebrook.

Kim and Jack Klinger.

Mandy and Braden Vance.

My first impression was that the piece read like a paid promotion for Gananoque. I knew the town, just across the border from New York state, and not just because it was where Tim and I had decided to get our wedding cake. Gananoque had a well-respected performing arts playhouse and enviable restaurant scene, and the newspaper story touted the town's many benefits for travelers from the US:

> *The couples share a love of adventure; some scuba dive, while others prefer to go cliff jumping. When they were in their early twenties, they decided to add an annual weekend retreat to their bucket list. Upon every visit, the group golfs, kayaks, and enjoys leisurely swims in the river, unwinding together in a Thousand Islands oasis just a few miles from home.*

There were several quotes too. 'It's a time for bonding,' Geena Colebrook wrote. 'As much as we love our kids and jobs and everyday life, our days in Gananoque are always a welcome break.'

'We cook and eat and play games,' added Mandy Vance. 'And we always come back knowing a little more about each other than we did before.'

'A decade of trips together,' I said. 'No wonder Kim Klinger said she and Ford were close.'

Around a colossal bite of his breakfast sandwich, Cunningham said, 'Did she?'

'Yeah. I don't know a thing about Mandy Vance though.' If Mandy was really with Geena Colebrook when she died, Valerie would have to look into her.

'Hey, I don't know what I don't know,' Cunningham said as he flicked a crumb off his beige V-neck sweater, 'but a mother drowns in a dive accident, someone claims it's homicide, and a few years later someone drowns her kid in the very same river? Seems a little suspicious to me. Then again,' he added with a shrug, 'you know what James Bond was told in *Goldfinger*, right? Once is happenstance. Twice is coincidence. The third time it's enemy action.'

'Enemy action,' I repeated, folding my napkin into a tight square.

I didn't disagree with Cunningham – or Ian Fleming, for that matter. The similarities between these two deaths were strange.

I just wished I could see who the enemy was.

# TWENTY-SIX

I didn't intend to visit Kim again. But Walton Street was on the way to work, and after talking to Cunningham, I couldn't stay away. The news that Kim had been with Geena when she drowned was alarming. That her daughter had been with Geena's son when he too lost his life confounded me even more. Something shady was going on with these people, and if I wanted Valerie to take that claim seriously, I needed to provide her with as much evidence as I could get.

Kim wasn't visible in her storefront window when I rolled by. What I did see was Ford Colebrook's black pickup parked half a block up the street. With that *Proud Dad* sticker and covered bed, the truck's ownership was unmistakable. Was Ford here for Kim? I glanced around, but there was no sign of him. There wasn't much to see past Kim's building – a few more houses, most pretty run-down. A corner store that sold beer and kindling. The church.

I took my chances and followed the bend in the road toward the Walton Street Cemetery.

This was one of the tour stops, per the Island Death tri-fold brochure I'd swiped the previous night, now creased from its time in my pocket. As it turned out, Kim was too smart to mention Bram by name, but the flyer did promise to 'guide visitors to sites of historic haunts and recent horrors in one of America's most notorious murder towns.'

Murder towns. Christ.

The graveyard on Walton was an altogether different attraction. According to the brochure, it was home to the ghost of a girl who froze to death in her own bedroom somewhere in town. She could often be seen lingering by her grave, supposedly looking for a way to get warm. I could easily picture Mia in her black cape, pointing out the ghost 'orbs' conveniently cast by the nearby street lamp.

The weather had turned while I was talking to Cunningham,

dull alloy clouds filling up the sky, and when the sun clawed its way through the light wasn't warm but stark white, its glare off the tombstones blinding. This was the grittiest part of A-Bay, far enough removed from the tourist traps that beautification was the last thing on the mayor's mind. Both the street and sidewalk were cracked, the latter forking off toward empty, overgrown lots like roads to nowhere. Those homes that still stood must have been stunning once, the cut of their porches and gables indicative of hidden treasures now obscured by beige vinyl siding, a quick fix to deal with chipped paint and rotting wood. Since Tim and I had started working on our place I'd developed a new understanding of home restoration, and as much as I disliked the thought of all that history moldering in a plastic shell, part of me could understand why owners chose to slap on a cover and call it a day.

The cemetery was slightly elevated from the street, hemmed in by a low stone wall. No wrought-iron fence, no elaborate gate, no sign. Just a man, standing alone by a headstone. Even with his back to me, I knew it was Ford.

I watched him for a while, his expansive shoulders hunched as he studied the grave. I was no stranger to sorrow and had grown familiar with the desolation in his stance, but there was something more to the way he stood there. He had the aura of a stone statue, a hushed but mighty presence that rooted me in place. When he looked up, I startled and raised my hand in an awkward wave. He smiled at me. After that, there was nothing to do but join him.

'I'm so sorry,' I told him. 'I didn't mean to intrude.'

'You're not. I could use the company. Were you looking for me?' He spoke in that same molten voice I'd heard at the dive site, all honey and cream. 'Is it about Leif?'

I faltered, unsure how to proceed. What the hell was I doing, trespassing on this man's private pain? My questions could wait.

'Don't worry about it,' I said, heat rushing to my cheeks. 'We can talk another time.'

'No, please. If it's about Leif, I don't want to wait. It's killing me, not knowing what happened. Who hurt him. If there's anything I can do to help, I want to try.'

I drew in a breath. Ford's presence here and now was an

opportunity. This wasn't my case. But weren't Valerie and I on the same team? 'My colleague's trying to find out how Leif got to the island that night,' I said. 'We know he didn't come on the Jet Ski with the others.'

'I wondered about that too. Someone must have dropped him off,' said Ford. 'But they haven't come forward?'

'No – which is a big part of why we're so eager to find them. Could it have been a friend of Leif's who brought him?'

Ford knuckled his bearded chin. 'Maybe. He had lots of friends. He was a popular kid.'

'You didn't overhear him making any plans for that evening?'

'I took a dive group out on Saturday, late afternoon. By the time I got home, Leif was already out for the night. That wasn't unusual,' he said. 'He was almost eighteen, basically an adult. Maybe I should have tried harder to keep track of where he spent his time, but there's only so much trouble a kid can get into in a town this small.'

As he absorbed the words he'd spoken, the bitter irony of them, Ford squeezed his eyes shut.

'What about the boys he's closest to?' I asked, careful to be gentle with him. 'Maybe someone with access to a Jet Ski or boat?'

As Ford thought about that, his expression quirked in a way I couldn't read. 'This kid you're looking for,' he said. 'Would he be . . .'

'A suspect? Just a person of interest for now.'

He nodded. 'There are a couple boys, yeah. You could try them.'

The first name was unfamiliar. The second stopped me short. 'Did you say Asher *Vance*?'

'He and Leif were pretty tight,' said Ford.

I contemplated asking him about Mandy. In a village the size of Alexandria Bay, it was likely every Vance was related. Who was Mandy to Asher, and what did it mean that he and Leif were close? I knew I was already on thin ice with my questions, that Valerie would soon be interviewing Ford herself and wouldn't appreciate me interfering. At the same time, she had her sights squarely set on Tristan. The more I could find out myself, the better.

'Do you know the Vance family well?' I asked.

Ford nodded. 'A group of us used to go up to a camp in Canada.'

*The River Rats.* I waited for him to speak the name, but Ford just said, 'But that was about us. The kids just knew each other through school. Any connection they made was their own.'

'How well do you know Mia?' I asked. 'And Tristan Laurier?'

'Tristan? Not at all. I don't know Mia all that well either. She's a year younger than Leif. Like your niece, right? Hen, is it?'

It felt odd, Hen's name on his lips again, and I realized hearing him talk about her made me nervous. Here was a man who had lost so much. Surely he was looking for someone to blame? Hen had been with Leif at the end. She'd been the only one.

'Can I ask you something?' I said. 'Did Leif have a girlfriend?'

'A girlfriend?' The idea seemed to sadden him. 'Not that I know of. He wouldn't necessarily tell me though. We've always been close, but I could feel him pulling away a bit lately.' Ford's eyes glazed over, but then he blinked, and he was back. 'I figured it had to do with graduation. Nerves, maybe, about leaving home. Growing up.'

Those last words were strangled. I looked away, feeling worse than ever for having approached the man at such a vulnerable time.

'I'm sorry,' I repeated, turning to go. 'I'll leave you alone.'

'Shana,' Ford said, his voice weak and low.

When I turned back, he was watching me with a look so intense it made me shiver. Under swaths of dark hair stirring in the wind, his eyes were ringed with red. Ford's gaze dropped just a little to my jaw, but he didn't mention my scar. 'I have to say something. It's probably not my place.'

'It's OK,' I told him as my mouth went dry. 'Go ahead.'

'I've been following you,' he said. 'Not the way you're thinking – God, pretend I didn't say that. What I mean is that I read about you in the paper. Your life. Your connection to Blake Bram.'

I felt the blood drain from my face. I would never escape Bram, never. It didn't matter how much time passed or where I went; I could move to New Zealand and somehow Bram would follow, his ghost nipping at my heels.

'I don't—' I began and found I had nothing to say. I liked

Ford, and a sliver of me felt disappointed to discover that he, like so many others in A-Bay, had a dark fascination with my ties to a killer.

'I know what happened to Carson Gates,' he went on. 'I know you weren't together when he died, but that can't have been easy for you. My wife.'

He nodded at the gravestone. *Geena Colebrook*, it read. *1975– 2014*. She'd been thirty-nine when she died. Just a few years older than me.

'She and I were together more than half our lives. We were practically babies when we started dating, still in high school. I come here sometimes to get her up to speed on what she left behind. I never thought I'd have to tell her that our son—'

Ford couldn't get the words out. He buried his face in his large hands and his shoulders shuddered, though he didn't make a sound. I had another apology cued up and ready to go when Ford said, 'Do you believe in ghosts? I'm not talking about like in the movies or Kim's stupid tours. I mean spirits. Of the dead.'

I didn't answer right away. If Ford wanted me to tell him paranormal phenomena had legs, that there was some truth to the stories and theories, he would be dissatisfied. My outlook was more pragmatic than that. At the same time, when I thought of what I'd felt standing at Bram's deathplace, and the chill that washed over me at Carson's grave, and the flurries in my stomach I felt now next to Geena's, I wavered. 'Honestly,' I said, 'I don't know.'

That was when Ford Colebrook's hand brushed my cheek, and he pulled me in for a kiss.

The wind kicked up, leaves pelting my ankles. My ears thundered with the beating of my own heart. I felt cold and too hot and sick and alive, prickling with something between pleasure and pain. A man who wasn't Tim was holding me, kissing me, his beard tickling my cheek and his chest firm and warm against my breasts.

Like waking from a dream that felt all too real I pulled back, panting, and Ford registered the expression on my face.

'Oh God,' he said, his woozy smile melting away. 'I'm sorry. I thought . . .' His cheeks burned pink above his beard. 'Jesus, you're not married, are you?'

'Engaged,' I croaked, looking down at my hand – but the ring I'd expected to see wasn't there, the diamond Tim had worked so hard to source from a Canadian mine just south of Alaska conspicuously absent. The ring was perfect and flawless, and I hadn't wanted to sully it with all that messy paintwork at the house. I'd been taking it off, reverently placing it in a lidded jelly jar on the kitchen windowsill to keep it safe. Why hadn't I put it back on? When was the last time I'd worn it? Had I left it behind the other times I'd spoken with Ford too?

Had the oversight been intentional?

'You're hurting,' I blurted, as much to excuse my behavior as his own, but the line sounded like a platitude out loud. 'I should go. Thanks for the names. I'll give those boys a call.'

A charged silence zipped back and forth between us until Ford spoke again. 'I wasn't going to say anything, but . . . I heard you're not working the case.'

'Not officially. With my niece involved, it's complicated. But I'm helping. I . . . want to help.'

With a nod, he said, 'I'm glad.'

'I should go,' I said for a second time, and then I was hurrying across the grass in the direction of the street and the safety of my SUV. I didn't look back, not until I was inside, and when I did, Ford Colebrook was gone too and I was alone, with my bare ring finger and Tim's favorite travel mug in the cup holder of my car and the weight of what had just happened tightening like a hammy fist around my heart.

It was wrong, what I'd enabled, and I couldn't understand it. Was it pity I felt for Ford Colebrook? Was it guilt? I knew Hen was still harboring secrets, my own niece hiding something that might provide this poor man with some answers. Is that what stopped me from immediately pushing Ford away?

There was another possibility, one that made my stomach lurch: I liked being close to the bold, alluring man so badly abraded by pain. Ford Colebrook was a magnet for death, and I was attracted to that.

Because he and I were the same.

# TWENTY-SEVEN

I was back at the barracks in a matter of minutes, driving too fast along Route 12. Craving the reliable shelter of my workplace like a drug. Tim wasn't around when I walked past his desk, and for that I was thankful. I needed to process my encounter with Ford. To reason out what it meant.

I paced my small office, hands still shaking hard. What the hell had I just done? Ford had it rough. It pained me to imagine him alone in his house, wandering rooms that had once brimmed with laughter and life. And yet, what I felt wasn't customary pity for a victim's family. The way Ford had reached for me, both down by the water and next to his wife's grave . . . it was like we'd shared a hundred embraces already, just as though he had every right to press his lips to mine. I hadn't stopped him. That was the part I couldn't get past. I'd allowed it to happen, and worst of all, it had given me a thrill.

I slammed my hand against the desktop, shook out my fingers, and reached for my phone.

'This is Courtney.'

Even though I was the one who'd placed the call, Tim's stepmother's voice on the line gave me a start. I stammered out a greeting and tried to put Ford Colebrook out of my mind. 'I'm sorry to bug you at work, but I need— Can you— I'd love your help with something.'

'Whatever you need, honey,' Courtney said. 'Just name it.'

Her kindness was a knife in my side, and I clamped my teeth against the pain.

'I know those boys,' she said once I'd explained the situation and given her the two names. 'Let me think. Dariel's not likely to be driving a boat these days. He's in a cast from the knee down – football injury, I believe, and right at the start of the season. Now Asher, he and Leif definitely hung out.'

As Courtney spoke, I rubbed my bare ring finger raw. Somehow,

I'd neglected to wear my ring. Somehow, I'd allowed a man who wasn't my fiancé to kiss me.

Courtney said, 'If there was someone else out there with Leif on Saturday night, I'd start with Asher Vance.'

'Thank you,' I replied, clasping my head in my hands.

I'd known Hen's arrival would bring changes. I'd even suspected it might put some strain on my relationship with Tim. The house was a source of stress too – but we were engaged and in love. What was happening here? Thoughts of Ford had me in their grip and were pulling me deeper. I was drowning. No hope of help in sight.

'Shana?' The door cracked open, and Tim's face appeared. 'Got a sec?' he asked, looking contrite. 'I was hoping we could talk about—'

'I need to find Valerie.' I was still in my jacket, I realized, the phone clutched in my hand. 'I'm sorry – later, OK?' I stammered, pushing past my fiancé and out the door.

I cornered Valerie at Bogle's old desk and filled her in on what I'd learned. Reluctantly, she reached for her coat.

'Due respect,' she said with a pointed look, 'I worry that you're muddying the waters. Since Sol's out canvassing the islands near Devil's Oven for witnesses, though . . . you might as well ride with me.'

'Thanks,' I said as we walked to the parking lot – and meant it.

The address was out toward Clayton, a long string of numbers followed by a street name I didn't know. Google Maps hadn't made it easy to locate. When I looked at my phone screen to give Valerie directions, the image associated with the Vance family's business was blurred. It was as if someone had rubbed a greasy thumb across the photo. Like they didn't want the place to be found.

A few dozen mobile homes that weren't at all mobile were situated too close together on a couple acres of clear-cut land. That was the extent of Camp Vance. There was a small beach though. Plenty of fire pits for roasting marshmallows and hot dogs. The trailer park was closed now, its summer residents long since returned to Syracuse, Rochester, Ottawa, but I'd called on the drive over. Mandy Vance, as it turned out, was Asher's mother, and she and her husband Braden lived in the park year-round. She told us to come right over. Apart from Valerie's, there were no other cars to be found.

'Shana,' Mandy Vance said when she opened the door, ignoring Valerie completely. I suppressed a sigh. I was getting a little tired of this routine, strangers calling me by my first name like we were pals. Undermining my authority by stripping me of the investigator title I'd bled to earn.

'Ash is still at school and Braden's at work – he's in sales at the winery – but I can try to help,' Mandy said as we settled on to the built-in couch. It was upholstered in red and green stripes that smacked of a nineties Christmas morning and matched the kitchen's berry-red laminate countertop. Mandy's trailer was only slightly bigger than the others, not much space for a couple and their high-school son, and I could sense her embarrassment. What I didn't register was surprise that we had called her up with regard to the investigation. It seemed Ford was right about Asher and Leif being friends.

Valerie asked what Mandy knew about Leif's death.

'Cried my eyes out when I heard,' the woman said, swiping at her hair – short, with a side part and stripy blonde streaks – as she spoke.

Between the haircut and her bee-stung lips, she had an impish look, but the way she held her body was flagrantly erotic, her sexiness palpable even through the leggings and oversized sweatshirt. The woman dressed just like Hen.

'Leif was such a good kid, such a good friend to Asher. I still can't believe it.'

'We're with the investigative team that's trying to reconstruct the events of that night,' Valerie said. 'We're hoping to find out who gave Leif a lift to Devil's Oven. Mrs Vance, do you know where Asher was on Saturday night?'

'Oh,' she said, running a finger under her right eye. 'I really don't? We're not, like, helicopter parents or whatever. Asher doesn't always tell us where he's going.'

Valerie said, 'Does Asher have access to a boat?'

The woman's eyes roved the room. She was deliberating. Strategizing.

'Shit,' she said at last, spitting the word like the flavorless shell of a chewed-up seed. 'OK, so the kids around here? They get bored sometimes. Not a lot to do in the off-season when the whole town's dead.' She made a face.

'What are you getting at?' Valerie asked.

Mandy sighed and looked down at the floor. She was barefoot, I noticed now, and there was a tattoo on the top of her foot. A stylized wave that must have represented the river flowing past her door.

'The kids, they sometimes borrow boats and Jet Skis.'

'Borrow.'

'Take. Whatever. It's just for fun. They do it at night, ride around the nearest islands, come back. No harm done. I used to do it too, when I was young, and nobody batted an eye, but I told Asher to lay off. Things are different these days, you know? Some people are pretty uptight.'

Suddenly, partying in the woods didn't feel so rebellious.

'Wouldn't they need a key?' I asked. 'To those Jet Skis and boats?' Tim's antique Lyman required one. The key was attached to a fish-shaped float, and Tim kept it in a dry bag at the house.

'Have you *seen* this town?' She said it with a snort. 'Nobody even locks their doors. Most folks leave their boat keys right in the ignition, especially this time of year.'

'OK,' Valerie said, 'so Leif had easy access to a boat. Where are we talking exactly?'

I knew she was thinking about Devil's Oven, its proximity to downtown A-Bay. I was too.

'The marina,' Mandy confirmed. 'Right in town. And Leif worked at Brooks, so he'd know what boats were out there.'

Brooks Hardware was as much a part of the downtown landscape as the public dock that tourists liked to walk in summer. Part general store and part lumber yard, Brooks was a few doors down from the marina, just across Otter's Creek from the house I shared with Tim. A quintessential small-town shop, it had all the supplies you could possibly need, from Christmas lights to concrete.

That Leif and his friend had access to an unlimited supply of boats was a significant find.

'Listen,' Mandy said, suddenly contrite, 'maybe forget I said anything about that, OK? It's not going to do anyone any good to hear the boss's kid was taking boats.'

'The boss's kid?' I said.

'Ford owns Brooks Hardware,' said Mandy. 'He inherited it from his dad.'

'I thought Ford owned a scuba-diving business?' Valerie said, looking to me for corroboration.

'He does,' I said, equally confused.

Mandy shook her head. 'That's just in summer. Not much diving around here in the snow and ice. Brooks is his main business. There's good money in that place, believe me.'

I had no doubt that was true. If I'd only asked Tim, he would have told me Ford ran it, but I'd been cagey with him about Ford from the start.

'Braden used to work there with Ford when they were in high school,' Mandy explained, 'stocking shelves and hauling lumber out to people's islands. He made a killing every summer. Now we do this.' A dramatic gesture at the mobile home park. A disdainful glint in her eye. 'Leif and Asher aren't the only ones, OK? Every kid around here does it. But if this gets out, a lot of locals are gonna be pissed. Customers,' she said, emphasizing the word. 'Ford's a good man, and he's had a rough go. Geena – his wife? She died too. It's been a few years now, but still.'

Mandy Vance was trying hard to downplay Leif's behavior, but his joyrides weren't just risky; they amounted to theft.

Valerie said, 'This is all very helpful, Mrs Vance. Tell me, could Leif and Asher have taken a boat late on Saturday night without anyone knowing?'

'Leif could have, maybe. Not Asher.'

'How can you be sure?' the investigator asked.

'Because Asher was home by midnight. I was still awake when he came in.'

*Midnight.* The time stamp on Mia's Instagram story, her glossy grin outshining Tristan, Hen, and Leif, had been 12:30. If Mandy was being honest with us, Asher was nowhere near the island when Leif died.

'Any idea where Asher was earlier in the evening?' I asked. Courtney had seemed so certain he was the most likely contender for transporting Leif.

'Sure,' Mandy said, casting me a puzzled look, 'he was out with his girlfriend.'

This was the way with investigations; leads scattered around like breadcrumbs, us like hungry birds pecking our way from one member of the community to the next and hoping to make a meal. I'd been optimistic that this visit to Asher's parents would confirm the kid's involvement. Instead, we now needed to hunt down a whole other suspect.

'If you could share the girl's name with us,' Valerie said, 'and phone number, if you have it, we'd love to talk to her. Just to confirm timing and such.'

'Phone number? Geez, if *she* doesn't have it, then I sure can't help you.'

Mandy Vance, when she said it, looked at me.

'What's she talking about?' Valerie asked me.

I inclined my head. 'Asher's girlfriend's number? Why would I have that?'

As Mandy studied me with pursed lips, a wave of realization pummeled me from all sides, rough and fierce and cold.

'You do know,' Mandy said with a quirk of her brow and a smug little smirk, 'that my son is dating your niece Henrietta?'

# TWENTY-EIGHT

The fury I felt was dazzling, a white-hot glare. Hen had lied to me. She'd known full well who else was on Devil's Oven the night Leif was killed. What's more, she had covered for him, no doubt aware his departure looked suspicious. I remembered the expression on her face when I showed up at the cave. It was fear I'd seen there, scrunching her features and squeezing her breath, but not just because Leif was dead. Hers had been the face of a girl who was worried someone she liked was about to be in deep shit. And that someone was Asher Vance.

'Right about the boyfriend,' Valerie had said when the interview with Mandy was done. 'Wrong about the boy.'

I had no response to that. Hen's duplicity had made me look stupid.

Worse than that, it made her look even more guilty.

The force with which I threw open the front door made the windowpanes shudder. Down the hall, Tim poked his head out from the kitchen, eyebrows hiked high. He wore an apron tied neatly at the waist and an expression of confusion so earnest I wanted to run to him, unburden myself of my sins and beg his forgiveness. Then I heard a creak on the floorboards above me and whipped my head toward the sound.

'Henrietta!' I yelled, staring hard at the ceiling. Was it possible to burn a hole through wood with the power of raw, unbridled rage? If so, I was at risk of setting the whole house on fire.

'What's up?' Hen asked, slinking casually down the stairs, and for the first time I knew who she reminded me of. Hen was Jade Byrd, the teenage hellion from Tern Island and one of the biggest obstacles I'd had to face on my first case with the BCI. Both girls came off as callous and selfish, not an ounce of empathy between them. Both had lied to protect someone they wanted for themselves. But as I prepared to lay into my brother's daughter, I reminded myself that there was a difference between Hen and Jade. Jade Byrd had been someone's pawn, a lost girl masquerading as a woman, stumbling through a life stacked with secrets in a house papered with deceit.

Could the same be said of Hen?

Tim didn't know what to make of my tirade, and I didn't blame him. All he could do was stand slack-jawed, dishtowel in hand, while I railed at my niece. *A boyfriend? A senior? And he was at the island? It's obstruction of justice. This is a homicide investigation, Hen!*

No matter what I said or how loudly I said it, she just stood there, every shot I lobbed pinging off her like she didn't feel a thing.

'You're grounded,' I told her, the words ridiculous on my lips, as if I was some high-strung mom in a movie trying futilely to keep my problem child in line. 'Go to your room,' I tried instead. No better.

'You heard your aunt,' Tim said softly. 'Upstairs, OK? We'll talk later.'

I didn't know if I should feel grateful for his help or undermined. In the moment, all I felt was incensed.

'I need some time alone,' I told him once Hen had taken her stony, shrugging self back up to her bedroom.

'I'll bring you some dinner,' Tim said. 'And a beer.'

The knife in my side pressed deeper, and though I thanked him, I couldn't quite meet his eyes.

I spent the rest of the evening holed up in the study, cursing and brooding and wondering when my life went off the rails. Things were supposed to be easier now, with Bram gone. Tim and I were supposed to get a fresh start. That we had this chance to build a life together felt miraculous, too lucky for words, and yet here I was. Adrift and alone, with no clue how to make things right.

Exactly how involved was Hen with Mia's depraved little gang? Was she an interloper, drawn by the need to feel like she belonged somewhere, anywhere, in this strange new place? Had she gone to Devil's Oven in search of acceptance, or was she a collaborator? Or worse still, was she the ringleader of this sick secret society, guiding Mia deeper into the darkness?

Abe and I had a club once too. Secret fun, designed just for us. The crimes my cousin manufactured and invited me to solve hurt people. They were built on thievery and violence, sometimes even death. They'd continued into adulthood, long after I'd stopped playing and we'd both left town – me to start my career in law enforcement, him to continue his career of evil as Blake Bram. *Good game*, he'd said when he finally exhausted every option. I wasn't sure how much Henrietta knew about all that, but she had to see her friendship with Mia was a colossal betrayal, that associating with a girl possessed by the need to know the killer in our family tree was an unforgivable act. But still, she'd gone to that island – and done it willingly.

From the moment she walked in the door, I'd been a little scared of Hen. I wanted so badly to believe Doug's stories and complaints about her reckless behavior was typical teenage nonsense, but how could I be sure when she, like me, came from a family that had birthed a ruthless butcher?

Since the night on Devil's Oven, I'd blamed Mia for everything: convincing Hen to search the house for signs of Bram, luring her out in the dead of night, bringing her to the island, forcing her to participate in some kind of ritual celebrating Blake Bram. Curled up on the love seat in the upstairs study, drained of the fight I needed to resist the pull of sleep, I remembered something Doug had said during one of his frantic late-night calls. When his voice was thick with liquor and grief, and I wanted nothing more than to help him fix his kid. 'I don't even know her anymore, Shay,' he'd told me in a desperate, desolate whisper.

'I swear to God, sometimes I'm afraid of what she might do.'

In the hush of the house, the haven where Tim and I planned to build a shared life, I couldn't remember feeling colder.

It was just before two when I woke up, still in my thin work clothes. Shivering and parched from all the shouting. Disoriented too. I'd had another dream, and this time it was Hen who was laughing. Her greenish hair shivered as she smashed Leif's head into the rocks and used the toe of her Converse to push his limp body into the river. In the dream, she turned from her victim to look straight at me, and though we were far from the fire, she had the eerie orange eyeshine of a coyote in the night.

Scrubbing my face with half-numb hands, I eased open the study door and crept out into the hall. The doors to both Hen's bedroom and the one I shared with Tim were closed, and both left me feeling equally relieved. I had no idea how Hen would react to my tirade once the scolding sank in, but it was Tim's response I was most frightened of. Instead of coming clean about Ford, heading potential disaster off at the pass, I'd spent hours cowering alone, too guilt-ridden and feeble to face him. *Tomorrow*, I told myself. *First chance I get.* As for tonight, I'd creep into bed and press up against him like always. Luxuriate in his musky, peppery scent and pretend my visit to the cemetery was just another bad dream. I didn't deserve that kind of reprieve, but damn did I need it right now.

I don't know what compelled me to peek into Hen's room. Apart from the night I found the earring on the floor, she'd been sleeping with the door closed, but now the silence behind it had a depth that was off-putting. Standing outside her room, I felt nothing but a gaping absence. I reached for the knob.

'Tim. Tim, wake up.'

I didn't whisper when, back in our own room, I crouched down next to him and shook him awake. Tim's eyes cracked open and he groaned.

'What time is it?'

'After two. Tim, Hen's gone.'

'What?' In a blink, he was upright, bracing his hands against the mattress and shaking the confusion from his matted head. 'What's going on?'

'Her bed is empty.'

'OK.' He squinted at me, weighing my panic in the dark. 'You sure she's not just in the bathroom?'

'I checked the whole house.'

'Could you have missed her? Maybe she's hiding. I talked to her a bit after your . . . speech. She was pretty upset.'

'She's not fucking here, Tim. I called her phone and there was no answer.' Hen's voice on the automated message had sounded uncharacteristically sweet. Impossibly young.

'OK, Shane. Deep breath.'

A hand on my arm. I pushed myself upright and backed away.

Hen's disappearance wasn't Tim's fault. If anything, it was mine, for failing to regulate my emotions and channeling the self-hate I felt over kissing Ford into an outburst worthy of reality

TV. There was no time to think about that now. Already Tim was up, sleep-blind and stumbling as he tugged on his work jeans, which still smelled faintly of paint. I ran into the hall and flicked on every light. I could hear Tim calling Hen's name as he struggled into the rest of his clothes, but the house only returned more silence.

'What the hell?' I said, first to myself, then louder. How could Hen pull another vanishing act? When Valerie Ott already saw her as a difficult witness in a homicide case? I was on the third floor, searching the dusty walk-up attic space we used for storage once more, when Tim's voice reached me from downstairs.

'Her shoes,' he said when I dashed to the foyer.

Hen had brought two pairs with her: chunky black ankle boots and off-white Converse that gaped at the toe like a dead pike's mouth. The sneakers from my dream were nowhere to be found.

'We'll find her,' Tim assured me. 'She's got to be with her friends, right?'

'Hen's friends are all murder suspects. How could she do this? *How?*' I asked, but I already knew. This was Hen's way of getting back at me, not just for the lecture but for the interview with Valerie, my refusal to believe her lies.

*I'm never having kids.* That's what Doug said all those years ago. He'd been so sure of it that night, so terrified by the calamity we'd narrowly averted, but he'd done it anyway. And now I'd gone and lost his daughter. I pictured her in an overturned car, head lolling against the bloodied wheel. Drunk in a field with a boy who'd just clocked their solitude.

Floating face-down in the river.

*Please God, let her be drunk in a field. Anything but in the river.*

'Let's check her room,' said Tim. 'See if she took her phone.'

'I'm responsible,' I said as we rushed back upstairs. 'Doug and Josie left her in *my* care. If something happens to her . . .'

Far as I knew, Hen had only been lost once before in earnest. I'd been there that time too. At the age of seven, she was separated from me and my mother in the new St Albans Walmart. It was opening weekend, shoppers packed in like sheep in a pen, and Hen had refused to stay close, preferring to zip from one display to the next. She was there and then she wasn't, the crowd swallowing her right up. Hundreds of strangers and an overly friendly kid, precocious and yet woefully naïve. Had a man offered her candy from a bag, she would have negotiated a bigger serving. By the time we found her, my mother was crying, and I was in a full-blown panic. Hen merely tipped her head and stared at us like we'd both lost our minds.

'I don't see the phone,' Tim said in her room. 'Man, it's hot in here.'

The house had cast-iron radiators that grumbled and clanged but kept out the cold, and Hen must have found the thermostat; between the temperature and her closed door, the room was a sauna. It was even more of a disaster than the last time I'd seen it, every item of clothing she owned tossed on to the dresser, the bed, the floor. She'd thrown a russet T-shirt over the lampshade, washing the walls in a blood-red hue, and it gave our former guest bedroom the air of a scarf-strewn harem. I felt dizzy standing in it, disoriented by the heat and foreign, fiery light.

And then it got worse.

'Oh, shit,' muttered Tim. 'Shana, look.'

He'd opened the drawers in the bedside table. Buried under a pile of library books was a slim stack of photos, every one of them of my cousin.

My hands shook as Tim handed them over. I'd be lying if I said I never wondered what the rest of my family had done with the evidence of Abe's existence. Home videos, school photos and, in the case of Felicia and Crissy, drawings and notes in his childish scrawl that any other mother or sister might have clutched like a priceless treasure. When the kid who created those drawings, and whom those photos portrayed, grew up to become one of New York state's most prolific killers, I had to think tradition would go by the wayside. But here were a handful of photos of Bram when he was just a child. In my house. In Hen's room.

'These aren't mine.' My voice was cold.

'Then who—'

'She must have brought them from home. From Doug. I didn't know he had these. Why the hell does *she* have these? What the *fuck?*' My voice was shrill, but I couldn't control it. 'She knows what he did to those women, to Carson, to me. She knows, and she's keeping pictures of him like some goddamn lovesick teen?' I braced my hands on my knees and leaned over. I was going to be sick.

'She is a teen though,' said Tim. 'We need to remember that. This is a lot for anyone to process, let alone a girl her age. The fact that someone in her family . . . that she's related to him . . . maybe it's normal, this fascination,' he said hopefully. 'Maybe that's all it is.'

It was possible Tim was right. Logic always prevailed with my fiancé; he had a way of clearing the grime to clean up the view. But this time, his rationale didn't hold water.

'She told us Mia made her search the house for objects related to Bram,' I said. 'That Mia created that fan club and mined Hen for information. But if she brought these pictures with her from home, that means she was thinking about him before she got here. If I know Doug, he didn't just have these lying around. Hen went looking for them, before she even met Mia.'

Tim looked pale. 'You don't think—'

'What I think,' I said, 'is that Hen tricked us. And the last time she snuck out like this, somebody died.'

# TWENTY-NINE

'D o you think she went back to Devil's Oven?' Tim asked as we raced to my SUV. Without asking, he'd grabbed the keys from me. I was in no condition to drive.

The thought had occurred to me too. But as we tore out of the driveway, past the marsh and crops dark with night, I was increasingly less convinced.

'Hen may be reckless, but she isn't stupid,' I said, watching the landscape for signs of movement and forcing Doug and Josie's faces from my mind. 'She has to know returning to the scene of the crime would only incriminate her further. Plus, she can't drive a boat.'

'Then where? What could possibly compel her to break curfew and risk getting caught all over again after the dressing down you gave her tonight?'

'Take a right,' I said when we got to Route 12. 'I have an idea.'

Tim listened as I explained what Valerie and I had learned from Mandy Vance the previous evening, and that Hen's boyfriend was, in fact, very much alive. Tim's expression turned grave when I told him Asher and Leif were close and that I suspected it was Asher who'd brought Leif out to the island the night he was killed. Minutes later, we pulled off the highway and into Camp Vance.

It looked different in the dark. The trailers loomed like boxy shadows against the backdrop of the river, night stripping them of detail and bestowing them with the obscure heft of shipping containers abandoned by the shore. Only one trailer was lit up, the blue of a TV screen coloring the grass outside its windows, but there was no car out front even now. Tim stood behind me when I banged on its flimsy door with the side of my fist.

'Is Henrietta here?' I asked when Mandy's bleary and astonished face appeared in the doorway. I tried to look past her into the tiny trailer that, despite the ungodly hour, thrummed with the manufactured hilarity of a game show.

'We're so sorry to bother you at this late hour,' Tim cut in, leaning toward her. 'I'm Tim Wellington, also with the New York State Police. We're here to—'

'What about Asher?' I asked. 'Is he home?'

'Asher?' Mandy looked puzzled then. She took a step toward us. Surveyed the empty park and quickly ducked back inside. 'He's not here,' she said. 'Must have gone out when I dozed off. He's been spending a lot of time with friends lately. Leif's death hit him really hard.'

In spite of her attempts to defend her son's clandestine actions, Mandy looked perturbed.

'Then where is he?' I asked. 'Where did he go?'

'Would you give us a minute?' said Tim.

It took me too long to realize he wasn't talking to Mandy, but to me. When I glared at him, he furrowed his brow. It was his warning look, or as close to one as Tim had.

Reluctantly, I stepped off the porch to linger, sullen, in the grass.

'It's really Hen we're looking for,' Tim clarified, turning back to Mandy. 'And there's a good chance they're together, so if you know Asher's hangouts and could point us in the right direction, we'd sure appreciate it.'

Mandy looked him up and down and dispensed a coy smile. 'I would love to help, but I honestly don't know where Ash is.'

'How about his cell number? Could you give us that? We could call him,' said Tim. 'We're really hoping Henrietta's with him. To be honest, she's not supposed to be out.'

'You know, I haven't met her yet,' Mandy said, 'but I hear she can be a handful.' Her eyes cut to where I brooded in the dark.

'Kids, right?' said Tim with a crooked smile, to which Mandy batted her lashes and laughed.

Back in the car, after slamming the door so hard a bracing vibration shot up my arm, I typed Asher's number into my phone. 'Straight to voicemail. Just like Hen's. What the hell do we do now?'

'We think,' said Tim. 'Where would Hen and Asher go?'

'Maybe it isn't just the two of them.' I remembered the photos in Hen's room, the way she kept defending Mia. Convinced that, without Mia Klinger, she was doomed to be friendless and alone.

As with Hen, I couldn't picture Mia returning to the island now. If the club needed an alternative to Devil's Oven, what location could Mia choose that matched it in isolation and creepiness alike?

A memory, loose and liquid, of Mia in the graveyard. *If we're lucky, we might even see a famous serial killer's ghost.*

'I think I know where they are.'

# THIRTY

T im's cottage was less than a thousand square feet, a tiny structure with a rocky yard that sloped down to the edge of Goose Bay. I had some great memories of the place, with its well-worn furniture, walls of hand-oiled knotty pine, and built-in bookshelves. We hadn't been inside in months, telling ourselves it would be better to sever the place from our lives like a necrotic limb. The whole town – hell, the nation – knew what had happened there, but they hadn't experienced the carnage like we had. I still had flashbacks of black blood arcing across my field of vision, and worse, of Tim, his lower half shredded by buckshot, face colorless as ice.

Where Bram was taken after he died here was a mystery to me. Aunt Fee would have told me if I'd asked, but that would imply I wanted to know. I would never visit his final resting place, though I did wonder if she'd reduced him to ash and scattered the cremains over the lake behind her house in Vermont, or mutely lowered him into an unmarked grave.

The two cars parked in the shadowy driveway were dark – but the moment Tim rolled on to the lot, one of them started up.

'Block it,' I said, leaning forward in the passenger seat.

Our SUV jerked to a stop, and the other vehicle, a dishwater-gray sedan that hadn't been in fashion for at least thirty years, did the same. Tim and I hurtled out of my car to surround it.

'Hey,' I said, rapping my knuckles on the driver's-side window.

The window came down to reveal a teenage boy. Bright blond curls in a mullet cut, tucked behind his ears. Barely there eyebrows and pillowy lips. The kid looked just like his mother. 'Asher Vance? What are you doing out here?'

Looking terrified, he mumbled a reply that I missed, then pointed toward the water.

'Out of the car. For Pete's sake, put down your hands,' I said when Asher scrambled out the door, raising his quivering arms to the sky as if held at gunpoint. In a way, it was reassuring to know our presence could actually instill respect in the youth of A-Bay. I had yet to see an ounce of this deference from Mia.

'This is private property, son,' Tim put in. 'Can you explain yourself?'

'Yes, sir. I–I'm here with Hen,' he stammered, standing very still. 'She told me to wait.'

'You pick her up at the house?'

A nod.

'You been drinking?' I asked, leaning in.

'No! No, ma'am. I swear it.'

'Where *is* Hen?' I was growing increasingly nervous. Aside from Asher, the car was clearly empty.

'We were going downtown – but then Mia texted. She wanted Hen to come out here.' He grimaced as he spoke.

'So why are you sitting here in your car?'

'I'm not into ghosts and shit,' he said, flushing. 'I told Hen I would wait.'

'So she's here?' I asked, and Asher nodded toward the river.

'Come on.' I motioned for him to follow me, and the three of us walked toward the cabin.

At the bottom of the pitched back yard, on a carpet of pine needles and toothy gray rocks, a fire was burning. Three figures sat beside it, their shadows long and twitchy, heads bowed and eyes lazy against the light. They were focused on something lying in the grass. I couldn't see what it was.

Mia, Tristan, Hen . . . with the exception of Leif, these were all the same kids who'd gathered on Devil's Oven. I imagined swooping down on them like a hawk with talons primed for an attack, tearing Hen away from the others and throwing her in my car and driving away as fast as I could. Tim's hand on my elbow was the only thing stopping me. Breaking up the gathering would do us no good, not when we didn't fully understand what we were witnessing. Why they were here. And so, instead of careening down the incline on my heels, I followed Tim's lead and pressed my body into the dark triangle cast by the side of the house.

'What is this?' Tim whispered, to which Asher shrugged.

'Mia does all kinds of weird sh— stuff,' he said.

Tucking myself even closer to the cabin, I dipped my head to the left and watched.

Against the backdrop of the carbon-black river, the three teens looked like a coven of witches. They might have been mistaken for a Satanic cult surrounding that baby of Rosemary's – only instead of obsessing over a child, they were staring at the object on the ground between them.

My searching gaze snagged on Hen, and I studied her expression. She held her body rigid, and her lips were pulled into a stoic line, but something in her eyes, black and orange in the flickering firelight, made me wonder if she wasn't just a little afraid. Last year, after Bram's death, I sometimes came to this place, always at night. Always alone. It had felt like the punishment I deserved, a kind of atonement for my cousin's many sins, but there was no denying the spot by the water had power and a devilry that scared me. I wondered if Hen could feel it too.

I held my breath and waited for Mia to speak, praying she'd issue some directive that would make it clear she, not Hen, was the leader here. For the occasion, Mia had dressed in the same dark clothes and cape she'd worn on her ghost tour, a cheerleader masquerading as a goth girl. She held some authority over the others, that much was evident; self-assurance emanated from her like a glow. *Say something*, I told myself, *so that I understand*.

It was Hen who spoke.

'Guardian of water, I invoke thee,' said my niece, her voice steady and clear. 'Bless us with your presence.'

'Come on already,' said Tristan. 'It's fucking freezing out here.'

'Fuck you. Just take another swig and shut your fucking face. Sorry, the demons.' Mia tossed back her head and laughed, painted lips distorted into a manic Joker grin. Reaching behind her, she retrieved a bottle – whiskey, maybe, already half-empty – from where it had been lying in the grass. When she passed it to Hen, the firelight caught its contents and turned the liquid into molten gold.

Hen took a swallow, cringed, and said, 'Shh, we need to focus. Close your eyes.'

'*Boo!*' Tristan laughed, and Mia gave his arm a swat. 'Seriously, guys. How does a person just *become* a psychopath?'

'Don't say psychopath,' said Hen. 'You'll piss off all the other psychopaths.'

'I feel like Bram would love to be called that,' said Mia. 'Like, he'd embrace it.'

'He probably would,' said Hen. 'But he didn't *become* a psychopath. He was born that way. Trust me, I know. I've been in the house he grew up in, inside his bedroom and everything. I touched his stuff with my own hands. I know almost everything there is to know about Bram,' she told them, eyes fulgid, cheeks ablaze. 'He was a brilliant, tortured soul, and the bloodlust was there from the start.'

'It always is.' Mia was nodding, her blonde curls quivering against the collar of her cape. 'Charles Manson went to juvie at age nine and the Menendez brothers robbed houses when they were in high school, even though their family was crazy rich. It's in the blood.'

'Enough. We need to focus.' Hen returned her gaze to the center of their circle. Once again, she closed her eyes. 'We call upon the spirit world. Spirits, we call to you. Oh, spirit,' she said, drawing a deep breath through her nose. 'Are you here now? Speak to us and—'

'Stop!'

Half-blind with fear and rage, I flew down the hill toward them, my State Police jacket flapping behind me. I was vaguely aware of Tim and Asher running too, but I had a singular focus, and that focus was Hen. I caught her by the arm and tore her away from Mia and Tristan and the Ouija board splayed between them. It was the same brand as the ones I'd seen on sale at Island Death Ghost Tours.

'Shit.' The word was sibilant on Tristan's lips. 'Shit, Mia, I told you this was a bad idea.'

'Shut the fuck up,' said Mia. Then, to Asher, 'Well, well. Look who decided not to be a chickenshit.'

'*What the hell is this?*' I barked, not just at Hen, who had the good sense to look embarrassed, but to all of them. 'You can't do this. You can't be here.'

'Actually, we can.' Mia's tone was insolent, her chin jutting out in defiance. The angle highlighted the point at which her makeup stopped and her natural skin tone, the angry pink of a

newborn, began. 'I have every right to be here – we all do. We're
buying this place,' she said, her lips curling into a smile. 'It's
going to be an official stop on the tour.'

I felt like I'd been dunked into icy water. Kim Klinger was
buying the cabin?

'Tim,' I said, his name a plea as I turned to face him.

Tim looked stricken. 'They never told me who made the offer.
I never knew. Jesus, I . . . it's . . . Shana, it's done.'

'No.' This couldn't be allowed to happen. Tim's beloved cabin
could not become a stop on the Klingers' twisted tour.

'You can't stop us,' Mia went on. 'We're not doing anything
illegal.' At that, she reached out for my niece's hand.

Hen looked from me to Mia.

She stepped toward her friend.

I don't know how Tim anticipated that act, above all others,
would finally make me snap, but suddenly his arms were looped
through mine and he was holding me back as I strained toward
this smug, horrid girl with the movie-star face.

'I can't stop you?' I said, shaking him off. 'This may become
your property, but the deal hasn't closed – which means you're
all trespassing. I've arrested kids your age for a lot less. A
criminal charge isn't like detention. It's going to put a serious
damper on your college applications. Or worse.'

'This was all her idea,' said Asher, pointing at Mia. 'Just like
that night at Devil's Oven.'

'Asshole,' Mia hissed.

'We were playing with the Ouija board,' said Hen.
'That's all.'

'My brother's going to fucking kill me,' said Tristan, repeat-
edly yanking his dark hair until it stood on end and adding,
'That shit's not mine,' when Tim picked up the Southern Comfort
from the grass.

Some perverse part of me wished Mia had dragged Hen here
against her will, but I knew better. She wanted to be part of this,
whatever this was. She'd come to Bram's deathplace freely, just
like she'd chosen to bring pictures of him into my house. I felt
ambushed, like Hen had laid a trap in the woods, sticks criss-
crossed over a deep hole, and watched from the pines while it
swallowed me whole.

'Asher, go straight home,' I said. 'The rest of you are coming with me.'

The group exchanged panicky glances until Mia said, 'No way.'

'That's my brother's car,' said Tristan, pointing at the beater parked atop the hill.

'You're drinking straight from the bottle,' I said. 'If you think we're letting you drive, you're crazy. Get in the car. We're taking you home.'

We waited as the kids reluctantly shuffled to my SUV. Before squeezing herself into the back with Mia and Tristan, Hen reached for Asher's hand. Their fingertips brushed and they exchanged shy smiles before Asher went on his way. Once he'd pulled out of the driveway and we'd closed the door on the others, Tim cleared his throat.

'Should we call Valerie?'

To say what exactly? If she'd shown no interest in my theory about Mia's gang of Bram fanatics, she wouldn't care about this bizarre rendezvous either. Suddenly I felt whipped, limbs bogged down with exhaustion, eyes itchy and dry. 'Later,' I said. 'Let's just get these kids home.'

'It'll be OK,' Tim assured me. 'I'm not excusing Hen's behavior, but just remember, they *are* kids. They're messing with stuff they shouldn't be, but it's a game to them. That's all.'

'You really believe that?' I asked.

'I do.'

As I walked to the car and slid into the driver's seat, I wished I could say the same.

# THIRTY-ONE

The route to Mia and Tristan's homes was indirect, the car as silent as a mossy grave.

Tristan Laurier was our first drop-off, and as we crunched down the gravel drive, all of us taking in the derelict house and pink plastic flamingos standing sentry by the front door, I saw the boy lower his gaze to the footwell, shame parading across his face in the form of angry red welts. The house was a hodge-podge of styles at the end of a long gravel driveway blocked from the street by a clutch of trees, its elaborate bay window with diamond-shaped mullions at odds with a barn-red metal roof. The property included a rickety shed and an equally rickety lean-to, the latter covering a trailer just big enough for a personal watercraft. I suspected it housed the Jet Ski Tristan had used to get out to the island. There was a distinct possibility that watercraft outvalued the entire home.

Tim walked the boy to the door, where Charles was already waiting, giving his kid brother a look of death. Through my open window, I heard Tim tell Tristan to stay out of trouble.

Would that it was so easy.

Mia's apartment above Island Death Ghost Tours was next. In the window of the Klingers' building, the ghost sign, which appeared to glow twenty-four-seven, sputtered. I debated waking Mia's mother, but at such an ugly hour and with no simple explanation for why Tim and I had charged the cabin – a cabin that would soon belong to her – I ruled against it. I didn't trust myself not to lose my cool with Kim. That confrontation could wait.

'I want you to stay away from my niece,' I told Mia as I walked her to the door, turning up my collar against the wind. 'Do you understand? I won't allow you to corrupt her with your sick obsessions.'

Mia's penciled eyebrows lifted. 'It was her idea to go out there tonight, not mine. Hen's not the angel you think she is.'

Angel? If only. 'I don't believe you,' I said. 'I think you organized the whole thing.'

'Ask her,' she said.

'Oh trust me, I will.'

A few more steps and we'd be at the door.

'I've talked to him you know,' Mia said suddenly. 'Blake Bram.'

I stopped, and Mia did the same, holding my gaze with her sultry stare. 'He was easy to contact actually. Almost like he'd been waiting for someone to communicate with him. Dark spirits often get ignored, so I think he was excited. He had a lot to say.'

Mia wanted me to lose it, like I had at the cabin. The statement was designed to provoke.

'Oh yeah? And what did he tell you?' I asked, wondering if she could see the heat rising up my neck.

'Two words.' Mia took out her house key, slipped it into the door and whispered, 'Good game.'

It was a good thirty seconds before I stopped seeing red.

'What did she say?' Tim asked when I was back in the car, but I didn't get a chance to answer. At the Klingers' place, commotion. We heard shouts coming from the apartment, and the violent slam of a door.

'What now?' I said as we peered through the windshield. What we saw left me stunned. The door to Kim's storefront had flown open and there stood a man in his boxers, a wad of balled-up clothes in his arms and the undone laces on his sneakers pooling around his feet. He was bald and bulky with a ropy neck like the trunk of an Eastern red cedar – and now he was running half-naked down Walton.

'What the hell am I looking at?' I asked as we watched the man careen on to Market Street. He seemed to be heading for a parked van.

'I think that's Asher's dad,' Hen said from the back.

'You've got to be kidding me. Kim and Braden Vance?'

Tim said, 'I guess Kim wasn't expecting Mia home tonight.'

'Guess not. Ford Colebrook said the River Rats used to be close.' Just speaking the man's name made me flush.

With a shake of his head, Tim said, 'He wasn't kidding.'

Braden's presence at the Klingers explained why there was no car at Camp Vance, but little else. Kim appeared to be sleeping with Mandy's husband, though Ford, when he described the dive trip that killed Geena, had called the women friends. I couldn't wrap my head around what, if anything, the discovery we'd just made meant. But I had a feeling it wasn't good.

# THIRTY-TWO

It was after three a.m. by the time we took the lane that branched off Route 12 toward our house. Hen had fallen asleep in the back of the car, her head lolling softly against the seat when jostled by the occasional bump in the road. I felt hollow-eyed and woozy with exhaustion. Spent.

'I need to talk to Doug and Josie again,' I told Tim as I caught a yawn in my cupped hand. 'We can't go on this way.'

'No,' he replied softly, muscles tense along his jaw as he looked at me. 'We can't.'

This was killing him, letting something as big as plans about our future drift untethered. I could see that now. 'I'm sorry about what I said on the boat,' I told him.

'Do you really have doubts? About having kids?'

I glanced over my shoulder at Hen where she dozed in the back and fell quiet. If I was honest, I wasn't sure how I felt. I could easily picture Tim as a father. He'd be brilliant at it, invested and engaged. Enthusiastic about every development and milestone, which I imagined he'd record in a book for posterity. He was close with all his siblings, J.C. especially; with two moms in the house, Tim had enlisted in the role of father figure. I knew he was eager to start a family of his own.

And me? I was close with my parents and Doug. My immediate family had always been stable, Wally and Della setting the ideal example of what a good marriage could be. But all the while, just across town, the Skiltons were skinning each other alive. It was as if Brett and Felicia were determined to create the most hostile, unstable environment a kid could have the misfortune of calling home. Just a mile away from my own childhood house, everything had gone horribly wrong for my cousins, and I would never be able to forget it.

More than anything though, I was tormented by the possibility that the rot spreading through the Skiltons might somehow still infect me. How could I even consider having a child with Tim when I shared Bram's DNA? It had been easier to dismiss that question before Leif was found dead.

Before Hen.

'Let's talk in the morning,' I said in lieu of answering his question. In the blue-black autumn night, our house was coming into view up ahead. 'It's been a long night.'

Reluctantly, Tim agreed we could all use some sleep.

But I didn't follow him to bed. Instead, I went to the kitchen. I needed a cold glass of water and a moment to gather my thoughts – about Tim, and Ford, and what the hell to do with Hen.

Doug wouldn't want to hear it, but he had to be told our current arrangement was no longer tenable. Having Hen live alone with me and Tim wasn't just an inconvenience; it was dangerous. She couldn't leave town, not until the investigation was closed, but maybe Doug or Josie could move in until then.

In a few hours, I'd insist Hen confess everything to her parents. Sit with her to make sure she didn't skimp on details. At sixteen, she was accountable for her actions, and my job was to protect her, not act as a buffer between the kid and her folks.

And as soon as we got a solve on Leif's case, Doug and Josie would take Hen home.

When, water in hand, I turned from the kitchen sink back to the doorway, I saw that Hen hadn't gone to bed either. She was on the living-room couch with a nubbly blanket tucked under her chin. The girl looked bedraggled but alert. It was way too early to call Doug, but I could text him. Let him know we needed to talk as soon as he woke up.

Watching his daughter from the doorway, I reached into my pocket for my cell phone and turned it over in my hand.

That's when I noticed the message on the screen.

There had been multiple attempts to reach me the previous night, all of which I'd missed in the bedlam. A voicemail from Mac and a couple texts too, one from an unknown number. It was the third message I homed in on, sent by Josie Merchant. It included a photo of my sister-in-law in a fitted tee and PJ bottoms, her belly gently rounded, hands folded protectively over the bump. The photo was accompanied by a message.

*Thank you so much for taking care of Hen. I know it hasn't been easy, but she's a good kid at heart. We'd be lost without you, Shay. PS It's a boy* :)

I darkened the screen, slid my phone on to the kitchen counter, and went to join Hen on the sofa.

'I'm done,' I told her, letting my shoulders sink into the cushions. 'This isn't a game, Hen. You're a witness to a murder, and your friends are suspects. There's a quote from Bram carved on a rock on Devil's Oven, and last night I found you all the way across town at Tim's cabin – a place you know is off-limits, a place you should never want to set foot – trying to summon Bram's ghost. This is my limit, Hen. I've reached it. This is it.'

'Are you going to send me home?'

The question was atypically meek, and for a second I felt Hen's hard outer shell give like the casing on a chocolate bonbon left too close to the fire.

'It's not only up to me,' I said, but how could I ship her back after seeing Josie's message? There was so much at stake. 'Your behavior since you got here . . . I don't know what to say.'

I was prepared for anything: the silent treatment, a screaming match. What I got instead left me stunned.

'It's my fault.'

'Damn straight it's your fault,' I said, flustered. 'You are darn right it is.'

'You don't get it.' Her voice quivered as she shook her head.

'Then explain it to me, Hen. I'm begging you. Make me understand.'

'I don't even know where to start.'

'Start with tonight,' I said, picturing her at the cabin. Brimming with confidence while summoning the dead.

'OK.' Hen drew a breath. 'Mia's into crime and ghosts and shit, and yeah, she's into Bram. But it wasn't Bram Mia was trying to contact tonight. It was Leif's mom.'

'Geena Colebrook?' I shook my head. 'But . . . why?'

'To find out how she died.' Hen let her head fall back against the couch. 'Mia's convinced that Asher's mom killed Leif's.'

'*What?*' My mind was frantically stitching together every scrap of information I had, desperate to quilt a picture that made sense. 'Mia believes Mandy Vance murdered Geena? Jesus,' I said, running a hand through my hair. 'I guess that explains why Asher keeps his distance. What's Mia basing this on exactly?'

'I'm not sure. But she says she's known it for years, and now she's trying to prove it.'

'By interviewing ghosts.'

'Not just that. She's been *looking into it*. I guess there's an old rumor that Kim did it, and Mia wants to prove her mom is innocent. That it was Asher's mom all along. Leif didn't believe it obviously. Asher and Leif were tight. But Mia kept saying she found something out. Kim's sleeping with Asher's dad, isn't she?'

Head spinning, I set down my glass and thought of Braden Vance half-naked in the street, along with the shouts coming from the apartment when Mia walked in and witnessed what she had. 'It looks like it,' I agreed. 'Where was Mia supposed to be staying last night? Kim obviously didn't think she was coming home.'

Hen's gaze shot away from me. 'Here. That's what Mia told her mom. But she and Tristan were going to sleep at the cabin.'

'The whole thing just sounds insane,' I said. 'I still don't understand why Leif was even on the island that night.'

'I mean, if it was my mom who died mysteriously, and someone told me they knew how, I'd want to hear it. Wouldn't you?'

Mia had insight into Geena Colebrook's death, and Leif wanted to know what it was. As unbelievable as it sounded, I could almost picture it. Hadn't Hen said in her interview that Mia and Leif were alone for a few minutes, behind a tree? Had Mia told him her theory then? Had that been what drove Leif to leave the group and head for the cave?

I thought of what Mandy Vance had said, about Leif and Asher taking Jet Skis and boats from the docks. How Asher had been *out with his girlfriend*. 'So Asher dropped Leif off at the island. Took a boat from shore and drove him over?'

'It was a Jet Ski,' said Hen. 'Leif asked him to. Like, begged him. There wasn't room on Tristan's, and Leif wanted to get to Devil's Oven to talk to Mia.'

'But Asher didn't stay on the island to be with you? His mother's convinced you two were together that night.'

'That was the original plan – before Mia invited me to the island. I think she was pissed that Asher and I clicked so fast at school.'

A flicker of a smile as she said it. Hen was smitten. From what I'd seen at the cabin, Asher was too.

'I spent lunch with Ash on Friday instead of her. She didn't like that and was bitchy with me all afternoon. I didn't want her to think I was choosing him over her, you know? So when Leif asked for Asher's help, I said I'd chill out there with Mia till Ash came back to pick Leif up. We were going to hang on the mainland after. But Ash never came back to the island, because . . .'

I nodded. Said, 'Because everything went to hell. But why didn't Leif just go to Devil's Oven by himself? If he had access to boats, he didn't need Asher to take him.'

'He did need Ash though. If Leif took a Jet Ski on his own, where would he leave it?'

'He could use an anchor,' I said. 'Like Tristan did.'

'Where the hell would Leif get that?'

My mouth fell open. Hen was right. Tristan and Mia had come prepared. They'd brought a weight and a line, probably from Tristan's place, so they could anchor near the island. But the Jet Skis at the marina were tied to the docks with boat lines.

'Jesus Christ, Hen, why didn't you tell me any of this sooner?'

'Because I didn't want them to get in trouble! Mia and Asher and Tristan, they had nothing to do with it.'

'Then who did, Hen? Who's left?'

Eyes squeezed shut, she said, 'I don't know.'

'Geena Colebrook's death was ruled accidental,' I told her. 'But if what you're saying is true, it explains a lot.'

As I spoke, I tried to picture the scene. Asher dropping Leif off and speeding back toward the boat dock. Mia, Tristan, Leif, and Hen pounding beers by the fire. Hen pulling up her photo of Bram's letter and reading it to the group. Mia taunting Leif with the promise of information about Geena's death and taking him aside to finally reveal what she knew. And Leif getting angry. Stalking off toward the cavern.

What had happened then? Before Hen started to worry and went looking for Asher's friend? Before she saw him face-down in the water, drifting a few feet from the mouth of the cave?

'You said this is your fault.' My skin went cold as I repeated her words. 'What do you mean by that, Hen?'

Hen blinked at me. 'When I met Mia and she asked about Bram, I could have ignored it, but I didn't. I told her everything I know. I talk about him all the time, and Mia and Tristan, they love it. And when Mia mentioned Geena's murder, I said I could help her solve it. I told her I knew how to spot a killer. That's why she's been digging for information on Geena – and that's what got Leif out to the island.'

'Oh, Hen.'

'I'm like him,' she said, her eyes shiny with tears. 'I'm just like Bram. I lured Leif out there, like Bram did with those women.'

'You didn't. You're not.' I reached for her and gripped her fingers tight. 'Christ, Hen, you're *nothing* like him.'

'We're related. We share DNA.'

'But you also share DNA with your dad, and your mom, and me, and we're nothing like him either. Bram, Abe . . . he's an anomaly,' I said. 'One in a million – just not in the good way. It doesn't matter that we're connected to him, not in the way you think.'

'But what if you're wrong?'

I couldn't fault her for asking. Hadn't I wondered the same when I found out that Abraham Skilton grew up to be a murderer? My cousin and I had been as close as two kids could be, until I finally understood what he was capable of. And when I did, I had asked myself the same question. I'd kept asking it until, two years ago, I'd posed it to Tim. *You're not like him. You never were*, he'd told me. And now, here I was telling Hen.

Nobody knows whether serial killers are predisposed to violence. No matter how many studies are conducted, how many experts convene to share their thoughts, society still can't pinpoint the genetic makeup, environmental factors, and unfortunate combination of personality disorders that lead to murder. By that logic, Henrietta and I shouldn't worry. If there was no blueprint a person could follow to become a violent criminal, the misfortune of being related to one shouldn't matter in the least. This was the theory I clung to like a life raft.

And yet, even as I reassured my niece, her words swirled around me like a fog. *It's my fault.*

*I'm just like Bram.*

# THIRTY-THREE

I sent Hen to bed then. Told her to rest and, crippled by bone-deep exhaustion myself, promptly fell asleep on the couch. Only two hours later I woke up with the bright autumn sun like a searchlight on my face. It made me feel exposed and raw as I rubbed my crusted eyes. Had something woken me? Whatever it was, the house was now quiet. I pawed the coffee table, searching for my phone, but it wasn't around, and I couldn't remember where I'd left it.

The clock in the kitchen read six a.m. The coffee maker spat and gurgled, and there was Tim, standing idly by while its contents inched ever higher inside the carafe. Leaning against the counter with an empty mug in hand, eyes boring into our ugly kitchen floor.

'You're up,' I said, my voice rough with exhaustion. 'Is Hen—'

'Still sleeping.'

'Good. I'm thinking about installing a deadbolt on her door. On the outside.'

I paused to give Tim a chance to chuckle or at least cast a weary, condoling glance my way, but he just stood there in his flannel PJ bottoms and favorite Bills tee, the one he'd had to explain when we first started dating (*I've never even been to Buffalo, but we don't have a lot of sports teams up here and my dad's a lifelong fan*). Tim's stare was unflinching as he studied the patterned linoleum flooring, the next thing on our demolition list to go. The machine finished its cycle with a hiss, and still he didn't budge.

'Tim?'

Another beat, and then he lifted the hand that had been hidden behind his leg.

'You left it in here,' he said, holding out my phone. 'Right on the counter. There's a message from Colebrook.'

The words sucked the air from my lungs as the weight of the phone met my hand.

My relationship with Tim wasn't without its complications. We were polar opposites. We worked together. Psychologically and emotionally, I'd been ravaged, mauled and shredded like a rabbit in the maw of a wolf. Our love though, that should have been simple. With Tim, there was no mistaking what he thought or felt or wanted, and after the missteps I'd made early on in the job and in our courtship, I'd done my best to be equally open with him.

And here was my phone with that missed text on the screen, just enough of the text visible to implicate me in the most terrible of crimes.

*Shana, it's ford. Maybe we shouldn't have done what we did, but the truth is, I'm not sorry. I can't stop thinking about—*

'Tim,' I said, frantic now. Desperate for him to understand. 'Ford – he kissed me, that's all, and—'

'*That's all?*'

'He was distraught over Leif. Tim, it's not—'

'Stop,' he said. 'Just . . . stop.' Making his hands into claws, he dug his fingers into his forehead. 'Valerie called me five minutes ago, when she couldn't reach you. There's a fire downtown.'

'A fire?' My mind went straight back to Bram. A year and a half ago, he'd set Smuggler's Cargo aflame to distract the authorities when he was on the run. 'Where?'

'Brooks Hardware.' Tim's muscles tensed as he turned his back on me, slamming his empty mug on the counter. 'We need to go.'

# THIRTY-FOUR

By the time we got downtown, Ford Colebrook's hardware store was engulfed in hellish thirty-foot flames, a pillar of murky black smoke sullying the morning light. There was already one engine on scene, more ladders arriving, and a small crowd of downtown residents and fellow business owners had gathered in the parking lot to shake their heads in awe.

'Looks like it started at the back of the building,' the fire chief said when I cornered him by his truck. 'Near the lumber yard.'

That part of the structure was still ablaze, and the siding around it looked like melted ice cream flecked with soot. We'd been warned to stay back and were keeping a safe distance, setting up camp by the rock wall that separated the business's two small parking lots. Hardware stores were stocked with hundreds of different chemicals, many of them both flammable and toxic.

'Any idea how it started?' Tim asked.

'Not yet, but we're gonna be here for hours.' The chief sounded exhausted already. It was not yet seven a.m.

This was going to be a devastating loss, not just for Ford but the whole town. The one consolation was that the fire could be contained. With the Brooks lumber yard backing up to the river, there was no need to worry about the blaze spreading to businesses nearby.

No sooner had the thought crossed my mind than the nature of the smoke, overwhelming the commercial building now, started to change. It poured out of the roof and windows like gray-green water running in reverse, and as Tim and I looked on, there was a colossal crash. Firefighters scattered like ants.

'Whoa! Major collapse,' the fire chief shouted, running toward his unit as smoke obscured the building, the sky, everything.

'Oh God, no.'

I swung around. Ford Colebrook stood a few feet behind us, his face a mask of horror and his hands sunk deep in his tussled hair.

'Ford's here,' I told Tim, who immediately stiffened but didn't make a move to turn away from the blaze. 'This place is going to be a total loss.' How would Ford withstand this too?

'By all means, go,' said Tim.

'It's not like that.'

'No, I get it. He needs you. Go comfort the guy. Why not grab some breakfast while you're at it? Diner's just around the corner.'

'What the hell, Tim?' I said under my breath. 'The man just lost his kid and now his family business is up in smoke.'

'And apparently you, my fiancée and a stranger to him, are the only woman in this whole fucking town who can make him feel better.'

'Please, just listen to me—'

But before I could say another word, he'd thundered off.

*Fuck.* I was sailing too close to the wind, and everything I said and did was making things worse. Tim wasn't going to put up with much more of this. Not an hour ago, he'd found Ford's text and learned his fiancée had kissed someone else. He had to feel stunned, and sick, and above all betrayed.

And still, when Ford Colebrook came to stand beside me, I let him.

Chemistry is the stuff of romance novels and Hollywood headlines. The concept has always felt artificial to me, a blurry explanation for something that can't be defined to begin with. Believing in lust so enormous and heady it raids our good senses to leave us quivering with sexual longing doesn't feel so different from believing in ghosts. I'd analyzed the evidence and found it to be lacking. And yet, there I was.

With Tim, I'd grown into my attraction. It hadn't been there from the start, when we first met. When we went out to Tern Island to investigate a missing man and Tim dismissed every one of my theories. The reason my body responded to his now was that my mind had done so first. It was a natural progression. A slow burn.

My body moved of its own accord with Ford, curling toward him like smoke to a draft. I didn't need Tim to tell me what a tremendous offense it was, making myself available to this man I hardly knew . . . but the chemistry.

God help me, if Ford ever pushed me further, it would take everything I had to resist.

'I'm sorry,' I told him now. 'I'm so sorry, Ford.'

All he could say, in that same soft, strangled voice, was, 'How?'

'They're still working that out, but they think the fire originated at the back of the building. Can you think of anything that could have started it?'

Ford shook his head. His eyes were wide and blank.

'The fire marshal's here,' I said. 'He'll figure things out. You'll need to talk to your insurance company. There's nothing you can do right now, not today. Ford, I think you should go home.'

'This place . . . it's been in my family for almost fifty years. I grew up working here. Leif too. I can't go home right now, Shana,' he said. 'I can't.'

No, he couldn't. I saw that now. Ford couldn't drive back to the home he'd shared with Leif and Geena, not in this condition. He needed someone to stay with him. Talk him through it and provide what little comfort they could.

My eyes trailed to his truck, and I felt a kick of hunger in my gut.

'Shana! Just the person I was looking for.'

Valerie Ott came out of nowhere. I hadn't seen her pull up or noticed her approach, yet she was right in front of me, hands clasped on her hips, her smile electric. The woman was dressed in a white button-down and trendy jeans, the last thing you wanted to wear to a fire, and between her outfit and her height and her ponytail, I nearly mistook her for a teenager.

Valerie looked from me to Ford and said, 'Mr Colebrook? Sir? I'm sorry about this – what a terrible mess. Come with me and I'll get you some coffee, take a statement. I know it all looks bleak right now, but this too shall pass.'

She'd been looking for me, she said. *Just the person I was looking for.*

But it was Ford that Valerie took by the arm, guiding the man from my side.

# THIRTY-FIVE

Tim liked to say that everything's connected. In a community like A-Bay, the words felt plain as a pikestaff, the most obvious statement in the world. There were bonds everywhere in this place, through work and school and daily life along the river. Friendships and feuds and romances took shape at the farmers' market and the Rotary club auction, the pond hockey classic and the summer street fest known as Pirate Days. Other connections, made decades prior, weren't so easy to trace, their origins long forgotten. It was those links I was interested in now, ready to follow the chain hand over hand until I found its anchor.

When Valerie and Sol brought Asher in for an interview, along with his mother Mandy Vance, I once again observed from behind the glass. I was desperate to know what this kid Hen was supposedly dating was like, and whether or not he could be trusted. The boy had lost a friend, and had been sitting on key information about the night of that friend's death. The only thing he had going for him, besides his beach-blond looks, was the fact that he kept his distance from Mia Klinger.

'Why didn't you come forward when you found out what happened to Leif?' Valerie asked. There was a smear of ash on her snow-white collar. On her right cheek too.

The boy looked to his mother, who gave an encouraging nod.

'I was scared, I guess,' said Asher. 'All I did was drop him off out there. I came right back to the mainland after. But when I heard that he drowned, and that it wasn't an accident, I knew it would look bad, me taking off like that.'

Hen had drawn the same conclusion.

'Why was Leif so eager to get out there that night?'

Asher's eyes, the blue of worn denim, narrowed. 'Mia was fu—' He paused. Glanced at his mom and flushed scarlet. 'She was messing with him. She was obsessed with this idea that Leif's mom was murdered.'

'By who?'

For an instant his face grew stormy, but the emotion passed quickly, flitting away. 'She never said, at least not to me. But it was just her mom and mine on that dive with Leif's, and it's not like she was gonna point the finger at Kim.'

'The whole thing's ridiculous,' Mandy said loudly, flipping her hair from her eyes. 'Everyone knows Geena's regulator failed. I was *there* – I saw it for myself. I tried to help her, but my best friend drowned right in front of me – and you're saying Kim's kid is out there spreading rumors that I'm a murderer? Who do I talk to about pressing charges? This is decimation of character.'

Suppressing a smirk at Mandy's blunder, Valerie said, 'You're welcome to call a lawyer, but we need to finish up here first. Asher, are you saying that Mia thinks your mother killed Geena Colebrook?'

'She wouldn't shut up about *foul play* and *suspicious circumstances*,' he said. 'So yeah, that's what I think. That's why I didn't want to go out there with Leif.'

'Did you talk to Leif about Mia's theory?'

'That Mia thinks my mom offed his? Um, no. That's kind of awkward.'

'This is insane,' Mandy told Valerie. 'Are you even sure you have your facts straight? I really don't think Kim would stand for this.'

'Mrs Vance, please. Did Mia talk to Leif, Asher? About her belief that your mom was involved?'

'I don't know,' he said. 'But a few days ago, she stopped us at school and said she knew something about Geena. Some big secret. She wouldn't tell Leif unless he went out to the island. I figured that's what it was.'

'Any thoughts on why Mia wanted him on that island in particular?'

Pondering Valerie's question, Asher said, 'It wasn't the first time she partied out there, I know that. We all have.'

Mandy stiffened, but he went on. 'I think she liked the name. She was into some dark shit, serial killers and evil spirits or whatever. I told Leif not to go. Mia's bad news. I don't think Hen should be hanging out with her either,' he added, looking away. 'But Mia kept dangling that secret in front of him. I was like, don't waste your time, man, she's just fucking with you. Sorry,' he said, shamefaced. 'But Leif asked me to take him out there. I was supposed to pick him up later. He was going to call me. I was waiting for him on the mainland, right by the marina. But when he didn't call, I walked the pier and saw the coast guard in the water.'

'Son,' Sol said, 'what did you think had happened?'

That was my question too. Had Asher known right away that something was terribly wrong?

'I thought they all got caught drinking,' he said with a shrug. 'That the coast guard was out patrolling and saw the fire. They come around sometimes. At night.'

I nodded to myself behind the glass. I'd seen the boats on patrol many times, cruising up and down the river. Ensuring boaters returning from dinners or trips to Canada or visits to friends made it home safe and sound. I'd seen them shut down boat parties too. Teens partying too loudly for the late hour.

When Valerie asked Asher what he did while waiting for Leif's call, I leaned into the glass. I was hoping he'd say he stayed on the dock, which would afford him a good view of the other boats – boats that might have made a trip out to the island that night too. But Asher, who was looking increasingly pasty, told Valerie he'd sat in his car in the parking lot of the pizza place, scrolling through social media. Waiting for Leif to summon him so he could finally spend some time with Hen. There was no river view from that lot at all, and even when Valerie pressed him, Asher insisted he hadn't seen anyone else come or go from the town dock all night.

'Arson,' Tim said when we all reconvened in the conference room. 'The fire marshal just called. He found some empty cans of wood stain near the back doors. That, plus the burn pattern, has him thinking someone set that fire at Colebrook's store. The question is why.'

It was all I could do not to drag Tim into the hall and beg him to hear me out. He jogged his knee under the table as he briefed us, and he was wearing my favorite shirt, white with a small check that brought out the cadet blue in his eyes. He wouldn't look at me.

'Colebrook has a surveillance system,' he went on, wincing a little every time he spoke Ford's name, 'including a camera facing the lumber yard and dock that would have caught the arsonist in action.'

'Would have,' I said.

'System's old school. The footage was all on-site. From the office, anyone could watch the shoppers and workers on monitors in real time or look through the tapes up to a few days back. But that whole situation's a steaming pile of shit now.' Tim picked up the coffee he'd poured in the break room, grabbing the mug so roughly that it splashed on the table before him.

'In other words, nothing's stored in the cloud for us to access after the fact,' said Sol.

'Not a thing.'

'So where does that leave us?' asked Valerie. 'Obviously this is somehow connected to the homicide. The business belonged to our vic's father.'

I cleared my throat. 'I don't know if this is helpful,' I said, 'but I talked to Henrietta again this morning. I think it's possible we've had this all wrong. Up until now, we've been focused on Mia, Tristan, and Hen. But those kids didn't set this fire. Mia Klinger might have the balls to call a school with a bomb threat, and Tristan Laurier might be rash enough to get in the occasional fight, but to light that store up so strategically? Knock out the whole surveillance system? Neither one of them is capable of that. On top of which, Mia and Tristan were drinking heavily last night – Tim and I saw it for ourselves. Tristan's brother was so mad the kid'll probably be grounded for a month, and Mia . . .' I took a breath and told Valerie and Sol about Braden Vance. 'I'd bet my badge that, after we got them home, neither of those kids so much as set foot outside let alone ignited a four-alarm blaze.'

'You're saying we're looking at someone else entirely?' said Valerie.

'Leif, Mia, Asher . . . they're all connected. Their parents are long-time friends. They call themselves the River Rats,' I told the group. 'The Colebrooks, Klingers, and Vances. They took summer vacations together, an annual weekend getaway to Gananoque. Ford Colebrook says they were close.'

'Some of them still are,' Valerie said with a snort, no doubt picturing Braden in his underwear.

Across from me, Tim dropped his gaze, and I knew he was still thinking about the text from Ford. What had happened between us. What this other man meant to me.

'One thing I don't understand,' I said. 'Ford told me the families went camping together. But the newspaper story my contact found says they rented a house.'

'Camping?' Tim repeated, not quite meeting my gaze. 'What were his exact words?'

'That they used to go up to a camp in Canada.' I pictured tents in a clearing, and my mind flashed to Camp Vance, those rusting trailers like a collection of old farm machinery abandoned in an overgrown field.

But Tim said, 'A *camp*. He doesn't mean camping like you think. A camp is a summer house, a property near the water where friends and family gather. You've never heard that expression?' Was there a note of self-righteousness in his voice? 'It's a North Country thing.'

'So these couples, they're all part of the same friend group?' Sol asked.

'They used to be. And they've had some rough times along the way. Five years ago, Geena Colebrook drowned on a dive trip with Kim and Mandy. And now, Ford and Geena's son Leif is dead too.'

'So's their family business. You could be on to something,' Valerie said. 'It looks like the Colebrook family may have made an enemy.'

'Right?' said Sol. 'The wife, the kid, and now this fire? Ford's clearly the target.'

I said, 'Here's where it gets complicated. Geena's drowning was ruled accidental – but during the investigation, someone sent an anonymous email to the press claiming it was murder and pointing the finger at Kim. Hen says Mia lured Leif out to the island with a secret about his mother. Hen thinks it might have had something to do with Geena's death – and when he was questioned, Asher said the same.'

'That drowning,' Valerie said. 'Was there an autopsy conducted? Any evidence at all of foul play?'

'No. Ford Colebrook pushed back against the ME. It's all hearsay.'

'Then look here. Mia and Leif may well believe Geena was murdered,' said Valerie, 'but they're kids. For all we know, one of *them* could have sent that email to the press. I do see your point, Shana. Leif's mother drowned, and that's a big red flag. But I'm guessing drownings aren't exactly uncommon around here.'

'You're right,' said Sol. 'I'd say we get one a season. Sometimes more.'

'See? I'm hearing a lot of speculation, when what I think we should be doing is focusing on the facts.'

One of those facts was that Asher Vance was no longer a suspect. Sol had managed to secure surveillance footage of Asher in his car from the pizza restaurant. Hen's boyfriend was officially in the clear.

'In addition to Leif,' Valerie said now, 'there were three other adolescents on the island that night. Mia, Tristan, and Henrietta.'

'Come on,' I said. Were we really back here again? 'Hen tried to *save* Leif. She pulled him out of the water.'

'She was the last person to have contact with the victim. Your trooper and the first responders may believe it was a rescue attempt, but how can we be sure?'

The tightness in my chest was spreading. I couldn't breathe. 'What possible motive could she have for killing a kid she hardly knew? How could Hen – skin-and-bones Hen – cause that kind of bruising to a boy as big as Leif? We need to look at the River Rats,' I said, not just because I was certain the lead had legs but because I couldn't allow Valerie to turn her sights back to Hen.

'Your boy Owen, the forensic tech, found nothing of value at the island, and the fire will likely be more of the same. It's going to be difficult, if not impossible, to recover fingerprints or DNA from the hardware store. And without that surveillance footage,' Valerie said, 'we've got no suspects. We can't put any of the parents at Brooks Hardware or the island. Which brings us back to the kids, I'm afraid.'

'What about Ford Colebrook?' said Tim.

'You think Ford killed his own son?' The words were out before I could question the wisdom of speaking them.

'I'm saying the man's highly suspicious. First his wife dies, then his son, and now his business goes up in smoke? Come on,' Tim scoffed. 'Ford – what kind of name is that anyway, huh? – he may not have been around when his wife took that fatal dive, but he could easily have tampered with her equipment.'

'For what possible reason?' I asked.

'And his son?' Valerie said it slowly. 'What's his motive for killing Leif?'

'The guy could be out of his mind for all we know. Shattered – isn't that how you described him, Shana?' He shot me a heated look. 'Maybe Colebrook wanted to reunite Leif with his mother. And let's not forget that the kid stole a Jet Ski,' he said. 'Right next door to his dad's business. If I ever pulled something like that at seventeen, my dad would have killed me too.'

The room fell silent, everyone a little shocked by Tim's overt display of rage.

'I don't like this situation any more than you do,' Valerie told me, her voice dripping with pity, 'but we have to look at the facts. There was nobody else on that island.'

'That we know of.' I felt a niggle as I said it. A memory maybe, or half-formed thought. Whatever it was, the idea spun away like a leaf in the current. Already gone.

'It's a pretty small island,' she said. 'They would have noticed if someone else was around.'

'There aren't many places to make landfall,' Sol put in.

'Wait.' I forced my mind back to that night. Pictured coasting up to Devil's Oven and not immediately seeing the rescue boats in the water.

'Leif was found by the cave,' I said. 'And whatever happened to him there, the others didn't hear it. Isn't it possible someone else came to the island without the kids noticing? Not Asher on the Jet Ski, but another boat that somehow came and went unseen?'

'You've been out there at night,' said Tim. 'Noise travels for miles on the river.'

I knew that to be true. There were loon calls, and I'd hear the occasional howl of a coyote, but apart from that, the St Lawrence was eerily silent.

'What about a rowboat?' I said. 'Something really quiet?' It was the legend of Bill Johnston that made me think of it, on the run from the British. He'd hidden in the cave for days, or so the story went. I knew that, in reality, no boat could fit inside. But wasn't it possible a noiseless vessel could have approached the island without being detected?

'Jeremy,' Valerie said, turning to Sol. 'You talked to the neighbors, right?'

'Sure did. The closest islands were already closed for the winter – summer residences, every one – but I found a few year-rounders on the mainland. A couple folks heard Jet Skis that night, but that was all.'

'But if the boat had no engine, or a motor that runs really quiet—'

'We'll look into it,' Valerie said, her voice flat as a skipping stone, and that was it. The end of her charity. She'd let me into the investigation thus far, inviting me to attend the odd interview and looking the other way when I got too involved, but all of that was over now. Her annoyance was plain as the frown on her face.

Hen and I were on our own.

# THIRTY-SIX

'It's all circumstantial,' Sol assured me in the hall outside my office.

I'd been surprised when he followed me, but grateful too. It was Tim who made a habit of talking me off the ledge, but he'd stayed behind to speak with Valerie.

'She's making assumptions. Don't worry too much,' said Sol.

'The thing is, I'm making assumptions too. I don't know that Geena was murdered, or that there's any connection between the kids' parents and Leif's death at all. The difference is that Valerie's the lead on this case. If she decides to charge Hen, I don't know that I can stop her.'

Sol forced me to meet his eyes. 'Not gonna happen,' he said. 'We'll find out who did this. Just stay on her good side. It'll be OK.'

What I would have given to believe him.

After talking to Sol, I wanted to leave. Storm out of the barracks and interrogate each of these families until I found the one harboring a killer. Instead, I retreated to my office, closed the door, and drew the shade to block the sunlight reflecting on my computer.

If I wanted to know more about these people, I had to start with Ford Colebrook's wife.

When I looked up Geena's case, I was dismayed to discover it was Don Bogle's name on the file. Five years ago, when that case crossed the former Troop D investigator's desk, I was still with the NYPD in New York. Tim was still a trooper with aspirations of making investigator. All I had to work with now were the notes Bogle had taken.

That, and a video file.

The details of the death were in line with what I'd learned from Ford. Geena, Mandy, and Kim had been diving the *A.E. Vickery*, just like he'd said. It was a popular dive site, from what I'd read online, a mid-nineteenth-century ship not far from Clayton.

The determination Bogle had made was consistent with Ford's account too. *Equipment failure.* Bogle reported that Geena's regulator had failed while she was exploring the wreck. *Victim attempted to return to the surface, receiving air (buddy breath) from Kim Klinger and Mandy Vance. Victim's mask was knocked off along the way, causing her to swallow water and drop off the line.* Kim and Mandy had attempted to locate her in the deep water, but visibility was poor. By the time Mandy found her and pulled her to the surface, Geena had drowned.

The file contained no startling revelations. Still, I hadn't expected that video. Geena had worn a GoPro on the dive that appeared to be mounted to her head, and I suspected the resulting footage was what had led Bogle to close the investigation.

Cuing up the digital file on my computer, I settled in to watch.

The screen went emerald, and the sound of scattered bubbles filled my office. Masks and neoprene hoods obscured the divers' faces and hair, but here were three people clad in deep-water drysuits, their fins and multicolored tanks glowing neon in the water. After a moment, the wreck came into view, its mass misshapen by rot and softened by clots of bright-green algae, clumps of knife-sharp zebra mussels that looked like swarms of bees. For several minutes, the scene was calm as the three women studied the wreck, shining their flashlights into the hull. It was mesmerizing to watch the gentle wag of their fins, the occasional fish darting across the screen. Everything bathed in that warm teal light.

At the ten-minute point, the divers made their way back to the line, preparing to ascend to the surface. Geena took a quick look at her diving gauge, which a cursory Google search revealed measured the air pressure in her tank. She gave the others the 'OK' sign with her gloved hand and gestured for the group to ascend.

They were fighting a current; that much was clear. The video captured their hard kicks and Geena's hands gripping the line to steady herself, the chain slipping slowly downward through her fingers as her body inched toward the surface.

That was when it all went wrong. An explosion of bubbles, a jolt, and the GoPro swung back and forth. Geena grabbed for her gauge, and then the diver with the pink tank unclipped a bright yellow regulator from the side of her dive harness and pushed it in Geena's direction. Bogle's notes called the device an 'octopus,' which allowed two divers to breathe from the same air source. Geena took a few pulls and signaled for them to move up the line. Another jolt, and then the camera was falling, past the wreck and into the cloudy gloom. I watched in horror as the realization of what had happened struck. The GoPro had been mounted to Geena's mask. A mask that, along with Geena, had spiraled down to the river's silty bottom, sinking like the wreck itself.

What had happened in the moments between those octopus breaths and Geena's deadly descent? Both Mandy and Kim had been questioned. Both had told Bogle they didn't know. The camera had shown both women right next to the victim on that line, willing and eager to help. Mandy had said the same during her interview. Yet somehow, Geena was dead.

I could see why a loved one might question the circumstances surrounding the accident. But it hadn't been Ford who'd requested the investigation. To the contrary, the case files included a statement from Jack Klinger. Kim's ex, Mia's father and another one of Ford's old friends. That was interesting. It was Jack – whose own wife had been on that dive with Geena – who'd been convinced of foul play. Despite all that, there was no autopsy conducted on Geena Colebrook. Like Cunningham said, Ford had declined to allow it.

That wasn't necessarily strange. Geena had drowned. Her equipment had failed, and she'd run out of air. Vanished in the dark before she could be saved. It was all caught on camera. According to the witness statements, Geena had not been drinking or on drugs or struggling with her health.

Conducting an autopsy after a drowning was standard procedure, in some cases even required by law. Opposing one would have required Ford to visit the medical examiner's office in Watertown and fill out a form, at which point the medical investigator would review the request and make a determination. It was a cumbersome process, but Ford had made the effort, and now that was a problem. The lack of an autopsy muddied the waters when it came to determining an official cause of death. In other words, no one could say for certain whether Geena's death was an accident, or whether Jack's warning and Mia's theory about Mandy Vance was right.

Staring at the black screen before me, I reached for my phone.

# THIRTY-SEVEN

Tracking down Jack Klinger was surprisingly easy. Kim's ex-husband, I knew, had long since moved to Rhode Island, but he was now superintendent of the Providence Public School district. I found his office number, navigated the automated system, worked my way through a directory of names, and hit six. A moment later, I was talking to Mia's father.

'Not to say school over here isn't without its complications,' he told me after we'd exchanged pleasantries. Jack Klinger was North Country born, no question; his was one of the thicker accents I'd heard. 'There aren't as many four a.m. wake ups to call snow days though.'

Before relocating to Providence, Jack Klinger had been assistant principal at the pre-K through twelve school in Alexandria Bay. That was before Courtney's time there. Jack had been in Rhode Island for six years now, having moved out of town and away from his ex and daughter about a year before Geena's death.

I wondered if he knew that Kim was now with Braden Vance.

'This won't take long,' I explained. 'But I'm afraid I need to relay some bad news.'

When I told him about Leif, Jack went quiet. I don't particularly like phone calls when I'm working a case. Tim's the opposite, constantly talking up the importance of 'checking in' and 'touching base,' particularly if the alternative is email. While I'll grant him that email, with its lack of context and social cues, is terrible, phone calls are a close second. There's too much room for pretense. It was impossible for me to tell, when Jack Klinger got the news that his old friend's son was dead, whether he was choked up or checking his socials or in a dangerous state of shock.

'The reason I'm calling,' I went on, 'is that I understand you and your wife were once close with the Colebrooks. The Vance family too. With Leif's death a suspected homicidal drowning, we're taking another look at his mother's dive accident as well.

According to my records, you weren't entirely convinced Geena's death was an accident. You can imagine why I'm eager to speak with you.'

'Leif Colebrook,' he said, sounding genuinely distraught. 'My God. He couldn't have been more than, what, seventeen?'

'That's right. A high school senior.'

'Christ. What Ford must be going through right now, after everything else.'

There was another stretch of silence, and then he said, 'I want to help, but I haven't talked to Ford in years. To any of them really, with the exception of Kim – and that's only because I have to. Sure, me and Ford used to be close, but I didn't really keep in touch after the move.'

'I understand. You moved a year before Geena's death, correct?'

'That sounds right. I took a principal position here; I was only elected superintendent last summer. Kim and I were already at the point of no return when I got the offer. I couldn't say no.'

'Geena's drowning,' I said. 'I'm told you advised Ford to concede to an autopsy, which he declined. What had you so convinced the death wasn't accidental?'

'Ah,' he said, sheepish now. 'I'm not proud of that. Kim called me when it happened, and I knew Ford was a wreck. I probably should have backed off, but Kim . . . she'd been dragging out the divorce and had started that godawful ghost business, and she wouldn't let me have any time with Mia on summer break. When she said that she and Mandy were with Geena when it happened . . .'

I'd been taking notes, but now I stopped, pen hovering unsteadily above the page. 'Mr Klinger, did you happen to send an email suggesting foul play to the *Watertown Daily Times*?'

'Yeah,' he sighed. 'Yeah, that was me.'

'And I'm sorry, I want to make sure I'm clear. Are you saying you accused your ex-wife of murder to try to get custody of your daughter?' It certainly sounded that way to me.

'No, no,' he said. 'Look, the fact is, nobody really knows what happened out there. According to Kim and Mandy, Geena's regulator failed and her mask fell off – right? But Geena was an expert diver. It was her *job*. I know there's a video out there somewhere, but you have to understand, Kim has issues. She's

flighty and unreliable and she holds a grudge like no one I've
ever seen. And look, it made no difference in the end. We've got
a long-distance custody arrangement now, which means Kim
sticks Mia on a bus every few weeks and I get to see her for a
truncated weekend. I'll go on the record as saying I never felt
good about leaving Mia with her, with those crazy tours and all.
All that talk about death.'

Part of me wanted to tell him his instincts were spot-on.
Mia was not OK, and that seemed to have a lot to do with the
environment in which she'd been raised.

'You said Kim holds grudges. Did she have anything against
Geena?'

'No idea,' Jack said. 'I was all the way out here, and me and
Kim only talked about Mia. All friendships have their ups and
downs though, right?'

'Even friendships between River Rats?'

This time, despite being encumbered by the phone, the man's
surprise was audible. His mouth mimicked the soft, pulsating
gasp of a beached fish.

'I read an article,' I explained.

'I remember that piece. The owner of the rental house had a
friend at the paper, I think. It was a stupid story, if you ask me.
Pointless.'

'Mm,' I said. 'Have you taken any trips lately, Mr Klinger?
Say, back up north?'

'I haven't been back to A-Bay since I left,' he said, and I
thought I detected a note of regret.

'If you need anything else,' he added, already on his way to
setting down the phone, 'I'm just a call away.'

# THIRTY-EIGHT

'So you're going to investigate this homicide,' Tim said, 'even though Henderson took you off the case. Even after what happened with Colebrook.'

Tim wasn't the one driving, but his eyes were riveted to the road home all the same. My own gaze flicked to the pulse in the tender flesh of his neck, its rapid throb like a flashing red light. He'd cut himself shaving this morning, and not just once. The bony front of Tim's throat was crosscut with nicks, a study of line art in crimson.

'I talked to Henderson after watching the video of Geena's fatal dive,' I said. 'He's agreed to let me reopen her case.'

It hadn't been as easy as I was making it sound, and I suspected the appeal had bombed the last bridge remaining between me and Henderson as a result, but I got what I came for.

'I think there's a connection between the wife's death and the son's – and Tim, you heard Valerie. She likes Hen for this crime. My niece. My brother's kid.'

'Don't pretend you haven't thought the same thing.'

I blinked at him. Had I? Hen lied to me, obscuring the truth and slowing the investigation. To some extent, I still thought of her as a rescue cat I couldn't quite trust, forever on edge around her claws. But had I ever really believed she was capable of murder?

'I have to explore this avenue,' I said, 'and not just for Hen's sake. It's the right thing to do.'

Tim's nod was unconvincing. 'Are we going to talk about it?'

'Ford kissed me.'

The words hung in the air between us like a putrid fog, wrinkling Tim's nose and deepening the crow's feet that fanned across his temples. It was the same face he made when he was in pain.

'I didn't instigate it.' Quietly, I added, 'But I didn't immediately stop it either. And I need to figure out what that means.'

By most measures, our relationship was still new. We'd only

known each other for two years and been dating for just fifteen months. While this wasn't the first rut on our road to marriage, I knew that, to Tim, it was nothing like the struggles we'd faced last year. Whether the kiss was my idea or not, it was a betrayal.

Ford was an attractive man, no question, but Tim . . . Tim was my partner, lover, friend. He'd been with me for some of the worst moments of my life, and as for the ones that happened before we met, he understood those better than anyone.

Since meeting Tim, in those early days when we worked the case on Tern Island, and later when Trey Hayes disappeared from under his teacher's nose and I suspected Bram might be to blame, I had put on an air of authority. I was a senior investigator after all, head of Troop D in A-Bay and Tim's direct superior. I'd earned a reputation for being hard-bitten, and I intended to keep it. But keeping up the appearance of strength required that I conceal my worries and fears, and that was exhausting. Even talking to Gil Gasko on the regular didn't ease the pressure I felt to pack down my every burden, foible, flaw.

I couldn't help but wonder if Ford's real appeal was in his weakness. The man didn't have his shit together any more than I did. He didn't know me at all – which meant he had no expectations about my behavior. With ravaged, rudderless Ford, I could be ravaged and rudderless too, and being with someone even more fucked up than me felt more freeing than I could have imagined. But was I really so weak myself that I couldn't resist him, knowing – then and now – what it would do to Tim?

'I'm a mess,' I confided to him in a quavering voice. 'I tell myself I'm fine, and sometimes I even believe it, but it's a lie. And the thing is, I'm going to *be* a mess for a long, long time. My abduction, Bram showing up here and terrorizing this town, Carson's murder, this stuff with Henrietta . . . I'm not in control of it, Tim, not any of it. I thought that being with you would fix things. Your life, everything about you as a person, is so stable. So *right.*'

'Not everything apparently,' Tim muttered, turning his hands into talons and digging them into his thighs.

'But that's just it.' I adjusted the wheel with small, deliberate movements. Watched the road. 'There's too much chaos in my world for me to be like that too. Bram's dead, he's *dead*, and I still look over my shoulder when I'm walking alone and get these violent, full-body shivers whenever I see movement from the corner of my eye. It feels like I've been through a war, but even though it's over, I'm still in the trenches ducking bullets and stepping over the dead.'

The swath of forehead between Tim's eyebrows and hairline was shiny now, and he was holding the rest of his body still. 'That's normal,' he said. 'It's the PTSD. Gasko tells you all the time you won't recover overnight. It could take years – and I understand that. I'm OK with that, Shana. What I don't understand is how you could make out with a total fucking stranger when we're months away from committing to each other for life.'

Tim didn't like to swear, would wince whenever a curse word slipped through. Not this time.

'I don't understand it either. I love you,' I told him. 'That hasn't changed. It never will.'

'Then why—'

'*I don't know.*' I hadn't intended to raise my voice, but my emotions were betraying me yet again. Friendly creatures who, when I wasn't looking, sank their teeth into my hand. The car was making me feel penned in. We were almost home.

'I'm going to Gananoque,' I said, doing my best to steady my voice. 'I did some digging on the rental place the River Rats used for their summer trips. I want to talk to the owner, see if he knows about any money problems or resentment that could have caused a rift within the group. I won't be late.'

We took the turn on to our road in silence. One of the things I liked about our street was that it was surrounded by farmland. On either side of us were meadows of yellowing grass that, as we drew closer to the water, morphed into brown marshland. The swampy area smelled like standing water with an undercurrent of rotting fish, but I didn't mind. Gradually, the funk had come to feel like home. And there it was: the house, its white trim aglow in the dwindling daylight. Tim's car was in the driveway. Hen was already inside.

He didn't answer until I'd pulled up next to it and turned off the engine.

'You know that I love you. In for a penny, in for a pound – that's how I've always felt about you. About *this*.' Tim gave a little wave as if my baggage was something tangible, built up around me like a drum tower wall. 'What I'm not going to do is be played for a fool. I had enough of that when I was a kid. I let Carson use and abuse me and said nothing, because I was too spineless. Too *nice*. I'm not that guy anymore, and I never want to be him again.'

If I'd been just a little bit closer to him, I could have heard Tim's heartbeat right through his chest. He was flushed to the point of looking ill.

'I need to know where you stand. With this marriage. With us.' Tim drew a shaky breath and said, 'You need to decide what you really want, Shana.'

*I want you*, I thought. *Your hands, rough and dry from working on our home, the home you found for us. Your seemingly random but totally relevant analogies, about choirs of crickets and bad wiring. I want you to call me Shane again, the way you did when things were easy.*

It wasn't fair for me to ask all this of Tim. I owed him an answer. I owed him a lot more than that.

The passenger door opened. Tim planted his foot on the asphalt. 'I need you to understand something,' he said, looking back. 'If you're not invested in this relationship – fully, doggedly, irrevocably invested – then I can't do this, Shana. I just can't.'

The door slammed shut with a clunk that jolted me like a shock. Tim crossed the driveway, mounted the steps, and disappeared into the house.

# THIRTY-NINE

The knock on the glass gave me a start. I'd been sitting in the driveway for nearly ten minutes, holding back tears and pressing my hand against Tim's still-warm seat wondering what the hell to do, when my niece's pale face appeared in the passenger window. Straightening up, I waved for her to open the door. Hen wore a nubby white fleece that was nearly worn through at the elbows, its trim and snaps the color of black plums, and as she slipped into Tim's vacated seat her eyes were keen, unyielding.

'Tim seems pissed.'

'I fucked up,' I told her.

'Yeah well,' Hen said. 'Join the club.'

A laugh escaped my lips, and in spite of everything, I found myself smiling. 'I have to go to Canada,' I said. 'Just over the border, to check out a lead. I'll be back in a couple of hours.'

Hen bit her lower lip. She seemed to be struggling with something, and the prospect of that made me antsy. I didn't have it in me to field another problem.

After a moment, she said, 'Can I come?'

'To Gananoque?'

'I already finished my homework.'

I blew out a breath. 'Hen, I don't know.'

'Why not? I don't want to sit around the house all night alone.'

'You won't be alone. Tim—'

Her expression stopped me short. Hen was right. Tim wouldn't be much company tonight, and it wasn't as if she had friends she could call. Not after I'd warned Mia to keep her distance.

'I know I'm grounded or whatever,' Hen said, 'but maybe I can help somehow? I can be like your spy. Poke around while you're doing your thing.' Her eyes lit up at the idea.

Almost two weeks. That's how long it had been since Hen's arrival, and we'd spent hardly any time together that didn't involve a police interview. Our interactions had largely revolved around lectures – understandable, considering I'd adopted the role of jailor with a vengeance, micromanaging her every move. Wasn't her visit supposed to be about bonding? Me and Tim setting a good example for Henrietta to follow so she'd be motivated to get her young life back on track? All I'd managed to do was doubt and berate her. And now I was leaving Tim in the cold too.

'Get your passport,' I told her, watching her mouth peel back into a childlike grin that put the gap left by her molar on full display. 'Let Tim know – and hurry, OK? I'd like to get home before dark.'

The Colebrook, Klinger, and Vance families' rental was off-market for the winter, but my suspicion that someone would man its email address year-round had been right. Frank Bouchard was expecting me and had suggested we meet at a building he owned right down the street from the wedding-cake bakery. The motel – cracked asphalt parking lot, fifties-style flat roof construction, horizontal blinds in the windows the color of crusted cream – was significantly less impressive than the photos I'd seen of his waterfront rental, but I supposed the man was wise to diversify. The house favored by the River Rats went for six hundred dollars a night, while the motel had a sign out front advertising clean rooms for forty-four bucks.

'Thanks for seeing me,' I said as I shook Bouchard's hand in the cramped, wood-paneled lobby. 'Or us, I guess. This is Henrietta.'

'Er,' he said, visibly flushing as he looked down at Hen. The man had a round face, a white goatee, and liver spots across his balding pate like a shower of nut-brown confetti.

'She's my niece,' I explained. 'Just along for the ride.'

'OK,' he replied, still looking ill at ease.

I took out my notebook. 'As I mentioned over the phone, I have some questions about your rental agreement with the couples who stayed at your waterfront rental. How many years would you say they did that?'

'Sixteen,' he said at once. 'I looked it up after you called. Even after I raised the price – there's a lot of upkeep on a property like that, a lot of expenses – they kept coming back. I guess they told you they were regulars?'

'I read an old article,' I said, 'about their time in Gananoque. Fun and friendship and all that.'

'I remember that story.' He said it with a grimace. 'A reporter friend of mine wrote it, as a favor, like. I thought it would help drive some business. I didn't know when it came out what I know now.'

True to her word, Henrietta had already wandered away, feigning innocence as she studied a bulletin board plastered with brochures for boat rentals. She strolled past the collection of vintage maps that hung unevenly along the motel lobby wall. At Bouchard's last words, I saw her head twitch.

'And what is it that you know now?' I asked.

'It's not my business what guests get up to.'

'Of course not.' I waited for him to say more.

'But.' Bouchard winced. 'You want to know what kind of people you're dealing with.'

I felt a flutter in my gut. 'What kind of people are these couples, Mr Bouchard?'

He hesitated, and I realized he was looking at Hen again. 'Hen, honey,' I said, turning her way, 'would you mind waiting in the next room?'

'Help yourself to some cocoa.' Bouchard waved at the tiny anteroom, where guests could make themselves a warm drink. 'It's the hot-water kind, but it's got marshmallows.'

Hen flashed him a smile and ducked through the door.

When I looked at Bouchard once more, his lips had turned in on themselves and disappeared under his white facial hair.

I said, 'That article talked about fun and games. Getting to know each other better.' I was scrabbling for purchase in the dark, unsure why Bouchard had clammed up. Had the River Rats caused irreversible damage to the house? Were they terrible renters, partying to Eurodance beats that echoed across the water for miles? Had one of them committed some kind of crime on the property? What?

'Games.' Bouchard coated the word in revulsion. 'Is that what they said?'

'Whatever you know, it could be vital to our investigation.' I'd told him very little about the cases, beyond the fact that two people were dead.

At length, the man took a breath. 'I don't know anything for certain. But I have my suspicions.'

'About?'

'About their *activities*. And they had families, they said. Kids.' He looked disgusted by the thought. 'Not at the beginning maybe, but later.'

Lost, I said, 'Who are we talking about exactly?'

'All of them. The four couples.'

'Four?' I only knew about the Colebrooks, Klingers, and Vances. *No. That's not true.* Cunningham's newspaper story had mentioned a fourth. I held my breath and hoped Bouchard would remember their names, but I needn't have worried.

'Fear,' he said at once. 'They were called the Fears. I make my renters give me the names of all their guests. They were only around for a couple of years, and then they disappeared and never came back. Can't say I blame them. Get out while you can.'

'I'm sorry, sir,' I said, 'I'm still not following. What do you think was going on in that house?'

He let out a sigh of resignation. 'My own place isn't far from the rental, see, and I fish in that area,' he said. 'Go out almost every day in the summer, real early. Sometimes before sunrise. Once, a few years into their routine, I was fishing nearby – not snooping, mind you, just doing my thing. They were hard to miss, right there out in the open. It was the man who always came to pick up the key. Ford was his name. I guess they didn't think anyone would see.'

Most couples outgrow the kind of partying they do in high school. They replace shared joints moist with saliva and urgent, drunken groping with more civilized behavior. Sex on Friday nights and Chardonnay by the glass. I was getting the sense that the River Rats were different. That, for one weekend a year, they went wild – Ford and his wife included.

'Like I said, not my business,' Bouchard went on. 'But then, a couple years later, I saw him again. Back out on the dock. This time, it was different.' He hung his snowy head. The man's face was the red of a roasted beet. There was more to this story than he was letting on. 'I understood then why they chose my place, and why they kept coming back. It was the privacy they wanted.

No neighbors for miles. Even so, he was out there for all the world to see.'

'Mr Bouchard, I don't . . .'

'I believe those people were having sexual relations,' he said in a fit of courage, drawing himself up to his full height.

*This time, it was different.* 'Who was having sexual relations, Mr Bouchard?' I asked.

With a final remorseful glance at the room into which Hen had disappeared, the man gritted his teeth.

'All of them.'

# FORTY

'They were hooking up,' Hen said, doing a poor job of containing her awe. 'Asher's parents, and Mia's, and Leif's. They were all f—'

'Yup, I heard.' My neck was hot. If you'd asked me two weeks ago about the conversation topics I was likely to broach with my niece, this would have been very low on the list.

*Doug's going to skin me alive.*

It had started to storm as we left Gananoque, and now the rain came down in sheets. I kept my eyes on the road, squinting through the wipers as we sped toward the US border. The last thing I wanted to find out was how much a high-school kid knew about swingers. From where I was sitting though, that's exactly what we were dealing with. For sixteen years, through their twenties and thirties, the birth of their children and the passing of years, all the way until Geena Colebrook's death, the River Rats had been meeting every summer for a weekend of free love. It boggled my mind.

It was also information that completely reframed my view of the investigation.

I knew why people did it, in theory. Open relationships weren't so uncommon. Some found partner-swapping exciting, while others wanted to keep their relationships fresh. I suspected there were plenty of couples who could live that way without significant problems. But two of the group – the Fears, Bouchard called them – had stopped coming, and another had moved out of state. A fourth drowned, two were having an affair, and now one of their kids was dead.

Whatever their former arrangement, and whatever had gone on inside that house, something about the River Rats wasn't right.

'If Bouchard's theory about what was happening at the rental holds water – and mind you, we don't have any evidence to corroborate it yet – it seems likely the River Rats' . . .

*relationships* could have something to do with these deaths,' I told Hen. 'But it's too early to say for sure.'

'You mean maybe Leif knew about the parents having freaky dock sex?'

I let out a groan. 'OK,' I said. 'It's possible.'

What would that do to a kid, finding out your parents and those of your friends had been getting it on for years behind your back? It wouldn't be easy to stomach, not for any of them.

'We know why the retreats stopped,' I said. 'Jack moved away, and then Geena died. It wouldn't have been the same after that. But that was five, six years ago. If there's a connection between the River Rats and Leif, what happened between then and now that would lead someone to murder him and target Ford Colebrook's business?'

'Maybe Leif knew something,' Hen said. 'He could have found out about Mia's mom and Asher's dad – Kim and Braden. They're having an affair. Maybe Leif knew it.'

I couldn't help but feel a flash of pride. Hen's powers of deduction weren't half bad. 'Jealousy's a strong motive for murder,' I agreed. What I didn't point out was that Hen's theory made Mia the most likely suspect. Asher and Leif had been friends, and Asher wasn't on the island at the time of death – but Mia was so determined to defend her mother against accusations of murder that she'd begun pointing the finger at Mandy Vance. Was it such a stretch to imagine Leif told her about Kim's involvement with Braden, and Mia got angry?

'Those kids,' I said. 'Mia, Asher, Leif. None of them ever mentioned the River Rats?'

'I was telling the truth about Leif,' Hen replied. 'I didn't know him at all. But Mia and Asher . . . no. They didn't mention their parents were swingers. Believe me, I would have remembered.'

'But Mia did tell you she was looking into Geena's death. And Asher said she had a secret to tell Leif. You have no inkling of what that was?'

She shook her head.

'We'll need to ask Mia – and soon.'

At the ends of her sleeves, Hen's fingers were busy fiddling with the fleece's purple trim. I could smell fabric softener on her clothes, a tender, cheering perfume that reminded me I'd been the one to do her laundry, that she was still just a girl.

'That Valerie woman,' she said, not looking at me. 'Does she think I killed Leif?'

The question stole the air from my lungs. I had to play this carefully. Maybe I was being overly optimistic, but it felt as though our trip to Canada, however brief, had altered something between us. We were finally starting to connect, and I didn't want to lose that. I didn't want to scare her either.

I said, 'You know that, based on the medical examiner's report, there was a struggle before Leif went in the water. Since you were the one who found him, the last person to be seen with Leif . . . any investigator worth their salt would take that into consideration. But you just met Leif a few days ago. What possible reason could you have for wanting to kill him? Valerie's considering that too, and she'll see it doesn't make sense. But she has to keep poking around until she understands what really went down. Until we can give Leif's dad some answers.'

'So Valerie needs proof that it wasn't me.'

'Process of elimination. Exactly. She needs to narrow the search for the suspect.'

'Or she needs proof of who *did* do it.'

'Yep.'

'But we don't know what that proof would be.'

I smiled a little. 'This is how it is sometimes. You don't know what you're looking for until you find it.'

In the passenger seat, Hen nibbled at the cuticles around her nails, black now, and pulled her knees to her chin. 'I know Mia isn't, like, your favorite person, but we're working on this project together for English. Could we maybe stop at her house real quick on the way home? I need to grab some notes.'

The wipers swept the rain from the windshield with a swoosh. When I thought about Mia, all I could see was her smug lipsticked mouth telling me she could say whatever she liked about Bram on her tour. I pictured her with the Ouija board by the fire, talking about natural born killers. *It's in the blood.*

'No,' I said. 'I'm sorry, Hen, but Mia's bad news. I really don't want you spending time with her.'

'I know, but she's the only person in the whole class who isn't either a total stranger or a total dick. She asked me to be her partner days ago, before . . . everything, and this project's worth, like, twenty percent of our grade.'

The idea of facilitating an ongoing relationship between Hen and Mia turned my stomach. At the same time, I didn't want to get in the way of school. Courtney had been checking up on Hen, and her grades were the one part of her life she seemed to be getting in order.

'Can't you FaceTime her or something? Get the notes that way?'

'Those first few days at school,' Hen said, 'I felt like I was in a fishbowl. Everyone staring. Everyone talking about me, and you, and Bram. But then Mia was nice to me, and she and Tristan introduced me to Asher, and I really like him, and they were all so interested in the Bram thing, and I didn't want to lose that. All my friends in Burlington ditched me because of Bram, and I finally had a life again. You know?'

I did know. A loss like that, being cast out like a social leper, these were things I knew well.

'Please,' Hen said. 'I'll be super quick. In and out.'

'Border up ahead.'

Hen knew to stay quiet. She'd crossed into Canada dozens of times to visit Quebec from her home in Vermont and understood it was best just to smile and let the grown-up do the talking, especially when the grown-up was a state investigator with a badge.

We breezed through the checkpoint and on to the Thousand Islands International Bridge. The incline was steep, the ground dropping away from us on both sides until we were 150 feet in the air. The darkness and rain obscured the view so that it felt like we were driving through a tunnel, no exit in sight.

I wanted to understand my niece, to really *get* her. And I was getting closer. There were some aspects of her character, though, that still baffled me.

'Hen,' I said, drawing out her name. 'When we were looking for you last night, Tim and I found something in your room. They were photos. Photos of Abe.'

I glanced at Hen and found her watching me through glazed eyes.

'I know it's wrong,' she said quietly, 'to be . . . interested in him. Why he did what he did. I can't help it. I know it makes me a sicko.'

'No, Hen,' I began, but then I realized that I did understand, at least a little. What Hen was feeling, it wasn't so far removed from my attraction to Ford and the comforting knowledge that, however fucked up, we were the same. 'Ah,' I said. 'Mia doesn't think you're a sicko, does she.'

Hen nibbled at the inside of her cheek.

When it came to female friendships, Hen's options were severely limited. If the other girls at school hadn't taken to her yet, they weren't going to be beating down our door now that they knew she'd been with Leif on the night of his death. Mia Klinger was all Hen had.

'In and out, OK?' I said, exhaling hard.

Henrietta replied, 'Cross my heart.'

# FORTY-ONE

The specter in the window of Island Death Ghost Tours bathed the wet sidewalk in light. The rain had intensified, and water gushed down Walton, the street alive with the hollow gurgle of swollen storm drains and pipes pushed to their limits. In the streaming window, Kim Klinger stood behind the ticket desk, head bent over the cell phone in her hand. She wore a man's black blazer over a tight purple shirt and she was smirking at something on the screen, eyes crinkled in a rinse of electric blue.

'No Mia,' I observed as we pulled up. Kim appeared to be alone.

'She's probably upstairs doing homework,' said Hen. 'Hey, is that the Snapchat ghost?' She pointed to the neon sign in the window.

'The what? That's from Pac-Man.'

'Pac-what?'

Rolling my eyes, I told her I'd wait in the car.

'Actually, can you come in with me? I promise it won't take long. Two minutes, tops.'

I studied the woman in the window. 'I don't think she'd like that.'

'Please,' Hen said. 'Kim creeps me out.'

I'd be lying if I said I didn't feel the same way. 'OK,' I told my niece, already regretting my decision. 'But hurry.'

Together, we stepped out into the squall, splashed across the street, and yanked open the door.

The place was creepier at night. I hadn't noticed before, but Kim had outfitted the glass on the sconces with frilly decals, and when the light filtered through them, it patterned the walls in shadowy lace. The black fringe on the chandelier shuddered in the breeze from the door. Kim's head jerked up at the creak of the hinges and rush of rain-swept air that followed us inside.

'Shana,' she said, and once again the sound of my name on

her tongue gave me a chill. The woman looked confused. 'Are you here for a tour? I cancelled them today. Weather's shit.'

'I just need to see Mia real quick,' said Hen. 'Is that OK?'

Kim looked from me to Hen. 'Go ahead, hon. Stairs are in the back.'

Flashing her an uncertain smile, Hen disappeared into the hall.

We stood in silence, Kim and I, listening to the rain beat at the window. As we waited for Hen to reappear, I thought about the River Rats. The secret Kim and all the others were keeping even now. I couldn't look at her without picturing Ford and Geena and Asher's parents at that rental house, swapping partners like restaurant entrées. Inviting one another to give their husband or wife a go. I couldn't imagine adopting their lifestyle, which felt tremendously risky in a town the size of A-Bay. Tremendously risky in general. It blew my mind that these couples had spent years building lives and relationships together, only to give themselves over to somebody else.

'How's Ford doing?' I asked. 'That was a real blow, losing his business.' I watched Kim's eyes behind her face-framing bangs, the way the skin above her lips crimped like tissue paper. She was watching me too.

'He's wrecked.' There was a faint rattle coming from her chest, like she'd been smoking. Or crying. Or both. 'He's lost everything. Every single thing he loved is gone.'

Outside, rain hammered at the window. The gap under the door emitted a pulsing, ghostly howl. I waited for Kim to say more, about Geena's death or Leif's. Instead, she drew the blazer across her chest.

'I want you to know, I have nothing but good intentions for that cabin. I know the kids were messing around out there, and maybe Mia told you some things. About the tour. What it is, see, is that I'm planning to build a shrine. Not to Bram,' she said when my eyes went wide, 'to his victims. Carson Gates, and all those women Bram killed over the years. To help their legacy live on.'

'Oh.' I wanted to tell her it was a terrible idea, point out that her so-called shrine would be a magnet for people feeding a sick obsession with Bram, people like her daughter. Upstairs, the floorboards creaked, and I heard voices. Mia's. Hen's. Right above my head, a door closed and then . . . silence. I wasn't going to make a scene here, in this woman's home, with her kid and Hen right upstairs. I wouldn't.

'So,' I said. 'You and Braden.'

'Just so you know, I've been divorced from my useless ex for years, and Braden and Mandy are planning to split up as soon as Asher leaves for college. They decided a long time ago. So if you're thinking I'm a husband-stealing whore or whatever,' Kim said, 'don't.'

'I wasn't thinking that.' In fact, I'd been trying to imagine Kim with Ford, and Jack with Mandy, and Braden with Geena, and which of them might have a reason to blow up Ford Colebrook's entire life.

Kim's shrug suggested she didn't actually care one way or the other.

A loud thump upstairs rattled the pendant lamp that hung from the ceiling, and the light gave the room a dizzying quality as it swung.

'I'm sorry,' I said. 'I don't know what's taking so long.'

'Probably gossiping about boys or something. Hen really likes Asher, huh?'

'Looks that way.' I was poorly equipped to discuss Hen's crush. It hadn't occurred to me to prod about the fledgling relationship, distracted as I was by a boy's murder.

'Asher's a good kid,' Kim said. 'Leif was too. Ford raised him well.'

As she looked away, I thought of Ford's gentle manner, that soft voice, and said, 'I believe it. I bet it's not easy raising kids in a town like this.'

'What do you mean?'

'There isn't much privacy, is there? Everyone knows everybody else's business. That has to be hard on a kid. On a parent too.'

I was trawling, hoping Kim would slip up and spill something about the River Rats. She said, 'No, you're right. All this stuff with Leif . . . I think it's hurting business. We always get some locals in the dead season, girls' nights out and such, but someone snitched about Mia getting questioned by the police and it's been crickets since. Around here, rumors stick like gnats to flypaper, and I can't have that.'

'I'm sure.' I felt some sympathy for the woman then, raising Mia alone on an income that was meager at best, all in the shadow of a rumor her husband had started to serve his own needs. Tiny towns defended their own to the death, but they weren't always forgiving of aberrant behavior.

I'd been quick to judge the River Rats, but there was another way of looking at things. How oppressive must it have felt to be these couples at twenty-one, living in a close community, the only home most of them had ever known? Maybe the need to get away, unfettered and unobserved, had nagged them like a recurrent muscle spasm.

When I thought of Ford Colebrook, I could almost understand it.

At last, the room filled with the sound of shoes clomping on the stairs. Hen appeared in the doorway to the back room like a breathless apparition, and for a second her eyes met mine. Was she getting sick? She was definitely pale. Behind her, Mia gnashed her teeth, blew a purple bubble with her gum and jeered.

'Did you get what you needed?' I asked.

The girls hazarded twin smiles, tentative expressions with a sweep of sweetness. Strawberry lip gloss on a fox.

'We'll get out of your hair,' I said. 'Have a nice night, Ms Klinger.'

'Bye,' Hen called over her shoulder as we stepped back into the rain.

'Two minutes? That took forever,' I told Hen as we dashed back to the car, dirty puddles soaking our shins and rain pouring down our faces.

'I got it,' she said.

Water in my eyes, my mouth. I dragged a sleeve across my face. 'Got what?'

Hen only smiled.

# FORTY-TWO

Same country road, same stretch of marshland, and then, blocking our path like a sentry, the house. The lights on the first floor glowed gold through the windows, and a stream of pale-gray smoke wafted up from the chimney. Tim had started a fire, the first of the season.

'What are you going to do?' Hen asked as we pulled into the driveway.

The question might have been about the homicide, or the cold case, or information we'd gleaned in Gananoque, or the problems between me and Tim. I didn't ask. Instead, I turned off the engine and faced her. 'Got any suggestions?'

Hen thought for a long time. 'There's something my mom always says. It's kind of dumb.'

'I'll be the judge of that.'

A glimmer of a grin. 'If you run from your problems,' Hen told me, 'they'll chase you.'

'Your mom's a smart woman. Come on,' I said. 'I'm starving.'

I steeled myself as we approached the front door. I was expecting utter silence. When last I spoke with Tim, he'd been angry and brooding, and I had no reason to think that would change until I gave him an answer.

The house – bright with the sizzle of searing food and jubilant voices – told a different story.

'You were right about that French place. The charcuterie board was to die for.'

The sound of Valerie Ott's voice echoing through my kitchen was a surprise – until I realized it was coming from Tim's phone. He had the woman on speaker while he spooned sauce over seared pork, a goofy look on his face.

'Right?' he said as he tipped the pan. There was smooth jazz playing on the little Wi-Fi stereo we kept in the kitchen. A glass of white wine sweating next to the stove. 'Chateau Gris's cuts are killer. I've tried to recreate that board at home, but Maynard

– he's the owner – cures the salami and prosciutto himself, and grocery-store meat just doesn't compare.'

'I used to be into sausage-making, but my ex is a vegan so that hobby fell by the wayside. It's the thing I resent about our marriage most.' Valerie's laugh was high and light. 'We should cook together sometime. I didn't pack my grinder, but I could show you some tricks for making a mean kielbasa. That's not a euphemism, I swear.'

'Uh, hi.'

Tim's head swung around at the sound of my voice. He'd taken off his dress shirt to cook, and the stark white tee he always wore underneath was pleasantly snug against his shoulders and chest.

'I've gotta run,' he told Valerie, picking up the phone from the counter. 'Talk later?'

'You bet.'

The contours of Hen's eyes and mouth told me I wasn't the only one who heard disappointment in Valerie's voice. It was hard not to feel a little intimidated by the woman, with her dark, conventional beauty and the self-possession that radiated off her like heat from a lit stove. I couldn't blame Tim for wanting to bask in her warmth.

That didn't mean I had to like it.

'How was Canada?' he asked.

'Interesting,' I said, resisting the urge to pour some wine of my own. 'And completely age inappropriate. Hen wants to show us something. We made a pit stop at the Klingers.'

With the spoon back in his hand, Tim idly pushed the chops around the pan, his eyebrows lifting as Hen took out her phone.

'So on the car ride back from Canada, I got to thinking,' she said, 'about snooping through your stuff.'

'That doesn't sound like an apology.'

'I'll get to that.' Beaming now, she cradled her phone against her chest. 'Point is, doing that? It wasn't my idea.'

'No?'

'Nope. Mia told me to. She said you probably had some souvenirs from those days. Personal stuff you kept from back when you and Bram were kids.'

I pictured Mia's face the way it must have looked when she

asked my niece to betray me and had to work hard to tamp down my rage.

Hen said, 'So I started wondering . . . why did she do that? Why did it even occur to her to make that suggestion? And then I realized.'

'Oh no,' I said.

'Because Mia found something in her *own* house. Something really juicy.' Puffed and triumphant, Hen flipped the phone around.

Part of me was afraid to see what she'd found. I knew kids Hen's age were exposed to more sex and violence than I could imagine, that preserving a sixteen-year-old's innocence was a lost cause, but Hen had set out to find evidence of a crime committed by her friend's swinger parents. That particular brand of sex and violence could cut to the quick.

When I saw the photo on Henrietta's phone, I forgot all about being worried.

'What the hell am I looking at?' Tim asked, aghast. 'How the hell did you get this?'

'I just told Mia Aunt Shay was in the store. You know how obsessed she is with crime. I told her she should hide on the stairs, and maybe she'd hear something about the investigation.'

'Geez, Hen, this isn't the movies,' I told her. 'What you did is really risky. Kim could be dangerous. Mia too.'

'Maybe – but that's why I brought my badass aunt.' When she raised her eyes to meet mine, I couldn't help but smile.

'They're all here,' I said, studying the picture Hen had managed to capture with her phone.

Four couples were represented, standing on the dock before the two-story rental. The picture was several years old; everyone looked younger, with slimmer middles and shinier hair. But here they were, the women in bikinis and men in bathing trunks. Arms slung over bronzed shoulders, hips cocked and teeth glinting in the sun. They'd taken the photo with a self-timer, it seemed, someone's mobile propped against a beer can or rock, and the low angle gave the group imposing height and an arresting demeanor. Every one of the River Rats had a blithe confidence, their easy sensuality impossible to miss.

Tim turned off the stove and listened as I explained what we'd learned from the owner of the rental. I had pressed Bouchard for details about what he witnessed on his fishing trips near the house. When I got to Bouchard's account about seeing Ford with a woman who wasn't his wife, drawing the conclusion that was now reinforced by the photo on Hen's phone, Tim stiffened. If he hadn't despised Ford before, he sure as hell did now.

'Did you know one in five American couples is non-monogamous? That's the same number of people who own a cat. I looked it up.' Hen's voice was high with excitement. 'There's this thing called a devil's three-way that—'

'Hen! Don't finish that sentence,' I said. 'Forget everything you read – and above all else, never mention this to your father.'

Laughing, she said, 'OK, but look. Look how they're standing.'

'Oh, I am.'

I was captivated by the image on the screen, all those hands on hips, butts, breasts. There were so many tangled, nearly naked limbs it took a second to make sense of them all. Geena was dead center, positioned next to Kim and Braden, and the way Kim clung to Braden's body, her breasts pressed hard against his chest, suggested their attraction was nothing new. On the other side of Geena was Jack Klinger – I recognized him from the photo I'd seen on his school district's website – along with an unfamiliar man and woman who must have been the Fears. They were the only couple who'd chosen to stand together, though the woman's body was angled slightly toward Jack's. In front of the group, Ford and Mandy kneeled side by side with clutched hands. My eyes returned to Geena. Apart from the dive video, it was my first time seeing what she'd looked like. With coffee-brown hair and olive skin, she was just as striking as Ford.

We were staring at the River Rats, every one of them, in their natural habitat.

'How long has this been going on?' Tim asked.

'Sixteen years, if you can believe it. It looks like they stopped after Geena's death. You found this photo awfully fast,' I said to Hen. 'Where was it?'

'Kim's bedroom. In a shoe box on her closet shelf.'

'So Mia could have found it too. And if she did, she could have shown the other kids.'

'Finding out my parents were screwing around with my friends' moms and dads?' Hen said. 'I would die.'

Tim said, 'But is that motive for murder? What does this . . . this *lifestyle* have to do with Leif?'

'I don't know,' I said, 'but let's not forget that Mandy and Kim were with Leif's mother when she drowned.'

'Oh, I asked Mia about that,' Hen said. 'The whole Geena–Mandy thing. I brought it up right before we left. She didn't want to talk about it though.'

'You mean at Kim's? You asked Mia about the secret she'd planned to tell Leif?' I'd been wondering how we were going to get Mia to open up about that. She'd made a point of omitting it from her interview. *Leave it to Hen*, I thought. The kid had a knack for this stuff. Only . . . 'She didn't tell you anything at all?'

'Sorry,' Hen said. 'Wouldn't say a word.'

'Well, thanks for trying – you probably stood a better chance than we did.'

I sighed and rocked back on my heels. 'There are a lot of overlapping threads here. Something must have happened – a fight, a grudge. We need to interview the other River Rats,' I said. 'Figure out how this is all connected. What about the fourth couple, the Fears? I bet Bouchard has their first names on file.'

'What we *need* to do,' said Tim, 'is tell Val.'

'Val,' I scoffed. Since when did the woman have a nickname? 'Yeah, I'll get right on that.'

'I'm serious, Shana.'

'Fine. But no way in hell am I sitting this out. This case is much bigger than we realized. Three local families involved in two suspicious deaths over five years? I'm doing my best to clear the runway for her, but so far *Val* has gotten nowhere. Who else is most likely to talk?' I said, half to myself. 'Kim had a chance today and didn't so much as hint at her wild weekends.'

'Asher's mom and dad?' offered Hen.

Questioning Mandy Vance about Geena's death was already on my to-do list, and I was dying to know what her relationship with Kim was like now. But would Mandy open up to me? Would Braden, whom I'd never even met?

When I was too slow to answer, Hen said, 'There's always Mr Colebrook.'

I felt Tim's gaze swing toward me and stay there.

'Text me that photo, would you?' I told her. 'I'll share it with Valerie right now.'

She nodded, but I could tell she felt deflated, no doubt disappointed that our game of whodunit had come to an end. I knew she could feel the tension between me and Tim seeping out at the edges. Our troubles were a slow leak dampening the carpet just enough to rouse suspicion. I could feel it too.

And when Tim backed into the kitchen, telling us dinner would be ready in five, Hen's cheerful reply sounded as labored as my own.

# FORTY-THREE

'I could come with you.'

Hen was all dressed for school, the last place on earth she wanted to be. My niece knew full well I was forming an alternative plan. A plan neither of us wanted to speak aloud.

'I think I stand the best chance of getting the truth out of him on my own,' I said.

'Probably. But what about Tim?'

Tim and I had tried to keep our voices hushed the previous night, resorting to a litany of stifled words and harsh whispers. Hen was everywhere and nowhere though, ears twitching just out of sight, and there was no hiding my red and puffy eyes this morning. Of course Hen knew. Of course.

'I love Tim very much,' I told her now.

'OK.'

'Relationships are complicated.'

'I know. Do you like him?' Hen asked. 'Leif's dad?'

'God no, not like that.' The denial had come fast. But was it the truth?

She nodded in a way that belied her inexperience and youth. 'Leif had this sadness to him. I only ever hung out with him once, on the island, but it was like he was under this dark cloud, you know? His whole vibe was heavy. I felt sorry for him.'

'His dad's like that too.' What stood out for me was our first encounter by the river. Ford had seemed so vulnerable that day, this big, beautiful mess with a voice like a secret. I'd chalked up the tingling in my limbs to empathy, pity for a widower who'd just learned that someone had murdered his son. But Hen had perceived that same bottomless misery in Leif.

'Go to school,' I told her. 'See what else you can find out from Mia and Tristan. But be careful.'

She lingered in the doorway for a moment before putting her thin hand on the knob and saying, 'You be careful too.'

\* \* \*

The text from Ford had been sitting unanswered on my phone for more than twenty-four hours. When at last I replied, before leaving the house, his response had been instantaneous. *I was about to do a dive, but that can wait. Meet at the museum?*

*On my way,* I wrote. As guilty as I felt for arranging a rendezvous, I had to see him.

Eight o'clock in the morning and there were already dive flags in the water, colorful triangles bobbing on the jewel-green river. The single dry bag on the shore indicated that Ford was alone. I spotted him sitting on a giant cement block behind one of A-Bay's oldest buildings, already stuffed into his wetsuit. Waiting.

On the drive over, I had thought about the River Rats. Four couples as close as couples could be, now fragmented and scattered like shards of smashed glass. Had their children been aware of what they'd done? Was their unusual lifestyle enough to drive someone to murder? Or was Leif's death about something else?

I pulled over and got out of the car.

'I didn't know if you'd want to see me again,' Ford said softly as I approached. 'I'm aware that I came on too strong at the cemetery. I was missing Geena, I think, and you just looked so beautiful—'

'It's OK,' I said, my stomach churning. 'Look, can we talk somewhere more private?' Tim's family lived in this town, his friends. Talking to Ford outside the confines of the investigation, so exposed beside the water, made me uneasy.

'My truck?'

'Fine.' A low-grade electricity hummed between us. I wondered if he felt it too.

Inside the truck, Ford said, 'I don't know what to say, or think, or do with my hands. You always do this to me.'

Heat flooded my mouth, and I forced myself to think of Tim. Tim's smooth bare chest under my hands. Tim's lips on mine. I sympathized with Ford Colebrook – that's all this was. When I looked at him, I saw Geena's grave and Leif's colorless skin. When I tried to quiet my mind though, my body still did things that were unexpected. The man was watching me with the same thinly veiled expression of lust I'd seen in the cemetery, and being so close to him again jangled my nerves.

'I can't tell you how sorry I am about the store.'

'If I didn't like you so much, I'd worry that you were a jinx. Things aren't great in my life right now.'

*Oh God.* 'I need to ask you something, Ford.'

'OK.'

'It's about the River Rats.'

Ford Colebrook searched my eyes. 'So you know about that. How?'

'I read an old article,' I said. 'Connected the dots.'

'Then you're good at your job.' His attention drifted toward the window and the wide river beyond. 'We thought we were pretty crafty, keeping it under wraps for as long as we did. What you must think of me. Of all of us.'

'I'm not here to judge. I just want to understand. Someone intentionally set that fire, and I think it might be the same person who killed Leif.'

'Do you really think so?'

'There's a good chance, yes. So the more you can tell me about all those trips to Gananoque, the better.'

He closed his eyes. 'It was never supposed to last. One and done, that's what we said. We were so young, and so . . . bored, I guess. There isn't much to do around here if you're a couple in your twenties – or thirties for that matter. It was the same thing day after day, working at the hardware store for my dad. Saving for my own house, a wedding, a kid. The options for my days off were severely limited. Get drunk on a boat, get drunk on a dock, rinse, repeat – and that's after years of the same routine in high school. It was Geena's idea to rent the house in Ontario. A weekend away, still close to home but far enough from A-Bay that it felt like a vacation. None of us had much money, but split the rental four ways . . . we made it work. And we had so much fun on that first trip. Someone said we should make it a tradition. It wasn't until the third year that things changed.

'That was Geena too,' he told me, leaning the back of his skull against the headrest and rubbing his thighs, up and down, with his palms. 'It was late, and we'd been drinking all damn day, and she said let's play spin the bottle. She went first, and it landed on Braden. And you know what? I was OK with it. I wasn't sure

I would be, but I was. You have to understand, we all grew up together. Geena and Braden dated for a whole year when they were thirteen, which was a lifetime by middle-school standards. I had it bad for Mandy in fifth grade. She was the first girl in our class with a chest, and man, did she flaunt it. We were always close, always up for a good time. What happened there, it felt like a natural progression. We could handle it. We did. Every year, we went back to that same spot, and eventually it was just . . . normal. We pitched in for groceries and took turns cooking. Took the kayaks out on the river and swam and lay around on the dock in the sun. And at night, Geena brought out the bowl.'

'The bowl?'

Ford said, 'For our wedding rings. Everyone took off their rings, closed their eyes, and made their choice. And it was a choice. You could tell the bands from the diamonds, and pretty soon their width and etchings were familiar too. It was less random that way. People had their favorites.'

The tips of my ears were on fire. Year after year, time and time again, Ford had watched his wife walk off with Braden, or Jack, or – later – the other man from the photograph. Men that Ford would bump into at the drug store, the diner, the school's parent night.

As if reading my mind, he said, 'It's not for everyone. Things changed a lot after Calvin and Maria joined.'

'Calvin and Maria Fear.'

He nodded. 'They weren't part of it from the beginning. Neither of them grew up here; they moved from Fort Worth in '07, when their oldest was in kindergarten, I think. Mandy met Maria through the school, and they got close. I don't know how she broached the subject, I really don't, but when Mandy floated the idea to me and the others, we were all skeptical. Nervous even. They didn't seem like the type.' His expression turned grim. 'I haven't seen either of them in years, not since they left town.'

'They don't live here anymore?'

'They're in Malone, I think. Calvin was in an accident,' Ford said. 'They were on vacation when it happened, in Maine. It was a car crash. Chemical and gas burns from the air bag.'

'How horrible. How long ago was this?'

'Nine years?' he said after a beat. 'More or less. About four years before Geena. Thank God Calvin was alone. He almost didn't survive it. He was in the hospital for weeks, and they tried to repair the damage with surgery, but . . .' He shook his head. 'When he came back, he was a totally different person.'

'How so?' I asked.

'Calvin was convinced God was punishing him,' Ford said, 'for what we did at the house. He and Maria only went twice, but after the accident, he wanted nothing to do with us. They moved shortly after that.'

'Weren't you worried he'd tell someone?' Nine years ago, the Colebrook, Vance, and Klinger kids would have been in third or fourth grade. It would have been hard on them, finding out about their parents' unorthodox sexual tastes. It was like Hen had said on the drive back from Gananoque: *Finding out my parents were screwing around with my friends' moms and dads? I would die.*

'We were freaking out,' Ford confirmed. 'The last thing we needed was for rumors to start flying. Our kids were still little, and we didn't want to confuse them. We'd all agreed they could never find out.'

'But you kept going?' I said. 'Back to the house?'

Ford drew a breath. 'Up until I lost Geena. Calvin did call me then – not out of sympathy but to tell me we brought Geena's death on ourselves. We were depraved adulterers, and now we were paying for our sins just like he had with the accident. But as far as I know,' he went on, 'Calvin never told anyone about the house, and neither did Maria. Why would they? They'd only be outing themselves. And after Geena died, we ended it. We all knew that phase of our lives was over. It was time.'

'Geena's death. Do you really believe it was an accident?'

Ford smiled briefly. 'You've been talking to Jack Klinger. Look,' he said, 'Jack's a good guy, but all that shit about the dive? Blaming Kim? That was totally self-serving. He took a job in Providence and was having second thoughts about leaving Mia behind. But what happened to Geena on that dive was nobody's fault. Just terrible, terrible luck. I know diving. There are always risks. Could Mandy and Kim have helped her if they'd been a little more experienced? Maybe. Should Geena have double-checked her equipment?' He inverted his lips and shook his head. 'I can't spend my life playing what if. I couldn't do that to Leif.'

'So you don't believe her death was foul play. What about Leif though? It sounds like Mia was trying to convince him it was murder.'

Ford went quiet. 'Is that true? Shit, is it?'

He buried his face in his hands. I watched the halting rise and fall of his chest.

'I always worried Mia would get wind of Jack's stupid theory. Wouldn't be hard, I guess. Jack thought he was so smart. He's the only one of us with a college degree, working that fancy job. But he didn't count on Kim raising hell when she found out he was trying to take Mia. I didn't know Mia had been talking to Leif about all of this.'

'Sounds that way. It may be the reason he went out to the island. That's our working theory as of now.' I considered recounting Hen's statement, but said, 'Valerie Ott, the lead on the case, interviewed Asher. He told her that Mia was dangling a secret over Leif's head, something about his mother. We think Mia might have told Leif that Mandy was responsible for your wife's death.'

'Oh for fuck—' Ford pressed his head against the car window, flattening his hair on the chilled glass. 'Just when I thought Jack was done screwing me. For the record,' he said, 'Leif would never buy that. Asher was one of his closest friends.'

'I don't know if Valerie's told you,' I said, 'but Asher's also the one who brought Leif to the island. He didn't want to stay and hear Mia's accusations about his mom.'

Ford thumbed his nose and stared hard at my mouth. 'If Asher thought that Mia was about to blame Mandy for Geena's death, he would have told Leif. So why would Leif go out there just to listen to Mia talk shit about his friend's mom?'

It was a valid question. In fact, it was the very question that had been plaguing me since observing Asher's interview.

'This fiancé of yours,' Ford said, shifting in his seat. 'Does he know you're here with me?'

Before I could answer, he reached across the console and closed his fingers over my own.

Slowly, I eased my hand out from under his. 'I'm sorry if I gave you the wrong impression.'

He thought about that, then said, 'Look, you may not want my advice, but let me tell you something I learned the hard way. Love? It doesn't conform. Not to rules, and not to rings. The heart wants what it wants, even when it's risky or inconvenient. Sometimes, that's when you feel its pull the most.'

I could give in to this, to him. It would be easy here, with his hands and mouth so close to mine. But when I pictured Tim, my brain screamed at me to move. *Get out of here. Shay, go.*

'Take care of yourself,' I told Ford, giving his arm a squeeze as I slid out the door. My footsteps echoed down the quiet street as I hurried back to my car. I felt flushed and queasy, but I'd earned the critical insight we'd been lacking. Wasn't that worth the risk?

It had to be. It was the only excuse I had.

The more Ford Colebrook talked about the Vances, Klingers, and Fears – their children and their checkered history – the more convinced I was that their past arrangement had played a part in Leif's death, and Geena's, and even the fire at the store. *Once is happenstance*, Cunningham had said. *Twice is coincidence. Three times is enemy action.* These families were so tied up with each other that I couldn't even make out the heart of the knot. And so, instead of trying, I grabbed my phone.

'Valerie,' I said. 'You busy?'

The information I'd included in my text the previous night had been minimal, so when I elaborated on the four couples from the photo, Valerie Ott needed a moment to process it all. Maybe she'd disbelieved that the River Rats' history had anything to do with our present-day crimes. Certainly, she hadn't expected them to be swingers. Either way, the woman was too stunned to speak – and that made her too stunned to argue with what I said next.

It was exactly what I'd been counting on.

# FORTY-FOUR

I f given the choice, I would have gone alone. Since I was low
on options, Valerie Ott sat in the passenger seat of my SUV,
eyes skimming the view through the window of a little place
called Malone.

The town was just two hours from Alexandria Bay, but Malone
felt more like Vermont than New York. Situated at the edge of
the Adirondacks, its downtown was all historic storefronts and
flowerbeds stuffed full of burgundy mums. A river cut straight
through its core, complete with a picturesque former wheat mill
and a border of lush green trees midway through their transformation to yellow and red.

There was no missing the First Congregational Church, just a
few blocks to the east. Russet-trimmed and built of stone, the
structure was enormous and boasted a gothic-looking bell tower
straight out of Paris's 4th arrondissement. According to my
research, Calvin Fear worked here as a church administrator.

Our visit was unannounced.

'Follow me,' Valerie said.

Inside, the church felt cool and dry. Its dark wood beams and
window trim were offset by creamy walls. Stained-glass windows
washed the pews in shades of candy blue and green.

'Do you know this place?' I asked, tailing her as she marched
with confidence toward the altar.

'Sunday school every week, bible camp every summer. I know
churches. There's an office around here somewhere. That's where
he'll be.'

We found it to the right of the altar, the door standing open,
a man sitting at the desk inside. He had his back to us, but he
was dressed in street clothes. This wasn't the pastor.

'Mr Fear?' Even making an effort to keep it low, Valerie's
voice rang throughout the vast space behind us. 'Can we have a
moment of your time? I'm Valerie Ott and this is—'

The man turned around. She only faltered for a moment

before recovering and completing her introductions, but there was no missing the flash of disappointment in Calvin Fear's eyes. This was a man accustomed to stares. That didn't mean he had to like them.

Ford Colebrook had mentioned an accident, but I hadn't been expecting this. In some ways, Calvin had the look of a country club regular; his sandy hair held the comb lines he'd pressed into it that morning, and he wore a smart polo shirt in shamrock green. But the skin. The lower half of his face was stretched out of shape, a too-shiny red-and-brown canvas of ravaged flesh. His nose was three sizes too small for his face, his lipless mouth stiff and unmoving, but what it lacked in expression, he made up with the glower he delivered now.

'Shana Merchant,' he repeated, eyes bulging. Even here, two hours from home, news of my connection to Blake Bram had oozed into the community like noxious gas. What we didn't know was whether the news about Leif had reached Calvin too.

Valerie broke it gently, studying his expression all the while. 'Mr Fear,' she said when she was done, 'we're aware that you were once close with the Colebrooks. The Klinger and Vance families too.'

'I'm very sorry,' said Calvin, struggling to swallow. 'I don't know what you're talking about.'

'Look, we get it,' she said. 'You were young. Adventurous. We don't care about what happened in Gananoque way back when. All we're interested in is the dynamics between the couples, and anything you know about problems within the group.'

Calvin studied us, his confusion over our presence long since replaced with dread. Moving quickly, he jumped to his feet and shut the door behind us.

'This is my community,' he said under his breath. 'My home. I'm a prominent member of the congregation, the face of this church.' His forehead blanched at his own choice of words. 'You can't just come in here and accuse me of . . . of . . .'

'As we understand it, you and Maria Fear were River Rats for two years,' I said. 'If we have our facts wrong, by all means—'

'Please,' he hissed, the skin around his mouth taut as a tanned hide. 'That was a mistake, a horrible misstep I've spent the past decade of my life trying to erase.'

'There's no reason why it can't stay a secret,' said Valerie, 'if you're able to help us out.'

It was a lie. Neither of us could promise the activities at the house near Gananoque would stay under wraps, not if they were connected to Leif and Geena's deaths, but Valerie's reassurances seemed to appease him a bit. He slumped into his chair and motioned for us to take a seat on the wooden bench along the wall.

'What do you need to know?' asked Calvin Fear.

I let Valerie do the rest of the talking, listening as she explained our theory that the deaths were related to those wild weekends on the river.

'Whether or not Geena Colebrook's drowning was accidental, we're treating her son's death as a homicide. What we're wondering,' she went on, 'is if there's any chance the kids – Leif, but also Mia Klinger and Asher Vance – could have known about what went on at that house. There's a photograph.' Here she paused and, as expected, terror flooded Calvin's face. 'Are you aware of any knowledge the kids might have had of those activities?'

He brought his hands up to what remained of his lips. 'I don't know them,' he said. 'We didn't talk much about our children. I saw pictures once or twice, but that's all. Leif, is it?' His eyes turned lazy then. Unfocused. 'I'm sorry for that young man. I am. But this horrible business has nothing to do with us.'

'We'll need to know where you and your wife were last Saturday night all the same.'

'Saturday.' His eyes lit up. 'Maria and I took the kids to an apple orchard in Quebec. We stayed the night in Covey Hill. I got an email when we checked out. I can show you.'

'That would be very helpful, thanks,' said Valerie. Proof of a hotel stay across the border was as good an alibi as a man could get.

'Strange,' she added thoughtfully while Calvin scrolled through his cell phone in search of the email. 'That so many of you have faced such hardships.' She wrested her gaze from his face.

Calvin looked up from the screen. 'I help out with the youth group here,' he told us, 'supporting the pastor. There's something he tells them sometimes. Something I wish I'd heard sooner.'

'Oh yeah? What's that?'

'When the devil knocks,' he said, his deformed face a mask of pain, 'send Jesus to the door.'

The indignity this man felt. The torment. What he'd done in Gananoque haunted him and probably always would.

'There's something I heard too,' Valerie said. 'We are either slaves to sin or slaves to righteousness. Isn't that right, Mr Fear?'

Calvin's eyes widened, but he nodded. 'It is.'

'Then you've already been set free.'

'Maybe so. But sins have consequences.' He brought a hand to his cheek. 'That poor boy,' he said with a slow shake of his head. 'Maybe they can finally be free now too. Confess it all at last.' He seemed to be weighing something. Making up his mind.

Valerie and I traded a look.

'Is there something you're not telling us, Mr Fear?'

There was that expression again, Calvin's face distorted with bone-deep dismay. 'Talk to Mandy Vance,' he said. 'She knew Geena best.

'I suspect she knows everything.'

# FORTY-FIVE

'Here's what I don't get,' Valerie said on the drive back to A-Bay. 'Everything we're hearing is scandalous, yes. Potentially, there's a motive in there somewhere for murder. But it's all old news. The River Rats are over. Three of the eight don't live in town anymore. Two others are having an affair – a poorly concealed one at that – which suggests they don't much care about hiding their indiscretions. Mia may have believed Jack Klinger's claim that Geena's death was foul play, even after the case was closed, but that drowning happened years ago too. What could Mia have needed to tell Leif? What information about a years-old death could be so urgent that she had to share it on Saturday night?'

'Something must have happened to set this all in motion,' I agreed, adjusting my hands on the wheel. 'We can't discount the fact that, with the exception of Hen, it was all River Rat kids at the death scene. The only recent development I know of that involves them is Mia's club.'

'Ah. Serial killer central.'

'Yeah. Except that's not exactly what it is,' I said, reminding her what Tim and I had witnessed in the yard behind the cabin.

Valerie said, 'Mia's obsessed with ghosts, especially those with ties to murder. So maybe Geena's ghost fessed up about who killed her.' She said it with a wink.

'At this point, nothing would shock me.'

'Hey. Did it feel to you like the sins Calvin Fear was referring to went beyond couple-swapping?'

As she asked it, she tucked a strand of shiny hair behind her ear. Valerie had an enviable profile, with her pert nose and graceful jawline, and her elegance reminded me I hadn't showered in days.

'All that talk about consequences,' she went on. 'What was that about?'

'With any luck,' I said through a yawn, 'Mandy will tell us.'

But Mandy wasn't at Camp Vance.

'She went out a couple hours ago,' Braden explained when he opened the flimsy trailer door. The sleeves of his flannel were rolled up past his forearms, revealing tattoos of waves like the one I'd seen on Mandy's foot. Across them, in swirly script, was the word *Family*. 'Didn't say where she was going.'

'It's important that we speak with her,' said Valerie.

Braden shrugged. 'She probably won't be back for a while.'

It was then that I noticed the state of the trailer. Broken glass on the floor by the kitchen counter. On the window near the sagging couch, a curtain rod dangled from its bracket.

'You and your wife have an argument, Mr Vance?' I asked.

Braden glanced behind him. 'She's fine, if that's what you're worried about. Mandy can be dramatic. I'll be sure to let her know you stopped by.'

'Mandy knows about Braden and Kim,' I told Valerie on our walk back to the car.

'Looks that way. It's late,' she said. 'Let's grab a bite. Bring her in for an interview in the morning.'

'Pizza at my place?'

Surprised, Valerie met my gaze. 'You're inviting me over?'

I hadn't planned to, but I also wasn't ready to abandon the case for the night.

'I guess I am,' I said.

There were two cars in the driveway when Valerie and I pulled up to the house, and neither belonged to me or Tim. One was Maureen McIntyre's. The second, I recognized from the night I'd found Hen and her friends at the cabin. Mac was here. And so was Asher Vance.

Hen hadn't invited a friend over since moving in with us, and I found that I was happy to hear another teenage voice inside. Valerie and I hung our jackets on the hook in the foyer and made our way to the living room.

'Oh,' Hen said when the investigator walked in behind me. 'Hey. Asher's here, and also Mac. Is that OK? That Asher came over?'

'Of course,' I said, studying the boy in the Nike sweatpants and Purple Pirates hockey sweatshirt as he turned on a tentative smile. Asher looked considerably calmer now than during his interview. I hadn't spoken with him much yet, apart from scaring the shit out of the poor kid at the cabin. Now that I knew he wasn't a suspect in his friend's murder, I liked Asher a lot more.

'Tim went out to get pizza,' Hen said, which I'd already suspected. Pizza Fridays had become our routine. 'Maybe we could hang in my room till he gets back?' She looked from me to Valerie. There was something in her expression, something she was trying to tell us, but I couldn't parse the message in her eyes.

'Door stays open,' I told her firmly.

'Obviously.' Hen flashed a grin and, taking Asher's hand, pulled the boy to his feet.

'Don't worry, I kept an eye on them the whole time,' Mac said, appearing in the kitchen doorway with an open bottle of wine.

'I owe you for that. Mac, meet Valerie. Mac's the sheriff of Jefferson County, and a former BCI investigator herself.'

'Former investigator, huh? Then boy,' Valerie said, rubbing her hands together, 'have we got a story for you.'

# FORTY-SIX

In the two years that I'd known her, I couldn't remember ever going so long without talking to Mac. I felt a pang of guilt about neglecting to return her call, buttressed by my failure to keep her abreast of the investigation. Since I first arrived in A-Bay, Mac had become my dearest friend and the closest person to family within two hundred miles. Technically, with Hen here, that wasn't the case anymore, but my relationship with Sheriff Maureen McIntyre remained as steady as the river that flowed through my back yard.

Two years ago, Mac was still the only person in town besides Carson who knew about my abduction and the psychological trauma I'd hauled with me from New York City like a bulging suitcase, straining the zipper and weighing me down. I was sure she'd recommend termination when she found out. Instead, she'd put her faith in my skills and advised me to talk to Tim. He was a stranger to me then, and worse, an old friend of Carson's. The last thing I'd wanted to do was appear weak or incapable of doing the job. But because of Mac, I'd fessed up. Because of Mac, I'd put my faith in Tim. I owed the woman a lot.

I reached for the wine, retrieved three glasses, and started to pour. Waited until I heard the kids laughing so I could make sure they were up in Hen's room, and told Mac everything about Leif's death, and Hen's presence on the island, and the River Rats, while she sipped her Pinot Noir and took it all in.

'Our working theory,' Valerie said after a long, deep swallow from her own glass, 'is that Mia found the same photo Hen did in the apartment, and it jogged her memory about Geena's bizarre death.'

'Blocking out memories is a common way for kids to cope with trauma,' I added, remembering my conversation with Gasko. 'Mia might have experienced some memory loss when Geena died and she heard her dad saying such awful things about her mom, but that could have come back to her when she saw the picture.'

'She knew the rumor about foul play on the dive because her father, Jack, was responsible for spreading it,' said Valerie. 'It's likely she overheard Kim talking about Jack's accusation of murder all those years ago.'

'Kim would have tried to convince her daughter otherwise of course, but Mia glommed on to the story. She'd been trying to convince Leif of it too,' I pointed out. 'Mia wanted to solve the mystery. Apparently, she likes to play detective.' *Just like I did as a kid*, I thought. *Just like Abe.*

'What we don't yet know,' Valerie told Mac, 'is why Mia didn't find the photo sooner. It took Hen no time at all, and Shana, didn't you say the apartment is small?'

'Tiny,' I confirmed. 'Why was it there all these years after it was taken? Why would Kim risk leaving it around for Mia to find?'

Valerie said, 'I think you're right that we need to expand our suspect list – starting with what's left of the River Rats. Bathroom?' She got to her feet.

I pointed her in the right direction, and turned my attention to Mac.

'Sorry I've been MIA,' I told the sheriff once Valerie was gone. 'Things haven't been great. With Hen. With Tim.'

'First of all, the fact that Hen cramped your style isn't surprising,' Mac said, not missing a beat. 'Nothing like a moody teen to put a damper on the romance.'

'It isn't just that. Ford kissed me.' I took out my phone and showed her the text. It was all surprisingly easy to sum up: somehow, this man was irresistible to me, and I'd given in to his siren song. 'It was nothing, a stupid moment of weakness, but I'm worried, Mac. I don't know what to do.'

McIntyre could have cast judgment on me, and I wouldn't have blamed her if she did. Tim was her friend too, and she'd known him much longer than I had. But Mac also knew what I'd been through. It wasn't an excuse, but maybe it served as an explanation.

She said, 'Did you kiss him back?'

'I didn't stop him. Not fast enough.'

'Look, Tim's not an idiot,' she told me. 'You're an attractive woman. But more than that, you're a local celebrity.'

'Oh, please.'

'It's true – and it's probably time you started acknowledging that. Allow me to psychoanalyze for a moment, if you will.'

'Be my guest,' I said with a half-smile.

'Some people are drawn to trauma. I think Carson was like that,' said Mac. 'He fed off his power to heal people – but to do that, he needed them to stay wounded. Convince them they couldn't survive without his help. Now, Ford Colebrook . . . this is a man whose life has been turned upside down, his wife and his son both taken from him in the worst possible way. He looks at you, and he sees someone who's hurting. That's something he can relate to. Is it such a stretch to imagine he's attracted to you because you've been through the wringer too?'

When I didn't answer right away, Mac leaned over and put her hand on mine. 'Tim feels betrayed, and rightfully so. But Tim is a rational person. There's nothing between you and Ford that could possibly get in the way of your marriage. If he doesn't understand that yet, it's only a matter of time.'

'All this stuff about the River Rats,' I said, 'it makes me question the whole idea of marriage. I love Tim more than anything . . . but didn't Ford and Geena and all the others once feel that way too? What if Tim isn't enough? What if this is a sign?'

We were quiet for a while, Mac sipping her wine and me turning my untouched glass on the table. Upstairs, Hen and Asher laughed. I could hear a car in the distance. Tim, back with the pizza.

'Here's a theory,' Mac said, fluffing her hair.

I'd always thought short hair suited her, the layered pixie style exaggerating her pale blue eyes and bright teeth, but suddenly it reminded me of Mandy. I shook the image away.

'This trauma attraction, it goes both ways,' she said. 'Ford Colebrook is a broken man, right? Maybe you want to fix him.'

'What? No.'

'Ever hear of a savior complex?'

'Come on. Really?'

'A lot of detectives have it,' Mac said.

'Well I don't.'

Her blonde head tilted. 'No? Your cousin hurt people – a lot of people, badly. He grew up to become a ruthless killer, and you grew up to be a cop. I'm no Gil Gasko,' she said, 'but is it possible you're subconsciously compensating for Bram's godless behavior? Someone else may have committed the crime this time around, but part of you still feels responsible. And now that Bram's gone, and Ford Colebrook needs rebuilding, you're all over him like flies on—'

'OK.' I raised my hand and realized I felt a little ill. When was the last time I'd eaten? I pushed the glass of wine aside. 'What concerns me are the people who are *dropping* like flies.'

A door closed down the hall, and we heard Valerie's footsteps, followed by an exclamation of surprise. She and Tim had found each other in the living room and were saying their hellos.

Mac let her head flop back, the swoopy seventies wings above her ears exposing her finely lined forehead.

'Swingers, huh?' She let out a low whistle. 'Don't see that every day. You hear rumors, of course. Someone once told me pineapple paraphernalia is a sure-fire sign that you're one of them. Putting two Adirondack chairs on your front lawn too.'

'Seriously? My parents had chairs like that.'

'Probably just an urban legend,' she assured me. 'But man, a lifestyle like that, you've got to think things can get messy.'

'I'm going to assume you're talking about relationships,' I said with a look of disgust. 'And I agree. Open marriage, swapping partners . . . you'd have to be the type who doesn't get jealous.'

'And you'd have to be all-in – especially if you're committing to an annual retreat. One person opts out, or gets protective of their spouse, and it could put a damper on the whole event. Or worse.'

I could feel her yearning for the challenge of the case, its sizzling energy like a struck match. 'For argument's sake,' she went on, 'let's say that's what we're dealing with. We've got one victim – Leif – and a question mark on Geena. Both of them are linked to Ford. Could he be covering something up? Could that be why he's trying to seduce you?'

'I thought you said it was because I'm attractive?' I gave her a playful shove.

Another laugh, this time from the living room. We looked to where Tim and Valerie stood close together by the front door.

'What is it Tim's always telling you?' Mac whispered as they began to walk our way. 'Us against them?'

I nodded. Tim said that on Tern Island, when my PTSD had me losing my shit and the only way to survive the night was to share my burden with him.

*Us against them.*

'Evening, ladies.'

Shadowed by Valerie, Tim stood in the doorway with a stack of pizza boxes in his arms. Immediately, the air in the room was filled with the scent of hot tomato sauce, peppers, melted cheese. 'What did I miss?' he asked.

Mac tossed a look of encouragement my way.

'Let's bring a pizza up to the kids,' I told Tim. 'We need to get you up to speed.'

# FORTY-SEVEN

It was after eleven when Hen and Asher wandered back downstairs with an empty pizza box in hand.

'Thanks for having me, Ms Merchant,' Asher said. 'Your house is really cool.'

'Call me Shana.' If everyone else in town was doing it, I supposed it couldn't hurt for Asher to join in. 'And say hi to your parents for us, OK?'

I waited for a reaction. A tell. 'Right,' he said simply, lowering his gaze to the floor before turning to go.

All four of us watched Hen and Asher as they headed for the door.

'Think he'll kiss her?' Mac asked once they were outside.

'Maybe she'll kiss him,' said Valerie.

I groaned and said, 'My vote's for no kissing at all.'

When Hen reappeared a few minutes later, looking pink and embarrassed, Mac hopped to her feet. 'I should head out too,' she told us, helping Tim collect plates and crumpled paper napkins from the table.

'I'm right behind you,' said Valerie. 'Any chance you could drop me at my hotel?'

Mac said she'd be glad to, and I walked them both out to her car.

As we crossed the wide porch, Valerie said, 'With any luck, we can talk to Mandy tomorrow and finally put this case to bed. Hey, I meant to tell you. Your niece seems like a good egg.'

'Does that mean she's off the hook?' I asked it playfully, but Valerie called my bluff.

'I truly hope it does.'

When we got to the car, we came to a stop.

'I have to hand it to you, taking in your brother's girl like this. Kids are hard,' said Valerie, 'especially at this age.'

'I tried to tell her,' Mac said. 'Last week, one of my nieces flipped her truck on the highway.'

I reached for her, panicked. 'What? Is he OK? Mac, why didn't you tell me?'

'You had enough going on – and yeah, he's fine. Point is, it was broad daylight, and the road was dry as dog poop in the desert. The kid screwed up. They do that. Parents too. But according to my sister, most parents wouldn't trade anger and heartache for all the gold in Ford Knox.'

'I can vouch for that,' said Valerie. 'My girl, Bobby? Drives me bonkers on the regular. She could screw up every way possible, though, and I'd still do it all over again.'

After seeing Mac and Valerie off and saying goodnight to Henrietta inside, I rejoined Tim in the kitchen. He was tidying, loading glasses into the machine, and for a second, as I idled there, I felt like a ghost myself. Invisible. Intangible. Incapable of enacting change. It was like all I could do was stand by and watch as my fiancé moved farther away from me.

Taking my future with him.

I awoke to the sound of someone beating on the ceiling. It was raining again, a precursor of the deep fall to come, but it still took a minute for me to get my bearings. The noise was relentless, the house straining against the wind. I felt something else in the cold, loud darkness too.

I was alone.

After running through my usual bedtime routine, which involved a toothbrush, a washcloth, and little else, I'd hauled myself into bed and waited for Tim to join me. He hadn't. Finally, after a long time, I'd managed to fall asleep, but now the digital clock at the bedside read one a.m. and Tim's side of the bed was empty.

The hardwood was chilly and coarse under my bare feet. Sanding down the old floors was on our list too, but for now the boards still pulled apart in places, nicked and scratched, the varnish slowly chipping away.

I crossed the room and shivered as the windows rattled and a slithering current of cold air found me where I stood. Tim must have fallen asleep on the love seat in the study.

*That's wrong*, I thought. That sounded too much like chance, as if he'd peacefully drifted off when I knew he had made a decision. That his absence was the product of intent.

I used the bathroom, hoping the sound would be swallowed up by the rain, and stepped back into the hall.

Driven by impulse, I pushed open Henrietta's bedroom door.

It felt like dreaming or déjà vu, with one exception: the note that lay on Hen's vacant bed.

> *I snuck out. I'm OK. You can punish me later.*
> *PS I think I know who killed Leif.*

The note was impossibly light in my hands. *Hen. No.*

I did the only thing I could think of then.

I called Valerie Ott.

# FORTY-EIGHT

Tim was up and dressed in minutes, no questions asked, when I told him Hen was gone again and that, this time, she could be in serious trouble. Ten minutes later, Valerie arrived at our door.

'Where the heck would she go?' she asked as she yanked her damp, tangled ponytail tighter.

'I don't know. God, I should have known this would happen. She was all excited when we talked to that property owner, and then she went and sniffed out the photo at the Klingers. She's playing detective with no earthly idea how dangerous it is.'

'Hen wouldn't do anything stupid though.' One of Tim's thick eyebrows had been mashed down by sleep in a way that flooded my chest with heat. 'Wherever she is, she'll be smart out there – right?'

I didn't want to think too hard about the answer.

'We'll check everywhere she knows,' Valerie said. 'She's new here, like me. Her knowledge of town is limited.'

'Even with my car she can't have gotten far,' Tim agreed.

Valerie followed close behind my SUV, bumping through swampy ruts in the road. But we didn't find Hen at the cabin, and the trailer at Camp Vance was dark too, no other vehicles to be found.

'Doesn't look like Asher's here. Where are Mandy and Braden?' asked Tim.

'I don't know,' I said, thinking of the broken glass Valerie and I had seen inside their trailer. 'I don't like this.'

Our third stop was Kim Klinger's. As much as I disliked Mia, I hoped we'd find Hen with her now.

'I haven't seen her since yesterday,' Kim said when she finally answered the door. 'And Mia's asleep upstairs.'

The sound of the TV through the floor gave me pause, and when I commented on Kim's late night, her eyebrows pulled together.

'Braden's here,' she said without apology. 'Mia can sleep through damn near anything.'

Braden. Mia. Kim. If Hen thought she'd identified Leif's killer and had gone off to find them, it seemed these three were in the clear.

'And Mandy?' Valerie asked.

Kim stiffened then. 'Try Ford's.'

'Ford?' The suggestion surprised me, but I only needed a moment to grasp that it added up. Hadn't Ford told us his relationship with Mandy went back to grade school? Maybe Kim and Braden weren't the only ones who'd been lured back to old habits by grief. It was impossible to say how much of the River Rats' current decisions were affected by their summer weekends at that rental house considering the group's history preceded those days by a decade or more, but there was comfort in a shared past. It made sense to me that, after what happened to Leif, they'd sought emotional safety in the familiar once again.

It hadn't occurred to me to wonder where Ford spent his time when he wasn't in the river. I didn't even know where Ford Colebrook lived – but Tim did. He'd been the one to deliver the death notification almost a week ago, and he was the one who drove us there now.

Ford's house, I discovered when we arrived, was just a few blocks from the dive site, in a quiet neighborhood on the edge of downtown. It looked almost as old as our place, except Ford's renovation was complete, every crack patched and flake of peeling paint buffed away. The porch was dwarfed by two massive rhododendrons that must have been glorious when in bloom. While the exterior of the main floor was constructed with thick gray stones, the upstairs had siding the same bright green as Calvin Fear's polo shirt.

'Let's just see if Hen's here and go,' I told Tim, who was looking at the house like he'd rather be anywhere else. Finding Hen was all that mattered now.

'Shana?' Ford said when he opened the door.

His eyes lingered on Tim next to me, and I felt a zip of fear race up my back. I had a sightline to the living room, a large octagonal space paneled with shiny dark wood. The TV was on here too, two open bottles of Labatt Blue on the table. None of the River Rats seemed to be getting much sleep these days. I could understand why. I met Ford's gaze, and after a moment, he made a quick gesture with his right hand.

From the entrance to what must have been the kitchen, Mandy Vance stepped out into the hall.

'We're not here in an official capacity,' I said. 'This isn't about Leif.' Speaking the name in the presence of the man who'd survived him, knowing what I knew about the group of friends now and how much Ford had lost, drove home the enormity of the crime all over again. A father had lost his son, a boy his mother, and we were running out of suspects. 'We're looking for Henrietta. She snuck out, and we think she might be with Asher. Any chance they're here?'

'No,' said Mandy, stepping toward me. Already concerned. It was the first time I'd seen her without lipstick, though smudges of it remained around her rosy mouth. 'We haven't seen either of them.'

'We're worried,' Valerie told her, stepping forward. 'Hen thinks she knows something about what happened to Leif. She knows about the River Rats.'

Tim said, 'Which means Asher might too.'

'Oh my God.' Mandy's breath hitched as she moved toward Ford and hooked an arm through his.

'Whoever killed Leif is still out there,' I said. 'That puts both Asher and Hen at risk.'

Mandy and Ford locked eyes, and then it was just the two of them, the rest of the world falling away like a pillar of ash. 'If Ash already knows . . .' she said to Ford.

'He might not.'

'But what if he does? We have to do something.'

Ford said, 'It'll change things.'

'But Asher's out there.' Mandy turned to me. 'Will it help? If we tell you everything?'

'It might,' I said.

The woman clasped her hands behind her neck, while Ford slumped his shoulders, his gaze on the floor.

'You might as well all come in out of the rain,' he said.

# FORTY-NINE

'God, I miss her,' Mandy said. 'She was the life of the party, Geena, up for anything. Raring to go. She called us the River Rats because we were all locals, born and raised.'

'We're told the rental in Gananoque was her idea too,' I said, not looking at Ford.

Mandy nodded. 'Life of the party, like I said. But it was also her idea to have ground rules. She knew it was risky. We were friends. The thing was, we'd *been* friends for a long time, most of us since high school. If anyone could make it work, it was us. We knew each other so well, and more importantly, we trusted each other. So, she made a list. No hookups off the property.' Mandy raised one nail-bitten finger, then a second. 'No secrets. No lies. It worked – for a few years anyway. We'd go out there and have a great time. Head home and live our normal lives till the next year.'

Mandy paused to nibble at her lower lip. Pursed that way, I could see fine lines above her mouth that matched the ones framing her eyes.

'We were careful, obviously,' she went on, 'all of us. But I guess not careful enough.'

The five of us were seated in Ford's living room, me, Tim, and Valerie facing the couple on Ford's tuxedo couch. It hadn't taken much coercion to get Mandy to open up. Not once we told her we feared for Asher's safety.

'I really didn't think all that could have anything to do with Leif's death,' Mandy told us. She turned to Ford. 'Did you?'

Shaking his ruffled head, he said, 'It was so long ago. And when Geena died, it felt like that part of our lives died too.'

When Mandy's breath hitched and her eyes went glassy, Ford put a consoling hand on her knee.

'It wasn't some big orgy, you know,' he said as she cried

silently beside him. 'We each picked one person, and they were it for the whole weekend.'

I'd heard this from him before, and it struck me that Ford might be covering for me. Pretending our talk in the truck hadn't happened, now that Tim was in the room. Deflecting for the sake of my engagement.

'I almost always ended up with Mandy,' he went on. When he looked at her, the corner of Mandy's mouth convulsed.

'I've known this man since preschool. We're a good fit. The others weren't always so consistent – but we were careful,' Mandy repeated. 'That was the important part. So a few years in, when we met up like always and went home to our lives and Geena found out she was pregnant, no one thought twice about it. She and Ford had been talking about having kids. We all had, really, but they were the most serious about trying.'

*Careful. Pregnant.* The realization trickled over me, thin and cold. I looked at Ford and said, 'You're not Leif's biological father.' *Sins have consequences.* Wasn't that what Calvin told us in the church? 'It's one of the others.'

Closing his eyes, Ford gave a single nod.

'Did Leif know?' Valerie asked.

Flexing his fingers, Ford said, 'No. No, we made sure of it.'

'But there was a close call once,' said Mandy. 'When Leif was twelve. Right before we took that dive.'

Together Valerie, Tim, and I listened as Ford and Mandy spoke in listless tones, reaching for each other often. The day before Geena Colebrook dove the *A.E. Vickery*, Leif had come home from school with a bundle of questions. His class had been doing a unit on genetics, the students tasked with bringing in photos of their parents. They'd been talking about how genes are passed down through families.

'Chromosomes. Observable traits. My kid did the same thing,' Valerie said.

'Yeah well, I guess Leif's teacher pointed out he didn't look much like me or Geena,' said Ford. 'She suggested he get some more pictures. Grandparents. Uncles and aunts. She was going to help him trace his blond hair and green eyes, whatever it took.

Geena freaked. After Leif went to bed that night, she told me.'
He paused to swallow. 'That Leif wasn't mine.'

'You didn't know until Leif was twelve?' Tim said, looking
stunned.

Ford only shook his head.

'Could she have been wrong?' I asked.

'No. She had taken one of those home paternity tests. She
showed me the results.'

I tried to visualize the scene inside the very house we sat
in now. Geena, confessing a life-changing secret she'd been
hiding from her husband for their son's entire life. Ford,
learning one of his friends had fathered the child he'd raised
as his own.

Ford said, 'I was angry. I felt so . . . so *betrayed*. I knew it
could have happened to any of us – we all took the same risks
– but I still felt completely blindsided, and I blamed Geena.
God help me, I blamed her for the whole thing, and we fought
about it. It was the most horrible night of my life.'

A fight, the night before the dive. I braced myself for what I
might hear next. I hadn't wanted to listen when Tim suggested
Ford could have tampered with Geena's regulator, or admit he
could be involved in his son's death, but now my mind was
skipping ahead. If Ford was about to tell us he killed his wife,
it likely meant he'd killed Leif too.

'By the morning,' Ford said, 'we'd come to a decision. We
would move on. Pretend it never happened. Leif didn't have to
know. We could come up with some explanation for the science
project, and Leif would accept it – because why wouldn't
he trust us to tell him the truth about something like that? By
the weekend, he'd have forgotten all about it. We sent Leif
off to school like usual that day, and I begged Geena to stay
home, but she wouldn't. She was upset and scared, and she
wanted to meet Mandy and Kim like they planned.'

'She was a basket case when she showed up,' said Mandy. 'It
was obvious she'd been crying. She told us what happened.'

Here, Ford stared at Mandy in a way that made me wonder if
he knew how long she'd been aware of the truth. Ford may have
confided in Mandy after Leif's death, but his wife had already
opened up to her friends years ago, the day of the dive.

'We told Geena that Ford would settle down and realize Leif was his kid in all the ways that mattered,' said Mandy, pushing that variegated hair from her eyes. 'We said Ford was probably feeling hurt, but it's not like he didn't know Geena had slept with other guys – I mean, the weekend she got pregnant, Ford had been with *me*.' They traded another complicated look. 'Eventually, Geena calmed down and we did the dive. And that's the part I'll regret for as long as I live.'

'I don't know much about scuba diving,' said Valerie, 'but it seems like a bad idea to dive a wreck when your life just blew up.'

'It is. It's a terrible idea,' Ford replied. 'But Geena had this thing about the river. She believed it was healing.'

Ford had implied the same thing the day I met him, when he'd spoken about how diving soothed him. About how much it reminded him of his wife.

'She insisted,' Mandy explained. 'And it seemed to be helping, at first. And then it all went wrong. But it *was* an accident.' She wiped a tear from her cheek and said, 'I was right there. She was fine, and then she had no air, and then she panicked. That wreck is in the channel. It's deep, and dark, and she disappeared on us so fast. There was nothing we could do. Jack tried to blame Kim, but we all knew that was about wanting custody of Mia. Kim and I both did everything in our power to save Geena. It was an accident. That's all it was.'

'You were angry with your wife,' Tim said, giving Ford a hard look. 'You had access to the dive equipment.'

'An *accident*,' Mandy repeated, holding Tim's accusatory stare. 'I know Ford.' As she said it, she took his hand and clasped so hard the effort whitened her knuckles. 'He would never have hurt her. He loved Geena more than anything.'

'I would never have hurt my wife,' Ford echoed, covering Mandy's hand with his own. 'It was an accident.'

Afterward, when the first responders failed to revive Geena and Don Bogle documented the drowning and Ford arrived to discover he was too late, Mandy and Kim had been slack-jawed and shaky, numb with shock.

'We didn't need to discuss it,' Mandy said. 'Both me and Kim knew we could never tell anyone about Leif. It could have happened to any of us, like Ford said. We picked one partner and stuck with them all weekend.'

Braden Vance. Jack Klinger. Calvin Fear. Any one of them could be Leif's father. Swapping couples for one weekend a year had been harmless, until it wasn't. And when the system started to fail, the destruction was unimaginable.

I said, 'Who was Geena with the summer Leif was conceived?'

Ford and Mandy exchanged a loaded glance.

# FIFTY

'**W**e'll split up,' Valerie said as the three of us ran to the cars. 'Drive past all the inns and hotels in town. I'll call Sol in to help.'

'If he's still here, his car is too.' And that would be easy to spot, because this time of year, when the tourists had long since gone home and only locals remained, it would be the only vehicle in town with plates from Rhode Island.

*Jack Klinger.* The moment the name tripped off Ford's tongue, it all made sense. Jack was Leif Colebrook's father. He was the only member of the core group to move out of town. He'd taken a prestigious, high-profile job in Providence and never returned, only seeing his daughter when she rode the bus south. Jack had put as much distance between himself and A-Bay as he could, all in an effort to conceal his involvement with the River Rats.

Rarely had I seen Tim look so shocked as when he learned Kim's husband had fathered her friend's child.

'*Ex*-husband,' Mandy had clarified. 'It was one of the reasons Kim stopped fighting the divorce. Once she knew the truth, she couldn't get past it. And she was terrified someone in town would pick out the resemblance between them. You'd never know to look at them that Leif and Mia were related, but Jack's a different story.'

'So Jack knows?'

Valerie's tone was charged with urgency, and I had felt it too. Providence was six hours from Alexandria Bay. I'd spoken with Jack on the phone just yesterday, assumed he'd been in his office, but couldn't he have transferred his calls to his cell phone? Until we contacted his wireless network provider and tracked that call, we couldn't be sure of his location at the time of Leif's death.

'We never told him,' Mandy assured us.

But the paternity test. I had turned to Ford then. 'Didn't you say Geena had proof?'

'It was a home test. The kind you send off in the mail. Geena had a printout.'

'Then Jack must have known,' said Tim. 'Geena needed a DNA sample.'

'It's just a mouth swab though, right?' I said. 'If you were still doing your weekends in Gananoque, and Geena was still sleeping with Jack . . .'

'You mean she could have gotten the sample without him even knowing?' Mandy brought a hand to her lips.

'Where's the paternity test report now?' I'd asked.

Ford had narrowed his eyes until I could hardly see the blue at all. 'I never saw it again after she died.'

'I can't believe it,' Tim said as we drove. 'How could a man kill his own son?'

That was what remained to be discovered. Leif's death was complicated by the nature of his injuries. The boy had died an unnatural death, that much was impossible to deny. What we didn't know was what led up to that. I'd never been sold on the idea of premeditation, not out there on the island with Mia and her friends so close by. Devil's Oven lacked the privacy most killers preferred, along with a getaway route that would allow them to escape unseen. It was more likely the person who killed Leif didn't intend for him to die, had attacked because they felt cornered. *Involuntary manslaughter.* An accidental death caused by some unlawful act committed outside that cavern.

I couldn't see the cave when Tim pulled into the parking lot of the pizza place, not even when we hurried on to the dock. But I could see Devil's Oven, dead ahead, along with the Thousand Islands International Bridge that Hen and I had driven. The bridge to Canada. The car with the blue plates that read *Ocean State* had been abandoned in the very same lot Asher sat in last Saturday night, waiting for the call from Leif that wouldn't come.

The car meant Jack was here, in A-Bay.

He couldn't have gotten far.

In my pocket, my phone emitted a buzz. It was Valerie, who'd been combing the other side of town. 'We found the car by the public dock,' I told her in a rush of breath.

'That makes sense, because I just got a call from Kim. Mandy phoned and told her everything. She's freaking out about Asher being MIA. Sounds like Kim got all worked up too and called Mia, only Mia's not answering.'

'Wait, what? But Mia was at the apartment an hour ago,' I said, nonplussed. 'Kim told me she was fast asleep upstairs.'

'Well, Kim told *me* she just walked Braden to his car and when she got back, Mia was gone. Is sneaking out an epidemic in this place or what? Oh, and don't ask me how, but Kim knows Jack's in town. Says she *fears for Mia's safety.*'

I said, 'What would Jack do if Mia found out he's the one who killed Leif?'

'His career would be over,' said Tim, who'd been listening in. 'His relationship with his daughter, too. The man's entire future would be toast.'

'Which means he'd run,' added Valerie. 'Get the hell out of town.' She paused. 'But how? You just found his car.'

'He could take a boat.' Tim nodded at the river. 'He's done it before, right? To get to Devil's Oven? Jack could steal a boat and go to Canada.'

'And if he was making a run for the border,' I said, 'he might take Mia with him.'

At night, in the fall when there were fewer patrols on the water, it would be easy enough to do. Boaters making landfall in Canada were expected to check in with border patrol, call a number to report their plans and share their passport numbers. It was an honor system, easy to follow. Even easier to evade.

'I'll call the coast guard,' said Tim once Valerie had assured us she was on her way.

Standing on the dock, I surveyed the river. Downtown Alexandria Bay was deserted. The pizza joint had long since closed for the night. The ice cream stand too. So when I heard voices, agitated and growing louder, I spun around with a start. What I saw made my stomach bottom out. Hen and Asher were running toward us at a full sprint. And Jack Klinger was between them.

The man looked nothing like the photo I'd seen on the school district website. This version of Jack was a boiled ham, his cheeks and forehead glazed with sweat. We hurried toward them.

'Stop right there,' Tim said when they began to slow their pace.

All three were breathless, and Jack's wild eyes skipped right over us to keep scanning the streets, the water. While Hen and Asher were clearly ill at ease, Mia's father looked frantic, his mouth yanked into a fierce line.

'Hen. Asher. Come stand by me.' Tim modulated his tone in the way we'd both been taught at the academy. It was a de-escalation tactic, one of many in our arsenal: start low, avoid curse words, issue simple commands.

'Mr Klinger, are you armed?' Yes or no questions. Another strategy designed to keep a suspect calm.

'Am I *armed*? No,' he said. 'No, of course not.'

Hen and Asher looked confused, but as Jack spoke, they did as they were told. When both kids were next to us, we all faced Kim's ex-husband. The man who'd tried to take Mia from her mother and accused Kim of having a hand in Geena's death. He was here, in Alexandria Bay, six hours north of Providence. He'd killed Leif and now, worried he'd been found out, he'd snatched his daughter from her home and was preparing to flee.

But if all that was true, where was Mia?

'Tim.' It was mayhem in my head, thoughts and memories all competing for attention. The paternity test, Kim's call to Valerie, her mention of Jack moments before we found him. The fact that Hen and Asher had been with him, all three of them sweaty and short of breath. I said, 'I think we have this wrong.'

'What?' Tim was still paying heed to Jack's every labored gasp and muscle twitch.

'Mr Klinger, where's Mia?' I asked him, but I was already certain I knew.

'I called her,' he said through gulps of air. 'Said I'd pick her up. Kim grabbed the phone away.'

'They're gone,' said Hen, her eyes wide as plates. 'Mia and her mom. We just came from the apartment.'

'The place looked like it had been robbed,' added Asher. 'Like they grabbed whatever they could carry and took off.'

'It was her,' I said, turning my dazed eyes to Tim. 'Kim killed Leif.'

'Mia found out Jack was Leif's dad,' Hen said. 'The secret

– *that's* what she was going to tell Leif. Kim knew and followed Mia to the island.'

'Kim's been blackmailing me,' said Jack. 'It's been going on for years. She has . . . sensitive information about me, and she threatened to take it public.'

'We know about the River Rats,' I told him.

Jack blanched. 'Then you know why I can't let that get out.'

'We do. We know a lot of things now.' Like that Kim had been about to lose her only reliable source of income, because her daughter had been bound and determined to tell Leif the truth. Once the news about the swingers and Jack's illegitimate child was out, that would be the end of Jack's payments. I couldn't fathom how Hen and Asher had known Jack was in town and where to find him, but there would be time enough to unravel that later. Our prime concern was finding Mia and Kim.

'Think,' I told Jack. 'Where would they have gone?'

'Kim wouldn't drive,' he said. 'She knows it's too easy to track her car.'

'A boat then.'

Jack nodded. 'I own the building they live in. Kim has hardly any expenses. I think she's been hoarding the money. I'm afraid she has the means to make them both disappear.'

I looked back at the water. Devil's Oven. The bridge.

And beyond that, Gananoque. A house sitting empty for the season.

A house Kim Klinger knew well.

# FIFTY-ONE

On the river, all was dark. Even bumping through the chop alongside the coast guard, both their vessel and ours equipped with powerful search lights, the water was a starless sky. We'd left Hen and Asher on the mainland with Solomon, though they'd been reluctant to stay behind.

For his part, Jack couldn't be coerced. 'She's got Mia,' he said, wiping sweat and tears from his eyes. 'She already took one kid from me. I won't let her take another.'

'We sure about this?' Valerie whispered as we neared the shore.

'Kim knows we're close to piecing things together,' I said, 'thanks to that call she got from Mandy. Where else could she go?'

According to Jack, Kim's parents and older sister had long since moved out of town. She had no family in the area. What she did have was money, adrenaline, and a desperate need to get out of A-Bay. Meanwhile, the River Rats were at the forefront of her mind, powering her every decision. Driving her every move.

The rental house was a few miles west of Gananoque, just fifteen minutes from the invisible border that divvied the St Lawrence between Ontario and New York state. There were no lights on when we pulled up to the dock, but we did find a fishing boat. The fifteen-foot aluminum Starcraft had water on the hull, so we dimmed our own lights quick as we could, tying up to cleats cold to the touch in the night.

Led by Valerie, Tim and I crossed a lawn silvered with September moonlight. Valerie gestured to the sliding glass doors on the house's main floor. If Frank Bouchard planned to winterize the property, he hadn't done it yet. A welcome mat printed with a red anchor still lay outside the back entrance, and when Tim slid open the unlocked door, the air that flowed out felt warm.

Tim turned on the flashlight he'd snagged from the boat, and I did the same.

'Kim?' I kept my voice level, like Tim had with Jack at the town dock. If Kim Klinger didn't already know we were here, we didn't want to startle her. She'd fled the country, a temerarious act, but she'd taken Mia with her, which suggested she cared for the girl. That said, this was the same woman who, by all indications, was responsible for Leif's death. Our insight into her state of mind was piecemeal at best.

Upstairs, directly above us, a crash. I heard a yelp – Mia – and the lawn behind us was flooded with light from the second-floor windows.

'Mia!'

Jack's voice was shrill and desperate as he sprinted across the yard.

'Mr Klinger, get back!'

'I saw her! In the window! *Mia!*'

Tim was on him in seconds, bundling the man toward the side of the house before he could put up a fight.

'Come on down, Kim,' Valerie called. 'We just want to talk.'

Kim took the stairs at a run, and the beam of clean white light I shone in her direction glinted off the knife in her hand. It was a chef's knife, likely dulled by decades of renters, but she held it aloft in a tight grip. The woman beneath the blade looked completely unhinged. Valerie and I drew our sidearms and locked her in our sights.

Kim didn't want this: a showdown with the State Police while her teenage daughter was right upstairs, alone and terrified. Kim's trepidation was visible in the surprised tilt of her brows, a question mark punctuating a face contorted by fear. To Kim, everything about the situation was unjust. It was she who was the victim, at the mercy of her ex and their friends. The command she thought she held over them all, the sway, long gone. Did she blame Mia for this colossal betrayal, or Jack? Did she know just how much Ford and Mandy had already revealed, or that Braden Vance would likely open up to us too, when we tracked him down tonight?

'Drop the weapon, Kim,' said Valerie. 'We don't want anyone getting hurt.'

'What's going to happen?' she asked, the knife trembling in her hand. She was shaking so hard I couldn't get a read on whether or not she planned to pounce.

'I won't lie to you. You're in trouble,' I said, 'but hurting us is going to make things a lot worse.'

Kim Klinger blinked as tears rivered her cheeks. This woman had roughed up a minor, pushed him on to the rocks and left him to die. Her regret seemed genuine, but I'd been fooled before. Real monsters can retract their claws.

Valerie took a step forward, elbow locked, sidearm steady. 'Drop the weapon.'

'Think of Mia,' I said.

At the mention of her daughter, Kim's swagger dissolved. 'I can't let him take her from me,' she said as the knife clattered to the floor. 'She's all I've got.'

*Leif was all Ford had too*, I thought. And now, thanks to Kim, he was gone.

# FIFTY-TWO

*It's my fault,* Hen had told me when she finally confessed what little she knew about Leif's death. She'd convinced herself she was the bait Mia had used to lure Leif to the island, when in fact my niece had assumed a different role, one she hadn't even known she was playing.

And Hen's arrival had started it all.

When Henrietta materialized in A-Bay, her connection to Bram was both a curse and a lodestone. To many, her affiliation with the killer made her divisive and strange, but those were traits that appealed to Mia Klinger. She was known for being a little strange herself.

Once she realized Mia was interested in her family history, Hen had used it to her advantage. And when she ran out of dirt on Blake Bram, she went looking for information about Abe. That's what led her to sift through my study. Why she found Bram's letter and shared it out on Devil's Oven so the group could speculate about how his past connected to his present-day crimes.

But something happened after Hen and Mia started meeting to talk about murder. Mia had long been interested in ghost stories and local lore, and being with Hen had reminded her about Geena Colebrook. Mia was only eleven when Geena died, most of her memories long since dissolved, but she knew Kim had something to do with the dive. She'd dug into her mother's cache of unusual deaths – the same scrapbook Kim had spoken of when we first met – in search of ghosts. What Mia found instead had altered the course of the remaining River Rats' lives.

'It wasn't the photo,' I said the next morning, sipping coffee in my office with Tim, Valerie, and Sol. 'It was that paternity test.' The second Ford told us he hadn't seen the test results since the day Geena died, I had wondered what became of the report. And so we'd put the question to Kim last night, once we had her secured on the mainland. Whatever happened to that incriminating test?

'Geena gave it to me,' Kim had told us. 'At the dive site. Right before she died. She knew Jack was trying to get custody of Mia. She told me to keep it, just in case.' Jack was smart, and he had money. Soon, he might have Mia too. Kim said, 'Geena wanted to help.'

'The test was collateral,' I told my team now. 'In case Kim needed to challenge her ex.'

'It was blackmail,' said Valerie. 'Kim used it to extort money from Jack. If news got out that he was Leif's father, the River Rats' swinging might be exposed, putting Jack's career in education at risk. So Kim held on to that test, and Mia found it. Evidence of a half-brother, right under her nose.'

'And when she asked her mom about it,' said Tim, 'Kim realized she couldn't let Leif find out. If he knew, any leverage she had with Jack went out the window.'

'In retrospect, the signs were there,' I said. 'I never understood how Kim could support both herself and a kid on the income from those ghost tours. The first time I met Mia, way before Leif's death, it was because a tour guest claimed they got robbed while on the tour. I thought maybe Mia had taken the money. More likely Kim was padding her nest egg saving up for a cursed cabin.'

Kim had been clever about a lot of things. It wasn't until we were docking the boats back on American soil that I noticed the burned-out remains of Brooks Hardware. I had a different perspective on the place, approaching from the water. The store had its own dock, and tied to it was a barge, the kind used to transport lumber, concrete, and appliances out to residential islands.

Ford's surveillance system had been reduced to a pile of melted plastic fused to the building's exterior wall. Had the camera in the lumber yard still been working, it would have captured Kim lapsing into behavior that had been displayed by two generations of A-Bay youth. Taking a boat that wasn't hers – that quiet barge this time – out to Devil's Oven Island in an attempt to stop her daughter from telling Leif what she'd learned. Later, when Valerie sent Sol to check the barge out, none of us had been surprised to discover a key in the outboard motor. Ford had no reason to think someone would steal a lumbering boat emblazoned with the name of his store, not when there were newer, faster options in the water. But that night, it proved to be the perfect vessel for Kim's needs.

'She intended to break up the party,' I said. 'Get between Mia and Leif, until she had a chance to reason with her daughter and convince her not to tell. Nothing strange about a mom who grew up on the river storming a bonfire and dragging her wayward kid back to shore. But when she got close to Devil's Oven, coming at the island from the east, it wasn't Mia she saw but Leif. He confronted her about Jack, desperate to know if what Mia told him was true. According to Kim's statement, she grabbed the boy and begged him to forget what he'd heard. And when Leif got upset, she pushed him down on to the rocks by the water's edge, panicked, and took off. Hen must have arrived shortly afterward.'

'She tried to throw us off the scent,' Valerie said, 'during our interview with Mia, when I asked whether she and Leif were close. All that stuff about high-school seniors not wanting to hang with juniors . . . she was trying to convince us they weren't linked in any way, when in fact the kids were half-siblings.'

'And remember what Mia said that day?' I added. 'We weren't close – *not like our parents*. Kim tried to deflect that too. She also made a point of casting doubt on her ex every chance she got.' Thinking back, each jab Kim had taken at 'useless' Jack, who'd left her a single mother, had made me distrust the guy more.

'I guess this means Mia's moving to Providence,' Sol said.

I nodded. 'Eventually. Sounds like Jack took a leave of absence and is letting her finish out the school year here. He didn't want to pull her out of her routine. Away from her friends.'

Friends that included Hen. I'd come to terms with that relationship, and even admired Mia for her insistence that Leif should know the truth about his father. I just wished she hadn't been so dramatic in the delivery of that life-altering news.

'What I'm still confused about is Geena,' said Sol. 'Are we really sure that was an accident? Considering Kim was with her when she died?'

'It does seem that way.' I'd been over the case from every

angle and still couldn't find evidence to the contrary. 'Kim had it out for Jack, but according to the other River Rats, she had a genuine friendship with Geena,' I said. 'We still need to confirm this with Jack of course, but I suspect Geena's death was the impetus for Kim to start blackmailing him. He came out swinging with that accusation of murder, but Kim had a bigger bat.'

We talked for a while about what was next and came to a mutual conclusion: the public didn't need to know about the River Rats. It wasn't just Calvin and Maria Fear who stood to suffer; Ford, Mandy, Jack, and Braden had all moved on too. Ford had a business to rebuild. A life to salvage. From our perspective, there was nothing to gain from sensationalizing a years-old private affair.

'Hey,' Valerie said once we'd finally dispersed, each of us heading to our respective desks to catch up on paperwork. 'Hold up a second, yeah?'

I did as she asked and doled out a patient smile. I couldn't say that Valerie Ott had managed to swoop in and close Leif's case like some infallible detective from a fiction novel. She, like the rest of us, had her flaws. But if I'd learned one thing while on the job in the North Country, it was that, from time to time, we all needed a hand.

I was puzzled, though, when Valerie ducked into the break room and gestured for me to follow. Once inside, she dragged the door closed and said, 'I don't think I've told you how my marriage ended.'

Where was she going with this? 'No,' I replied. 'I don't think you have.'

'I cheated,' she said simply. 'With a mutual friend. A friend of my husband's actually.'

'Oh.' *Oh.*

'We hadn't even been together all that long, my ex and I. Less than ten years' total which, when I think about my parents' marriage, isn't so much. But this other guy . . . I'd always had a thing for him. Never entertained it obviously. Until I did.'

I nodded, unsure of what to say. After a beat, Valerie shrugged. She'd said what she wanted to say – or so I thought.

'One more thing. Henderson called before. He offered me the open investigator job. I accepted.'

'What?'

'I'm your new investigator,' Valerie said in response to my dumbstruck stare. 'Are you surprised? I tick all of the agency's boxes – woman, ethnic minority, et cetera, but I'd like to think I earned the position too. It'll be a couple months before I can start. I've got a move to organize, some child custody issues to work through. With any luck though, I'll be back here by New Year's.'

Valerie Ott, my new investigator. Working at the barracks with me and Sol. And Tim.

'Congratulations,' I said, locking eyes with her while I shook her hand. 'And Val?'

'Hm?'

I smiled. 'Thank you.'

When I stepped out into the hallway, Tim bustled by on his way out the door. He was off to help the troopers with a criminal mischief charge, and I knew he might be gone for hours. For a fleeting moment I was surrounded by the smell of him, as familiar now as my own. I glanced behind me to see if we were alone, and there was Valerie. She raised her eyebrows at me. Jutted out her chin and disappeared into the break room once more.

I caught up with him, snagged his arm, and pulled him into my office.

'What?' Tim said. 'I've got stuff to do.' His eyes weren't moist exactly, but there was a redness to their edges. He slid his long fingers into the pockets of his pants, and that simple motion left me feeling gutted. Tim was nervous. Nervous around *me*.

I knew our relationship would change when we got married. The uncertainty of where our conjoined life would take us was one thing. Introducing children into the equation was another. We were trying to build a life in a house with rotten boards and wormy beams, the damage caused by termites left to roam free for too long at risk of becoming permanent. We'd sprayed for just such bugs when we bought our new home, but I'd seen the rivulets of eaten wood, knew the structure wasn't as strong as it should be. Eradicating the pests is only half the battle. They leave a labyrinth of holes behind.

'I've never understood why you put up with so much from me,' I told him. 'It shouldn't have to be that way.'

Tim's breaths came slow and steady. He didn't move.

'The guy lost everything,' I said. 'I felt bad for him, I think. That doesn't make it right.'

And still, Tim was paralyzed.

'I'm so sorry,' I told him, 'about what I did. About letting it happen. I don't know what else to say.'

Slowly, he met my gaze.

'You think I don't know what it's like,' he said, 'wanting something you can't have? Wanting things to be uncomplicated? I lived it for months, remember? You kept telling me we couldn't be together because of Bram. Believe me, I didn't understand why I wanted you either.'

My eyebrows shot up. Tim ignored my reaction and went on.

'We all feel things,' he said. 'We all have crushes. I think I had a crush on Val for a bit when she was talking about sausages.' When he paused, an invisible thread yanked up the corner of his mouth. 'But it's our job, when we're in a relationship, to separate the crushes from the deeper feelings. The feelings that we know will last even when things go to shit.'

*The heart wants what it wants*, Ford had said – *even when it's risky. Sometimes, that's when you feel its pull the most.* There was a pull, that much was true, present since the moment I met him. But it had nothing to do with my heart. I didn't understand the mechanics of love, but I knew it didn't operate the same way for everyone. Ford Colebrook's idea of love was friendship and fun, the nostalgia of youth and a means of escape. I'd seen the longing for it in his face when he'd talked about the River Rat weekends. In contrast, the pull I'd felt was a kick in my knees and a knot in my stomach, claws raking across my skin and tongue. It was purely physical. Animal lust.

My heart? That belonged to Tim, and always would.

There were questions we needed to answer. Issues to work through. But still, I knew.

'I want us to last,' I told him decisively, 'even when things go to shit. I want that more than anything.'

'I want it too,' Tim said, pinning me to his chest and holding on tight.

# FIFTY-THREE

'One week with us and she's the second coming of Jessica Fletcher.'

'Not what my brother had in mind, if I had to guess,' I reply with a withering smile.

Tim chuckles as we watch Henrietta, Asher, and Tristan where they stand on Market Street. The house in front of them, another bastardized historic building encased in vinyl siding, is the last stop on the tour. Mia Klinger wears a dress that pushes her cleavage halfway to her chin. Her dangly pewter earrings are shaped like skulls, and though the sun has only begun to set behind the Cornwall Brothers Museum across the street, she carries an LED lantern, swinging it idly as she speaks. Today's tour group includes a few pre-teen boys; a mother with twins who can't be older than eight; and us. A good-sized crowd for the season. The Klingers' customers are dwindling. Soon it will be too cold to run the tours, if they still exist by then. For the moment, Mia is back in her happy place, commanding the small but zealous flock.

'Historic towns like this have more stories and folk tales and legends than you can imagine,' she says, her long blonde curls trembling in the breeze. 'They grow and evolve as time marches on. This building you see behind me now was a funeral parlor, the town's first furniture store, and a multi-family home. It has lived many lives, and it's overrun with spirits of the dead. I want you to focus on the windows of the first floor, where the mortician did his work. Remember to snap two pictures so you have a reference photo for any ghostly presence you think you might have seen. The building sits vacant right now, but that doesn't mean there's no one home.' For a second she looks dazed, like she's forgotten her lines, but then Mia lifts her eyes to the crowd once more. 'There are secrets all around, if you know where to look.'

'That kid's tough as nails,' Tim says.

I nod, but in truth I have my doubts. If my experience with Hen has taught me anything, it's that kids are masters of disguise. I won't make the mistake of taking their moods at face value again. Behind their eyes and under their skin they're still babies, tiny fists clenching as they search for companionship and comfort. Expecting our protection from the devils at the door.

'It's nice that Jack's letting her keep up the tours,' I say. 'I hate to admit it, but she's good at this. The kid could have a career in acting.'

'Sure is. I can't believe this is my first ghost tour. So, Shane,' Tim says with a tilt of his head, 'you picking up what she's putting down? Do you *believe*?'

We're just a few yards from Ford Colebrook's dive site, but my eyes stay squarely on Tim. 'What I believe,' I say, 'is that the dead are never really gone.'

'For better or worse,' he replies with a sigh, placing a hand on the small of my back.

The fruitless search for ghosts in the windows complete, the group starts to break up, some handing tips to Mia as others wander toward the main drag while comparing photos on their phones. Hen, Asher, and Tristan wait for Mia to finish, then the foursome set off toward the ice-cream stand. Two young couples, walking hand in hand.

'Teenagers can be pretty cute,' Tim says as we turn away from them. The break in the rain has left the air feeling as fresh and cool as the river.

I smile a little as I think about the conversation I had with Hen that afternoon. She'd been begging to come downtown with her friends, even though she has school in the morning, and I'd almost put my foot in my mouth. 'Might as well live it up while you can, I guess,' I'd said. 'Things are going to be very different for you when—'

Shit, I'd thought. *Shit.*

'I know about the baby,' Hen had said.

I'd stared at her then, slack-jawed. 'You do? Since when?'

'Since before I left. I found a pregnancy test in the trash. My parents are idiots.'

'And you didn't say anything to them about it?' *Or wonder if that played a part in sending you away?*

She'd shrugged. 'They'll tell me when they're ready, and I'll act surprised when they do. Anyway, it might be fun to have a baby in the house. Someone to torture.'

'Hen . . .'

'Kidding, obvs.' She'd said it through a grin.

Tim's voice tugs me back to the present. 'Did you talk to Doug?'

'This afternoon. He and Josie are coming up next weekend. They're excited to meet Asher. Mia too,' I say.

We cross James Street. Walk past the Bean-In and the pizza place. The Chamber of Commerce, with its twin lion statues out front. The tree on the corner of Walton is halfway to golden, the grass underneath it starting to bleach.

'You really like kids, huh?' I ask.

Tim sighs. 'I really do. But I understand if you don't feel the same way.'

'I don't know. I think they're starting to grow on me.'

'Yeah?'

'Which I guess is good,' I go on, 'because Doug and Josie's baby is getting a cousin.'

*Cousin.* The word lodges in my throat for the briefest of seconds, but then I see Tim's face, a procession of emotions in his eyes as his brain unriddles what I'm trying to tell him.

'I'm pregnant, Tim. We're having a baby.'

I give him an encouraging nod and watch the man I love more than anything light up and grin with pure, wanton delight. I laugh when he blushes, asks *how?* and assure him I know what he means.

'I took a test,' I say. 'After talking to Hen about her baby brother. I've been feeling woozy and . . . off my game, but it didn't occur to me to check sooner.' Bushwhacked? Was that the right word to describe how I felt when I saw the results on that stick? Maybe, but the bewilderment had passed surprisingly quickly, and I'd found I was left with unalloyed joy. 'Some sleuth I am, huh?' I tell Tim.

'Don't be so hard on yourself,' he replies, pressing his hands against both my cheeks. 'You almost always get a solve in the end.'

Tim kisses me then, slow and deep, and my body goes molten. Hand in hand, we make our way home.

# ACKNOWLEDGMENTS

Whether you're new to Shana Merchant or a long-time reader, thank you for choosing to spend time with her. I hope this story satisfied.

To Rachel Slatter, Martin Brown, Tina Pietron, Laura Kincaid, Piers Tilbury, Joanne Grant, and the entire Severn House team, thank you for your enthusiasm, devotion, and my favorite cover yet.

To Marlene Stringer, thank you for piloting this series for so long. To Chris Bucci, thank you for embracing it now.

Writing crime fiction takes a team of subject matter experts, and I would be lost without mine. My deepest gratitude goes to Jordan Taylor, Michelle Sowden, Jun Takayasu, Dennis and Kathi McCarthy, Mike Girard, Aidin Repsher, Tom Ahern, and former Jefferson County Sheriff Colleen O'Neill. On the branding front, I am very lucky to work with Jessica Burnie.

As always, thank you to my wonderful early readers Leila Wegert, Dorinda Bonanno, Elise Hart Kipness, and Samantha Skal. To my dear writer friends (you know who you are), I treasure you more than I can express. A special thank-you to Samantha Downing, May Cobb, Nadine Matheson, Danielle Girard, Hannah Morrissey, and Sarah Stewart Taylor for your generous and ongoing support.

To the libraries, bookstores, and bookstagrammers that have hosted me over the years, and to Sisters in Crime CT, International Thriller Writers, and Mystery Writers of America, the support and sense of community you offer is invaluable.

Finally, thank you to Grant, Remi, and Schafer for welcoming Shana – a perpetual houseguest – into our lives.